THE
WARRIOR
OF CLAN
KINCAID

THE
WARRIOR
OF *CLAN*
KINCAID

LILY BLACKWOOD

St. Martin's Paperbacks

This is a work of fiction. All of the characters, organizations, and events portrayed in this novel are either products of the author's imagination or are used fictitiously.

THE WARRIOR OF CLAN KINCAID

Copyright © 2018 by Lily Blackwood.

All rights reserved.

For information address St. Martin's Press, 175 Fifth Avenue, New York, NY 10010.

ISBN: 978-1-250-08484-2

Our books may be purchased in bulk for promotional, educational, or business use. Please contact your local bookseller or the Macmillan Corporate and Premium Sales Department at 1-800-221-7945, ext. 5442, or by e-mail at MacmillanSpecialMarkets@macmillan.com.

Printed in the United States of America

St. Martin's Paperbacks edition / August 2018

St. Martin's Paperbacks are published by St. Martin's Press, 175 Fifth Avenue, New York, NY 10010.

10 9 8 7 6 5 4 3 2 1

For my agent—and friend—Kim Lionetti.

Thank you!

Acknowledgments

Acknowledgments

I want to express the most sincere thank you to Cindy Miles, Jeri Chatterley, Rachel Osborn and my wonderful mother, Ella Dawn. You wouldn't know it, but you said (or wrote) the words I needed to hear, just when I needed to hear them, and I'll never forget it.

Thank you to Lizzie Poteet for loving Highlanders, and romance, and for your editorial guidance. I was so lucky to have you work on these books! Thank you to Jennie Conway for your cheerful help in bringing this book to publication. John Simko, thank you for your excellent copy editing on the manuscript (and giving me the giggles, more than once).

All my affection to Eric, Jon and Tristan for your unfailing love and support. I couldn't ask for a better family!

Much love to my author lunch (and movie) group, who brings me endless smiles.

And thank you to the wonderful readers who read romance with an open and happy heart, for the joy of the love story and the adventure.

Prologue

At the master's command, the boy crept up from the pit of the vessel and squinted into the dim light. Because he had spent so long in darkness, the sky seemed as brilliant and painful to his eyes as the light of a blazing Mediterranean sun.

But there was no sun here, only thick fog, all around, and the blood-chilling cold that for the previous blur of days had crept into the hold of the ship and through his rags to claim his bones.

He struck away the stinging pain from his eyes—so akin to tears—though he had stopped crying a very long time ago, all emotion flayed from him by the master's punishing whip.

"Here, boy," called his black-eyed Venetian master, his voice sending a ripple of hatred through the boy.

For as long as he could remember, that hatred had consumed his heart. That hatred had kept him alive, while others had died, like his only friend, Omid, who one day had whispered stories of Trojans and Greeks, of Achilles and Hector, and the next had been still and cold . . . and before noonday, swallowed up by the sea.

The boy complied, his chains dragging against the wood as he moved to stand before his bearded master and another man, a stranger he had never seen before. But strangers were nothing new on this vessel. They came, and they chose, and they passed coins to the master, and they left with men and boys who had been deprived of their spirits and their souls.

"There he is," said the slaver. "Aye, just look at that pale hair . . . the blue eyes."

Dark eyes assessed him, from head to toe.

"A Scots boy among all these Greeks and Slavs? How uncommon. How strange." The man spoke as if amused, and leaned back upon the rail of the ship. "I cannot even imagine how that came to be."

The slaver grunted out a laugh.

Scots . . . the boy did not know what the word meant. Indeed, he could barely understand the man's foreign words. They bore a thick and unfamiliar accent, yet strangely, the accent matched the mysterious cadence of his dreams.

He kept his head bowed, as he had learned to do, but he saw that the man's boots were of the darkest, finest leather. That the hem of his heavy wool tunic was thickly embroidered with leaves and circular symbols.

The visitor sighed, as if burdened. Aggrieved. "How can I, if I have one fraction of conscience, allow a kinsman of mine, no matter how lowborn, to live the life of a slave?"

Would the man purchase him, and be his new master? Would he be taken off this vessel to live in this strange, cold land? He did not believe it. In the past, no price had ever been good enough.

The boots stepped closer. "How old now, tell me if my estimation is right . . ."

"Twelve I would say." The master strode forward then, dragging his whip along the planks. He seized one of the boy's wrists, wrenching his arm high. "Though he is as hearty and strong as a bull. Do you see his muscles? He has been fed well, and labors long, and he has not been overly mistreated."

Aye, he had been treated with favor. His punishment, more often than not, had come from a bruising club, and not from a cutting whip.

The Scot scrutinized him with dark eyes. "What is your name, boy?" the stranger commanded of him.

The boy searched the blackness of his mind. His name? He had never been called a name. Not a true name, like Omid or Ivar.

"Boy," he answered, his voice a croak.

The stranger laughed then, throwing his head back.

Dark eyes returned to him, alight with satisfaction. "*Boy*, how would you like to become a warrior for Scotland? How would you like to fight for me?"

Chapter 1

An Caisteal Hiaul, Inverhaven, March 1390

It was after midnight. Cold and raining.

"Doesn't it matter at all that I don't want to be sent away?" Derryth MacClaren sat atop her mount, gripping the reins in her mitten-covered hands, her chest tight with fear and dread.

Just moments ago, it seemed, she had been warm and asleep in her bed. The next she'd been hoisted by a Kincaid warrior into her saddle, as rain *pattered* on the stones all around. There was a wagon . . . and a group of Kincaid men gathered nearby, speaking quietly. They wore dark hoods and furs, with weapons glinting beneath. Clearly they were to be her escorts.

But she did not want to ride out of the castle gates, into the great darkness beyond, even if she *did* have an escort of the clan's largest and most skilled warriors to protect her along her way. Though sleep still muddled her mind, the frigid air quickly cleared the cobwebs away.

Her older half-sister, Elspeth Braewick, the Lady Kincaid, stood looking up at her in the shadows of the castle bailey, out of the dark frame of her cowl. Drops glittered on her face.

"Of course your wishes matter," Elspeth answered softly, in a conciliatory tone. "But sometimes you must trust that decisions are being made for your own good. I'm sorry, Derryth, but you have no say in this. You must go."

"Elspeth! What a paltry reply," Derryth said with a frown. "I am not an unquestioning child." She was nineteen, nearly twenty. "Tell me why you are sending me away."

Derryth had only a dim, sleepy memory of Elspeth rousing her from her sleep and urging her to dress in garments that were quickly laced by two silent castle maids. Now, beneath a thick fur cloak, she wore the costume of a peasant—layers of oilskin, leather, and wool, all roughly hewn—and underneath those, not one, but two pair of heavy woolen hose. A dagger had been strapped to her waist. Instead of riding her own gentle gray pony, she sat on a hardy young mule.

Derryth's grip on the reigns tightened, her gaze fixed unwaveringly on her sister. Why hadn't she been told the day before of this plan? Why would they send her away now, in the dead of night?

Then suddenly . . . she knew.

"It's the Wolf, isn't it?" she whispered, her heart sinking like a weighted stone in her chest. Just speaking his name caused her vision to blur and her throat to close. Though the last two years had passed peacefully, an enemy presence loomed like a dark shadow over Inverhaven, always. A threat that had never really gone away.

"No, of course not," Elspeth murmured with a shake of her head. Her gathered brows and half-smiling lips declared Derryth's suggestion to be the silliest thing. But tellingly, she'd glanced away as she spoke the words.

Derryth's pulse increased, knowing some unpleasant truth was being kept from her.

"I don't believe you. He has threatened the Kincaids again, hasn't he? Don't send me away. I choose to stay here with you and Niall. I'm not afraid."

It was a lie. She *was* afraid of the Wolf—Alexander Stewart, the Earl of Buchan—and the terrible destruction he'd all but promised to wreak upon the Kincaids. But love for her sister, and all those here at Inverhaven, made her brave.

Like Elspeth, Derryth was a MacClaren by birth. But since Elspeth had married Niall Braewick, the Laird Kincaid, two harvests ago, the Kincaids had become Derryth's family too. Once, their clans had been fierce enemies, but those times seemed a distant memory, all but forgotten.

Since early summer, Derryth had resided at *An Caisteal Niaul*, the Kincaid clan's legendary Castle in the Clouds, as a guest of her sister and brother-in-law. There'd been feasts and festivals, and she'd indulged in several exciting *near*-romances, though she had not settled her affections on any man, as none had satisfied the always changing requirements of her heart. In the meantime, Inverhaven had all but become her home.

But now they were sending her away, to her *other* home—to the MacClaren stronghold at Falranroch—over which her young, widowed stepmother, Bridget, presided.

"Of course you aren't afraid, and you shouldn't be, because there's nothing whatsoever to fear," her dark-haired sister replied lightly, though Derryth heard the uneasiness that she tried to hide. "But winter has passed, and Bridget deserves a bit of respite from tending to our little sisters, Mairi and Kat, who will be so happy to see you after you've been gone for so long."

She *did* miss Mairi and Kat. Their constant girlish chatter and fun. But she did *not* want to leave Elspeth, not when they had grown so close of late—since their father's passing the previous year. In their grief, it seemed they'd seen each other for the first time through different eyes. Before, Derryth had always thought of Elspeth as her bossy older sister, but now she considered Elspeth her dearest friend. The years had taken so much from them—both of their mothers and now their father, who had been far from perfect but they loved him still. For now, it seemed important that they stay together, no matter what.

If all was well and good at Inverhaven, as her sister claimed, and she was merely being sent to help her stepmother with her little sisters, she would be leaving Inverhaven on the next clear day, *not* under a black night sky, heavy with unspent rain.

Anxiety pooled like ice at the pit of her stomach. Derryth knew without a doubt they were sending her away to protect her from *something*, which could only mean they knew of some danger or threat.

"You'll arrive at Falranroch in two days," Elspeth continued. "And you'll be back in a comfortable bed before you even realize."

She offered a forced smile, but Derryth could plainly see that the dampness in her eyes came from tears, not the rain.

Derryth's eyes flooded in response, because Elspeth had always been the strong one, and hardly *ever* cried. But now her sister cried for some reason over her. Because she was afraid? Because they might never see each other again?

"I don't even know why we are crying!" Derryth exclaimed, reaching out her hand. "Because you will not tell me!"

Elspeth reached up and grasped Derryth's hand and sighed. Just like that, her lips lost the easy smile they'd attempted to hold.

"Oh, very well," she said resignedly. "You coax my secrets from me, as you always do." Elspeth's damp eyes warmed with sudden affection, and she squeezed Derryth's hand. "Yesterday, the old farmer, Carmag, came to the castle insisting on speaking to Niall. While working in his field, he claims to have seen three, perhaps four soldiers on a distant hill." Her voice dipped. "King's men."

Fear struck through Derryth's heart as she straightened in the saddle. Her heart beat more frantically. Her mind grasped quickly onto the words. The importance of the revelation. The air around them seemed to grow colder, and darker.

She'd been right, after all.

King's men.

They might as well be called "Buchan's men," at least here in this distant corner of the Highlands, so far away from Scone and Edinburgh. As the third son of King Robert, and some claimed, his favorite, the Wolf commanded a force of royal soldiers and private mercenaries, which he dispatched to do his bidding. Though two years ago he had lost much of his power, he had regained it over time and remained just as dangerous as before, though until now he had kept his distance.

Suddenly she wanted nothing more than to return to the castle, to her soft, warm bed, and go back to sleep, because maybe when she awakened in the morning she would find this had all been a bad dream.

Elspeth spoke again, a hand coming up—perhaps nervously—to touch the simple bronze brooch that fastened her cowl. "Of course, no one else saw this, and poor Carmag is not the best witness. You yourself must remember a fortnight ago when he arrived naked and drunk at the castle, claiming fairies has stolen his garments—and his cow. Today Niall himself rode out, along with a large company of men, and searched all day and found nothing. No camp. No soldiers. Not even the cold remains of a fire." Her voice softened. "So you see we don't know if they actually were soldiers, or"—she shrugged—"just a trick of the light in the shadows and trees. But if there were soldiers, it's possible they were scouts sent by Buchan. And if something should happen—"

"An attack." Derryth spoke the words bluntly, shivering from more than just the cold, damp air. Here, in this place, already stained by the blood Buchan's army had once spilled, nearly nineteen years ago.

Elspeth nodded, her skin paling a shade more in the night. "Or a siege. Then Niall and I want you to be safe and away from here, long before there is danger. Today, messengers will be sent to our allies, and all in the village will be informed and urged to come inside the walls, at least for now."

The truth, at last. Elspeth's words, and the fear she saw in her eyes, caused Derryth's stomach to clench tight, and she felt almost ill. Elspeth, always so strong and decisive. Always the caretaker. Perhaps for the first time, she realized Elspeth needed tender care too.

"I won't leave you," Derryth said firmly, shaking her head—moving as if to dismount. "Not in your condition."

Yet Elspeth, whose eight-month pregnant stomach could barely be discerned beneath her cloak, stilled her—reaching up and spreading a hand over hers where she clenched the saddle's horn. "This is Buchan of whom we speak. It matters not that you are a woman," Elspeth continued, and Derryth could see the worry and desperation in her eyes. "His actions led to the death of many innocent Kincaids. Not only Niall's father and his warriors, but Niall's mother and youngest brother as well. He would be no less ruthless with you or me."

Niall appeared then, tall and strong, to stand beside her sister. Dark-haired and striking, and wearing a *pladjer* over his shoulder, the air became charged anytime he came near. Warriors stood straighter. Castle servants moved faster. Not from fear, but because he carried himself with such presence and each day earned their respect, and they wished, in turn, to earn his approval and praise.

"Ye'll not be staying here, lass," he said in his rich, deep voice. "So cease your arguing, ye're just making your sister feel worse about it all. She'll be joining ye as soon as the bairn is born. I'll have ye all safe, until the danger—if it exists—has passed. Besides, ye know ye are too spoiled a lady to suffer through the hardship of a siege, should one occur."

He spoke the words in a low, teasing tone, but with enough gravity that she knew he was serious.

Hearing his words, Derryth's chest tightened with shame. She was indeed spoiled, and had always cared far too much for pretty things and amusements. Even now, her skin complained at the scratchiness of the rough garments she wore. Ugly, shapeless clothes she would never have chosen for herself.

She winced, regretting the pettiness of her complaints. It was why they sent her away, no doubt. They considered her a helpless creature they would only have to worry about. And why should they not? She had never proven herself to be of any *true* use or value to anyone other than to be marriageable, and thereby a useful tool in strengthening or gaining a new alliance.

The burden of her shortcomings weighted her heart. She knew they loved her, but unlike Elspeth she didn't know how to properly hold a sword or stitch a wound or even clean a goose. Most important, she had no experience assisting in the birth of a child. Instead she'd spent her hours learning every possible way to plait, curl, and otherwise arrange her hair, and how to stain her lips and cheeks with cherry juice without anyone knowing she'd applied anything at all. She had mastered decorative embroidery, because as a young girl, she'd always believed her simple gowns needed something *more*, but what good were fanciful patterns in thread at a time like this?

Tears stung her eyes. Tears of self-reproach. Why had it taken this moment—this threat against all she loved so dearly—to make her realize she ought to be more?

As if Elspeth saw straight into her heart, she said, "Derryth, you've done nothing wrong. We just couldn't bear it if something happened to you."

"But don't you see?" she replied, her voice unsteady. "Nor could I bear it if something happened to any of you."

"You must trust that I will protect her and our babe." Niall's arm went round her sister, and his large hand squeezed her shoulder gently—an offering of comfort.

Elspeth looked up at him, love plain in her eyes, seeming small and protected within the protection of his muscular arm. Niall was a famed warrior, and fearsome both in negotiation and in battle. And yet she had seen her sister fell him with just a glance. Silence him with a single word. A kiss.

How she envied them, in the most loving way. Would she ever find a love so deeply passionate? She craved a feeling of romantic . . . *mad* love in her heart, but thus far she had found no one to inspire wishes of forever.

Shifting his gaze to Derryth, Niall said, "So go ye

now. Prepare for your sister and our babe to join you, in perhaps a fortnight's time. Mayhap even a sennight, if the child is hearty as I expect he or she will be."

He grinned, but even here, in the dim light, Derryth perceived the dark shadows beneath his eyes, as if he had not slept since hearing of the soldiers' presence on his lands. He loved them all so much—his wife and his clan, and yes even her silly self, whom he called "little sister." Aye, she loved him like a brother too.

She forced herself to look past the hurt of being sent away, to the intent of his words. Niall had given her a task—to prepare for Elspeth and the bairn, and she must embrace that new purpose with enthusiasm. Whatever the future brought, she must make herself a useful part in it. As soon as she arrived at the Mac-Claren stronghold, she would set about educating herself on more important matters, and becoming a woman to be admired for more than a fetching braid or a pretty gown. She'd surprise them all, in the best possible way, the next time they met. Next time, they would not think of sending her away.

But what if their worst fears were realized, and she never saw them again? It was no overreaction. She had only to look at the past to know that danger was everywhere in the Highlands, and that death could strike at any moment. Trepidation filled her mind, consuming her thoughts, and causing her chest to constrict with each quickening breath.

"Oh, Elspeth," Derryth choked, as her emotions overtook her.

How she despised Buchan—a man she'd never even

seen with her own eyes—for the wrongs he had done, and for the fear he inspired. For tearing their families apart.

She leaned down, wrapping one arm around her sister's shoulders, inhaling the familiar, comforting sweetness of her skin and hair. Niall embraced them both in his strong arms. Enveloping them in his warmth, he kissed Derryth's temple and then his wife's.

"I love you both," she whispered.

Just then, a figure approached—one who became more familiar with each trundling step. The older woman smiled up at her.

"Hello, child." Bundled heavily in garments similar to hers, the woman appeared prepared for travel, carrying a large embroidered pouch and a covered basket. "Are ye ready? Ah, don't ye fret, my bairns. We'll all do just fine, and I've brought a big basket of bread, cheese, and ham, and oh, yes, honey cakes to satisfy our bellies along the way."

Niall moved quickly to relieve her of the burdens she carried.

Was Fiona to accompany her then? She gave a sigh of relief, and her tension lessened to some degree. Fiona always made everything seem better.

Elspeth smiled warmly at their former servant, who had always been a treasured friend, and her words confirmed what Derryth had already surmised. "Fiona has offered to journey with you. She wants to see Mairi and Kat, and she'll help with the bairn when I join you."

"The bairn!" exclaimed Fiona. "'Twill be a braw

lad, I've already told ye, and I cannae wait tae meet him, after the Lord—guiding Ina's capable hands—sees him safely into this world, without me hovering about as a distraction."

Elspeth and Niall's faces broke simultaneously into smiles. Fiona had once been Elspeth and Derryth's nursemaid. Though the old woman now lived in a small cottage at the edge of the village, she remained a constant and comforting part of their lives, acting also as midwife to many in the village. With her vision failing and the pain of age in her hands, she had trained Elspeth's maid, Ina, to take her place.

One of the younger warriors, Nathan, came forward to help Fiona into the wagon.

Glancing at the sky, Niall grew serious. "It is time. We can delay no more if you are to arrive at Falranroch tomorrow before nightfall. I've given instructions to the men. If you encounter anyone and there are questions, ye are merely common folk—MacClellans, traveling through on your way to work the spring fields with your Drummond kin." The two clans he named were not sworn allies, but friendly enough to claim them if questioned. Accompanying them would be nine warriors in all. "Ye'll take the Cairnmore road."

Deargh appeared then from the castle, his heavily tattooed skull and face making him just a shadow in the night—a terrifying one to anyone who did not know him. An older warrior with silver shimmering in his beard, he was Niall's fearsome second-in-command. He had also saved Niall's life that night many years ago when the Laird and Lady Kincaid had been killed, hastening him safely away and raising him to be the warrior he'd become. He wore a dark plaid, thick leather boots, and a fur draped from his shoulders. A sword glinted at his waist.

He grinned as he passed, his manner mischievous as always. "'Tis a perfect night for a ramble across these Highlands."

"Aye, 'tis." Derryth nodded, heartened by his good humor.

She knew she was very special indeed to her brother-in-law if he sent Deargh to protect her, and knowing he would escort her eased her fears a thousandfold.

As for the Cairnmore road—it was not the most direct path to Falranroch, but she knew without asking why that route had been chosen. It led in the opposite direction of Carmag's farm and the more commonly traveled Barradale road. If there were indeed soldiers, there'd be less likelihood of crossing paths on that road. There were also few settlements along the way, as the terrain was stony and rough and devoid of good farmland.

Niall added, "The men will return here, after delivering you so that we will know you and Fiona are safe and well."

And because they would be needed in the defense of Inverhaven, though the words went unspoken. A moment later Fiona was settled into the wagon, wrapped in layers of blankets and fur.

Elspeth reached for Derryth's hand and pressed a kiss to her wool-covered knuckles. "Farewell, sister. Until we see each other again. Very soon, I vow."

"You'll be a mother then!" Derryth exclaimed.

"Indeed!" Elspeth laughed.

Derryth saw tears rise again in her sister's eyes. Her own eyes blurred.

"Dinnae cry," she exclaimed. "Because then *I'll* cry. Aye, farewell. Until then."

Praying that she would see them again very soon, and that all this fear was for naught, Derryth pulled the reins of the mule and followed the wagon, which trundled toward the castle gates. The warriors all proceeded silently on foot.

Moments later came the heavy rattle of the gates closing behind them, gates that were normally left open so the villagers could move to and fro. High above, on the walls, Derryth perceived the outline of more sentries than usual, their faces turned out toward the night, watching.

She breathed deeply, doing her best to calm her anxiety over leaving, and her fear of the darkness that rose up all around them. Instead, she focused her thoughts on the future, and her duties at Falranroch, where she would throw herself into preparing for Elspeth's arrival. Aye, and she would be a better sister and friend to Katrin and Mairi, and become an example of strength to them, as Elspeth had been to her.

For the moment, it had stopped raining, but here in the open the cold wind gusted into her face. She wiped her cheeks, determined to shed no more tears, and brought her woven cowl high, to cover her nose. The village of Inverhaven lay quiet and sleeping, with smoke rising from countless chimneys. For a time, Niall had maintained a large army of cateran mercenaries for the defense of Inverhaven and the clan's surrounding lands. While many of those men and their families remained, having become a part of the clan, when spring had come, just as many had asked Niall's leave to go off again into the world, to pursue the same adventure that had brought them here.

The mule plodded forward, and Derryth relaxed as best she could. The dagger she wore at her waist dug into her ribs with the animal's jerky gait. She adjusted the blade on its leather strap so the hilt wouldn't poke her so annoyingly.

Rain fell, off and on, but bundled up as she was, she wasn't cold. Not really. The travel was tedious, a never-ending up-and-down over hill, berm, and stone. After a time, she could no longer look over her shoulder and see the castle tower looming in the dark. Eventually the road wasn't a road at all, but merely a worn path she could not discern.

For three hours . . . perhaps four . . . there was only the monotonous turning of the wagon wheels, soft noises from the animals, and the occasional cough or mutter from one of the men to break the silence. Eventually, her eyes became heavy . . . and she dozed . . .

She started awake to find the sky above had lightened to indigo blue, in vivid contrast to the inky shadows that now surrounded them—the trees of a forest.

And yet there had been a sound.

Indeed . . . she *had* heard a sound.

Had she not?

Chapter 2

Whatever the sound had been, the men had heard it too.

The wagon and the warriors came to a stop. Ahead, Deargh stood straight and motionless on the path, his body rigid, his hand raised for silence.

Instantly awake, Derryth straightened in the saddle, her gaze searching the shadows. Nathan moved silently over the earth, taking her mule's bridle in hand.

A *snap* sounded in the dark. A furtive rustling.

"Nathan," she whispered.

"Quiet," he hissed back, with a sharpness that only increased her fear. Underneath his cloak, his shoulder moved, and she knew he grasped the hilt of his sword.

The garments that had sheltered her from the cold and the rain now felt heavy and constricting. Taking Nathan's lead, she took possession of her dagger, slowly sliding it free of its leather sheath to hold at the ready under her cloak, all the while praying no one was out there, and that the sounds were made by a foraging animal.

She jumped when a voice spoke from the darkness.

"Well . . . who are ye then?" a man demanded.

"Travelers, passing through," Deargh answered evenly. "We wish nae trouble. Only tae be on our way."

"Why ur ye traveling at night, in the mirk an' the rain?" the voice asked slyly.

"We dinna want to draw the notice of the Kincaids," Deargh replied. "I hear they've got hundreds of murderous caterans protecting their lands and their castle." He paused. "Be ye one o' them?"

The voice chuckled. "Nay, peasant. We are not Kincaids."

The tone taunted. Threatened. Nathan stood taller, slowly shifted his stance outward, toward the darkness, as if prepared to engage and defend. The hair on the back of Derryth's neck stood on end. Something was about to happen.

Suddenly, the shadows along the edges of her vision moved . . . converged on them, revealing that not just one man stood there, but a score. Not soldiers, but Highlanders, by their plaids and bare feet, and the furs they wore. She knew as well as anyone, not all Highlanders were heroes.

All around her, they chuckled and breathed and growled, making a show of fearsomeness. In the dim light, their expressions were cold and cruel.

"Wot should we do w' them?" asked another voice.

A long silence passed. Everyone stood still, listening . . . waiting.

"Kill them," pronounced the man who'd spoken first, his words filling her with fear. "But not *her*." An arm extended from the darkness, pointing at her. "Aye, we've got use for her."

Her terror magnified at knowing they'd fixed their attention on her.

With a low growl, Nathan threw back his cloak, and lifted his sword. Ahead, Deargh did the same, as did the other Kincaids.

"Ye'll stand back," Deargh commanded. "Do y' hear?"

The men moved forward, creating a shield with their bodies. Derryth watched them, riveted . . . terrified.

Yet, in the next moment, a hand seized Derryth's thigh—gripping her there, tearing her attention away. Startled, she turned to confront whomever had come from behind, striking out at them with her dagger, but her arm tangled in her heavy garments, making the weapon useless.

Her pulse raced, as another figure appeared. Then another. Growling, muttering shadows. Hands pulled *hard* on her cloak, nearly dismounting her off the back of the mule.

"Deargh!" she cried, clutching the reins, clenching her thighs to remain seated. In doing so, she dropped the dagger.

Voices shouted. Swords clashed.

Afraid . . . she twisted in the saddle and wrenched the reins while jabbing her heels, trying to spur the animal away. The mule started, and turned, but did not run.

From the darkness, Deargh bellowed. "Don't touch her."

Two . . . three men pressed close, their feet stamping in mud, the acrid smell of them rising up to fill her nostrils.

"Get away!" she cried.

Fear consumed her. Fear for herself. Fear for Fiona and the men. Would they all die here, like this?

Her assailants pushed close, all around. Again, she jabbed her heels into the mule's side and at last the animal sprang forward, but shadows darted toward her. More hands reached . . . grabbing the bridle. Seizing her. Pulling her off.

"No!" She screamed and kicked, her boots striking flesh and mud.

She broke free. Twisting, she scrambled across the sodden earth, only to be captured by the ankles—

And dragged facedown through the cold mud, her cloak and skirts catching on stones, baring her legs to her thighs.

"No!" she cried again. Desperately, she clawed at the earth and grass, fighting with every bit of energy she possessed. A hard yank deprived her of the fur. Another, her cloak.

"She's spirited." One man chuckled deep in his throat.

"All the better," declared another.

Men still shouted. Fiona screamed. More feet thumped on the earth . . . distant, but growing closer. More attackers?

"*Stop!*" a man's voice thundered. "Do not move."

But nothing stopped.

Flipped onto her back . . . stones dug into her bottom, her shoulder blades. She saw the sky above, then numerous filthy faces with wide eyes, leering mouths, and crooked teeth. She struck at them . . . clawed at flesh, until her arms were seized, and she regretted that she had not used the dagger on herself in that moment when she could have saved herself from this. Again she screamed, and a muddied hand crushed her mouth, filling it with grit.

"Get off," the same man ordered, in a voice of command.

Several of the men disappeared, but others remained, as if they'd not heard, or ignored the order. Hands grabbed her bare calf—but when her other leg slid free, she screamed and smashed her heel against the nearest attacker's jaw. His head snapped back. Then, wild-eyed, he glared down at her and cursed, before grabbing her ankle and holding her immobile—and utterly defenseless. She screamed.

"*Now, I say*," the man's voice bellowed.

Boots crunched over the sodden earth, moving toward her, fast. There came a solid *thud*. A man groaned—as if struck.

"Damn you," the man giving orders growled. *Thud. Smack.* The sound of fists against flesh. The sudden *rip* of a tunic. "Damn you all. Filthy, undisciplined mongrels, every last one of you."

The man on top of her flew backward through the air, legs flailing as if hurled by a catapult.

In her terror, she saw only a blur of movement. The dim gleam of golden hair. Flashing ice-blue eyes. High, harsh cheekbones. The church priests had always described God's angels as beautiful, fearsome creatures. Her mind hazy with fear, she prayed that an angel had been sent to save her.

The others gone . . . he appeared, standing above her. The angel.

Her heartbeat staggered, caught . . . stunned, in her chest.

Oh, but he wasn't an angel. The thing that knelt beside her was a tautly constructed, oversized war machine. A frightening vision of fury and brawn. Shirtless, he wore only linen trews and unlaced boots, as if he'd been awakened from sleep. His muscled shoulder flexed as he reached for her.

Everything inside her recoiled at the thought of his touch. She cried out, and crawled backward—away from him—but her elbows and heels slid in the mud, and her spent muscles failed her. Any escape demanded more strength than she now possessed. She could only breathe heavily, and gape at him.

He had saved her from the others. But was he her savior, or just another animal hiding behind the mask of a man?

The blue, early morning light revealed his face, so severe and frightening it appeared to be hewn of stone. Cold eyes glanced at her dispassionately. His hair, though long and falling to his shoulders, was shaved close at the sides of his head, giving emphasis to the high slash of his cheekbones.

He reached for her again.

"No," she uttered, flinching. Her voice emitted only as a dry rasp.

He either did not hear, or did not care what she wanted.

The mud sucked at her garments as he lifted her, to hold her like a child. She pushed against his chest . . . his shoulders, and found them as unyielding as a castle wall, indisputable proof she was at his mercy. Any remaining hope inside her disappeared. She could not help but believe *this moment* was a prelude to the rest of her life . . . or her death—however it would come.

Her hair and her garments weighted with mud, Derryth looked *everywhere*, desperate to know her surroundings and how her companions fared. Over her captor's shoulder, she glimpsed Nathan standing, circled by soldiers, his shoulders hunched. Blood streamed from his nose, dark against his pale skin in the wane light, but he raised his head, and his burning gaze met hers as she was carried past. Another soldier brought Fiona by the arm, wide eyed and bright cheeked with distress, to stand nearer to the young warrior. Deargh and the others were herded together, no longer in possession of their weapons, their expressions seething and mutinous, all of them bruised and bloodied.

In the distance, nearly obscured by trees and mist, she saw rows of tents, small and rectangular, but also several larger circular ones bearing high peaks at their centers. There were wagons, mules, and horses, and many, many men, but no banners. Her heart sank, seeing so many. A cloud of silence hovered above it all. An air of secrecy.

The wild-eyed men who had attacked them belonged to an army, though they were the poorest examples of Highlanders that Derryth had ever seen. Filthy and rough, with grizzled, overgrown beards and hair, they wore tattered, mud-colored plaids and were bare of foot. The soldiers were visibly different, with trimmed hair and beards, and yellow tunics and leather boots. She could only assume the man who held her was their leader, for he did not have the look or speech of a Highlander.

He carried her, his boots crunching heavily on the ground, only to draw to a stop. He exhaled through his nose, and glared at all those who waited, silent and watching. A crowd of men surrounded them. Those who had been part of the attack, and those who had intervened.

He spoke. "Secure these men, who have defied my *explicit* orders, so that they may await my punishment. As for the travelers, hold them as well, separate and secure, until I decide what must be done with them."

They all awaited a sentence then. His judgment. Her as well. Their faces blurred as he carried her past.

"Child!" Fiona buried her face in her hands.

"But sir," murmured a man's voice, as he approached, his expression pleading. "I tried to stop them."

Her vision focused on the face of the man speaking—a face she recognized as one of her attackers. She stiffened, her hands clenching the arm of her captor. Her lips parted to confront his untruth, but the giant who carried her spoke first.

"Y' dare lie to me?" he said coldly—his voice, and the retribution it promised, sending a chill down Derryth's spine.

"I'm not tae blame for what happened—" the Highlander all but whined.

"Even now, you argue?" the warrior muttered in clipped syllables, his jaw taut and his eyes devoid of warmth. "Think again. Do you wish to say more?"

The man held silent. Tension blanketed the air.

"Go wait with the others," the man holding her said with frightening calm, his voice like a slow, cutting blade through the silence of the early morning. "I promise you, it won't be long until I return."

The man's face paled. Swallowing deeply, he lowered his gaze and stepped back, bowing his head in fearful reverence.

Her captor moved again, in the direction of the tents, carrying her past the men, who stepped back, allowing him to pass. Everything moved so fast, as with each step he carried her away from her companions. Roused to reaction, she elbowed at his arms. His chest.

A sudden murmuring rippled through the men, and in the distance, a man with shoulder-length dark hair and a long, prominent nose strode toward them, in a brocade dressing gown, which hung open over an embroidered tunic. Accompanying him were several armed warriors in fine metal-worked armor, such as Derryth had never seen. He exuded authority in the way he moved and held himself. He was young though— too young to be Buchan. Still, she ceased her struggles and averted her gaze, not wanting to draw more attention to herself than necessary.

"Cull. Answer me this. What has happened here?" he said, coming nearer, his words more a demand than a question.

Cull.

Cull—the man who carried her—slowed, coming to a stop.

"These men attacked a traveling party with the intention of killing everyone, to steal their possessions. They would have raped the girl."

The girl. *Her.* Tears blurred her eyes, for she still wasn't safe.

"And?" the man responded, his dark brows rising on his forehead—as if the crime that had almost occurred did not trouble him in the least.

Cull answered without hesitation. "They placed our entire mission in jeopardy. If one of the travelers had escaped this melee, they might very well have gone to the Kincaids for protection and we would have lost the entire element of surprise. The men defied the rules I plainly set forth, to hold back, silent and unseen, and immediately inform me of any passers-through. I will punish them for it so that all the others may know the consequences."

The words were spoken with an edge of arrogance, in a manner that reflected a certain ease with the man who questioned him. He did not sound the least bit defensive, but confident that his response would be accepted. Derryth listened, her limbs heavy with dread, for they all but confirmed a planned attack against the Kincaids. And consequences—what would the consequences be for her and the others who had stumbled upon the advancing forces?

The dark-haired man chuckled, as if amused.

"Well, for whatever reason my father did place you in charge of these men," he answered cuttingly.

Father. Did he mean Buchan?

"So indeed, punish them, if that is your decision." He nodded, his expression cold, and smiling. "Yes, punish them as harshly as you deem necessary to set an example." He lifted a hand and pointed a finger at Cull . . . before pressing it against his own lips, as if a sudden thought had occurred to him. "Though we do need *every* man for the undertaking before us, so I hope your punishment will leave them alive and able-bodied, at the least. I do believe Father would wish it so."

The undertaking before us. Derryth's heart beat as fast as a frightened bird's. He meant an attack upon the castle at Inverhaven. Frantic thoughts clamored inside her mind. How to get away? How to warn them?

"Of course," Cull replied.

Another man stepped forward then, from among those who had accompanied the one in the robe. Dressed in dark trousers, boots, and a leather hauberk, his appearance was very similar to the man in the robe, as far as his dark hair and eyes and his wide yet arched nose.

"As for our unfortunate travelers, what do you propose to do with them?" he asked, without the sarcasm of the man she presumed to be his brother.

"A fair question, Robert," the robed man declared. "It's not as if we can simply set them free, now that they've seen us. They could be Kincaids for all we know, and as Cull has already said, we can't have them rounding back and warning our enemies that we are here."

Derryth closed her eyes, listening to—memorizing—every word.

"Very true, Duncan," said his brother, for yes, she was now certain they were brothers. *And sons.*

Robert . . . Duncan . . .

Buchan had many illegitimate children, with many different women. He was famed for it. But Derryth knew he had two adult sons, who in the past had done his bidding in and about the Highlands, one being named Robert . . . the other, Duncan. She had also heard that Robert Stewart had once helped Faelan Kincaid's bride, Tara, escape the Wolf's custody so that she might reunite with her husband—yet clearly he remained loyal to his father because he was here, prepared to attack the Kincaids alongside the others.

Duncan added, "These peasants are inconsequential to our cause. It is imperative to preserve the advantage of surprise."

Inconsequential. The word sent a chill through her bones, because she knew that the unspoken alternative to keeping them would be to kill them.

"And we shall," Cull replied in a low, even tone. "They will remain in our camp, watched at all times, until our forces are in place and the attack moves forward."

"What . . . as our guests?" Duncan replied with a sarcastic laugh. "Eating our food, and drinking our ale, when we have none to spare?"

He all but argued for their deaths. Had she and the others just escaped murder at the hand of savages, only to be executed by men of higher power?

Cull answered. "They'll earn their keep, until we release them. The men are strong and capable. There is timber to be cut and transported for battle fortifications. One of the bakers was lost to illness last night. The older woman can take her place."

"And what of this one?" said Duncan, drawing nearer, his lip curling into a leer. He lifted a hand to her hair as if to lift it from her face, but as if thinking twice, drew the hand away. "This peasant's whelp? You've denied the men her company, only to keep her for yourself. How will *she* earn her keep?"

She knew what he insinuated, and inwardly she recoiled in equal parts fury and fear. Despite the cutting rebuke that hurtled up from her soul, Derryth kept her gaze lowered and her teeth clenched tight. Surrounded as she was by these dangerous, snapping wolves, she knew if she did one thing to draw their ire, they would tear her to shreds.

"What does it matter to you?" Cull replied, his voice low and sharp.

The two men stared at each other, and Derryth realized then that they did not like each other.

"It doesn't matter . . . not at all." Duncan laughed, but it was a mirthless sound that issued forth from his lips. "It's just that you must see something I don't. But by all means, keep her for yourself, if you must. She is yours. Your lowborn, stinking prize."

Beneath the layer of mud that painted her skin, Derryth's cheeks burned. The men all around chuckled. The man who held her did not.

Duncan stepped back, lifting the edge of his robe. His boots sloshed in the mud. "Go on about your duties then, as those in the service of higher powers must do. As for me, being born to that higher power . . . I'm going back to bed." He turned, and the hem of his robe swung heavily around his boots. Robert and Duncan moved away toward the furthest edge of the encampment, while Cull carried her toward the center of camp.

Derryth looked over his shoulder, growing more frantic with each step that separated her from her companions.

"Let me down," she insisted, her voice thick. "I can walk."

Abruptly, he complied. The moment her feet touched the ground, she spun round to return to the others—desperate not to be alone with him, and fearful she would never see Deargh or Fiona alive again.

But he seized her from behind and half slung her over his shoulder, with no more effort than a child would hold a doll.

"No! Please. Take me back!" she choked, fighting against him, pounding her fist to his shoulder as he carried her past one tent . . . two, his pace never faltering. All around, soldiers watched and laughed, as if her torment amused them.

Suddenly, he released her legs, and she kicked at him, only to find herself set free, and spinning into shadows. She stumbled across a darkly patterned carpet, only to come face-to-face with a terrifying figure—

Nay, 'twas not a man! But a full set of armor, gleaming on its wooden stand, and beside it, a brazier wavering orange and gold with the light from a small fire.

She backed away from it—and from the warrior still

standing in the tent opening behind her, now bare of foot, as he'd left his boots on the threshold. She peered at him warily, and he looked back at her, his face inscrutable for the shadows concealing it.

What would it mean to be this warrior's prize? She did not want to find out.

"Please. Release me—" she whispered earnestly, clenching her hands together, praying that there was some goodness in him, that he would show her and the others mercy. "Me *and* my kinsmen. I beg you! Let us all just go on our way, and ye'll never see us again—"

"*Quiet.*" One word commanded her to silence. He moved toward her.

Here, inside the close confines of the tent walls, he seemed even larger and more threatening than before. The light from the brazier cast the lines of his face into relief, making him appear more dragon than man, and his body—muscular, hard, lean—that of some ancient warrior god. A young warrior god. Seeing him like this, face-to-face, she realized he was younger than she'd first believed. The sight of him closing in on her dizzied her, and filled her with terror, for what did he intend?

"Careful!" he barked, looking to her feet.

She looked too, and only then saw the pallet, dressed with linens and furs, onto which she almost stepped in her retreat. Frantic, she scampered back and around, placing the pallet between them, retreating into the shadows. Her heart thumped with dread. She realized the danger of being alone with him. No matter how much she fought or resisted, she would not escape him.

But she would try! She would die before letting him take her.

He glared at her coldly.

"You needn't fear *that*, peasant. I have far finer taste than the likes of you."

Heat rose into her face. *Peasant!* Aye, she was glad he believed it, but . . . the words stung, nonetheless. The way he looked at her now, with such blatant disgust, she might as well be a toothless hag. At that very moment, a great clod of mud chose to fall from the front of her tunic, as if to confirm her pathetic state.

He rolled his eyes and let out an annoyed growl.

"Stop moving," he commanded, his nostrils flaring. "You're spreading your filth everywhere!"

Her cheeks burned with the sting of humiliation. She had never been "filthy" before, or looked upon with such derision.

"I'm not moving," she retorted. "I'm just standing here, breathing."

"Then stop breathing!" he shouted.

She winced. No one had ever shouted at her thusly before! As if she were undeserving of care and respect. Not even Elspeth, when they argued. Her face flamed hotter, which made her skin itch beneath its mask of mud. She wanted nothing more than to bathe, and to put on clean, soft, *warm* garments—and for him to stop looking at her as if she was a squirming, filthy worm.

But . . . how stupid she was. How childish a reaction! Her vanity and desire for comfort could have no place here in the *now*, not when her life could be snuffed out at any moment. Not when her Kincaid protectors and friends had fought and bled to try to save her.

Rage replaced fear, and she blurted, "If I offend y' so greatly, then stop looking at me."

She glared back at him, shivering as the coldness from her sodden garments seeped into her bones. More words crowded her mouth, but she bit down her teeth, holding them inside. She had no wish to reveal herself to be anything but the peasant he believed her to be, and mayhap her speech would give her away. She needed time to calm herself. To exert control over her thoughts and actions. To decide what she must do.

"That I will," he muttered.

Seizing up one of the blankets from the pallet, he tossed it against the center of her chest. "That is *your* blanket. Everything else in this room is mine. If I see that you've touched anything . . . anything at all, I will cut off your hands. Do you understand?"

She did not answer. She did not nod her head. Perhaps she could not fight him or escape, but she'd not *agree* with a single thing that he said.

His nostrils flared. "Ye'll be safe in this camp as long as y' remain in this tent. Your companions will *all* be safe, as long as they do as I say. If you can all do that, for just a few days, you will live and you will go free. Defy these orders, and I will not protect you again."

She clutched the blanket against her chest like a shield.

"Now sit and be still," he growled. "Do not move or make a sound or touch *one single thing* until I return."

Stepping back, he turned and moved toward his armor, where a wooden chest also sat on a stand, which, with a muttered curse, he opened. Her gaze settled on his bare back, and the muscles that bunched along his shoulders and striated his side . . . and scars? Aye, old ones, which had faded. She watched in silence as he angrily wrenched a tunic over his powerful shoulders, and pulled on another pair of boots, tying the straps at his calves. Scowling, he fastened a sword at his hip.

Taking up a leather hauberk, which he yanked onto his arms, he was gone.

Derryth stood frozen in place for a long moment, then dropped the blanket and ran to the opening of the tent, which she pushed open and peered outside, seeking a clear path back to Deargh and Fiona and the others. Instead, her gaze struck straight into Cull's blue eyes, where he stood just a stone's throw away, as he fastened the hauberk.

"Go ahead, little one," he said quietly, his eyes gleaming dangerously. The corner of his lip twitched into a smile. "Try me. Or should I say, try *them*?"

He cocked his head back.

Behind him . . . to his side . . . in the distance . . . all around him were soldiers. Sharpening blades. Cutting arrow shafts. Sewing their leathers. But most had stopped what they were doing, and stared now at her like hungry wolves.

She stepped back, and flung the flap back into place.

Chapter 3

Cull walked the line of stone-faced men. "And so, consider yourselves fortunate to be henceforth known as the masters of the latrines, rather than receiving lashes—or death—for defying me, your commander." He turned, and walked in the opposite direction, over earth and stone that would be brutal to dig. "Each time the camp moves, you will dig two pits—the locations to be chosen by my captain, who stands with me now. Memorize his face, for he is your commander in my stead. You will dig wide, and you will dig deep."

He turned and scrutinized their faces, looking for any sign of rebellion. Any hint of dissent. It was not his first command, but his largest, given the hoard of grizzled Highlanders whom Buchan had paid to bolster their numbers.

"If there is any confusion about what I mean by deep, then you will refer to the guide post there." A jerk of his chin directed their attention to his captain, who held a rod, some three feet taller than Cull's own head. The men's faces paled. Several groaned. "Good. You understand the task before you. You will dig quickly, through earth and stone, and through the night to ensure the latrines are ready for the use of your fellow warriors the first morning after our encampment. Because you are new to this very important responsibility, today you must dig faster and harder, so they will be complete by noonday."

"Noonday!" a man's voice exclaimed softly.

Cull's intentions did not waver. He felt no pity for these men. He had seen them at their worst, and knew them for what they were.

"Know this. . . . you will receive *no . . . further . . . warnings*. The next man to disobey my orders will be flogged . . . by me." He peered directly into their eyes as he passed again. "If you wish to serve in the king's army, as you've sworn an oath to do, then you will conduct yourselves as king's men. With honor. With discipline. You follow orders. My orders. Not your own impulsive, base desires. If you can do this, you will be rewarded. Perhaps not with wealth, but with the respect you will earn, as well as the appreciation of your king—and your commander."

He stepped back, looking at them—meeting their gazes, one by one. He crossed his arms over his chest. "D'ye ken?"

"Aye," the men answered as one.

He saw understanding in some faces—the realization they'd been given another chance to seek a different life, as well as his forgiveness. Others . . .

not. Indeed, he could almost predict the ones would suffer lashes in the coming days, which gave him no pleasure, and certainly no satisfaction, but he would not abide criminals in his ranks—especially those who would victimize innocents. Those were the worst crimes of all. Perhaps God could forgive such sins, but he would not.

"Very well," he said. "Because the day after tomorrow we move camp again, and again you will dig."

"Aye, sir," they shouted, many nodding.

His captain moved forward. "Each man, take yer spade and follow me."

Turning to another of his captains who waited behind them, arms crossed over his chest, Cull spoke again. "Take me to the travelers."

Graham, his second-in-command, nodded. "Aye, sir. This way."

Graham led him to a copse of trees, where underneath, the men he'd seen that morning, along with the old woman, waited, their clothes splattered with mud and their faces drawn. They sat or crouched, surrounded by their meager belongings, but one man paced, his gaze searching the encampment—before focusing on Cull as he approached.

Cull had noticed the man earlier. 'Twas difficult not to, as the entire surface of his skin was covered with tattoos, a startling collection of complex swirls and images. Beyond that, he was a powerful bull of a man with a thick, muscular neck and arms to match. Older than the others, he carried the air of a leader. Behind him, as the rest of the party became aware of Cull's arrival, they stood as well.

"My girl—" cried the old woman, her hands clasped together, looking as if she would fall to pieces if not given some assurance.

Seeing her fear, Cull's heart faltered—as much as his heart was capable of faltering.

"Is safe," he replied, lifting a hand. He took no pleasure in inflicting fear or pain on innocents. Indeed, he wished these innocents had not traveled into the face of the army gathered here. He looked at the tattooed man. "What is your name?"

Storms clouded the man's eyes, and he answered through clenched teeth. "Deargh."

"Deargh, tell me, what clan do you and your kinsmen claim?" He stared hard into the man's eyes—but the man did not look away. Indeed, his eyes challenged Cull.

Cull was younger than most of the King's Guards beside whom he served, and a good many of his warriors. He had learned to command respect from those who might be reluctant to give it.

He held the man's gaze. "I suggest you don't look at me like that, old man, unless you wish for me to treat you as an enemy, rather than a temporary guest in my camp."

"This is not how you treat guests," Deargh growled, his hands curling into fists at his side.

"I could show you how I treat my enemies, if you like," he replied, with a tilt of his head. "Then you can decide which you like best."

Deargh's lips pressed into a fine line, and his nostrils flared. He blinked, then lowered his gaze—a response that gave Cull immediate satisfaction, for he had no wish to be in conflict with this man. "We are . . . MacClellans, traveling to join our Drummond kin, to work the spring fields."

Several others nodded. Others tensed, as if waiting to see if the explanation would be accepted. But Cull had noted the man's pause in speaking the name of his clan, as if the answer did not come naturally.

"Or ye could be Kincaids," said Cull, with a lift of his shoulder. He shifted his gaze toward the camp.

It mattered not to him. It would not change his decision on how to proceed.

"Nay . . . *sir*," answered Deargh, with a curl of his lip, as if speaking the word "sir" went against his nature. "We were trying our best to avoid them, when we came upon your men." He gestured with his big, scarred hands. "We've no quarrel with either side, so if y'd just return our lass to us, and let us go, we'll not trooble y' further."

The urgency in the man's eyes flared when he spoke about the lass.

The lass. The filthy, wild creature that presently occupied his tent. Perhaps she was this man's daughter, or even his granddaughter. Cull did not want to know. He had learned long ago not to ask questions, for if he had to kill any of them later, it would only be more difficult and weigh more heavily on his conscience. He was a King's Guard, sworn to serve the Scottish king and those whom the monarch and the estates placed in command—not to ask questions. But there was no reason that he and this man could not be honest with each other.

Cull peered directly into the man's eyes. "I cannot allow you to continue on your way. Not yet."

"But sir—"

"Ye say ye are MacClellans, but I don't know who ye are, or where your loyalties lie. Because of this, I must keep you close for a while longer." They stared at him, hard-eyed and tense, yet without any true surprise, as if they'd known they wouldn't be released. "Ye'll serve me, and this army for a sennight perhaps, mayhap even less, and then ye'll go free, to continue on your journey if that is what you wish—or take up arms against us, in which case ye will die. Understand, 'tis no punishment that you must remain here, simply a necessary consequence. But you must earn your keep while you are here. Men, you will cut timber, and transport it to our next encampment. Mistress, do you bake?"

The woman looked at the tattooed man, and he nodded.

"Aye," she answered earnestly. "As does the lass. She would be a great help to me. To anyone."

"Nay, mistress, after what occurred this morning, the girl would only cause distraction and strife in my camp, and I fear, she would soon enough find herself in danger. She will keep my quarters in order, tend my fire and mend my garments, or whatever else my manservant can find for her to do." The pain reflected in the old woman's eyes struck him hard, in his chest. "Ye have no cause to fear for her person, nor her innocence. You must trust me in this, aye?" He met the woman's gaze squarely, before shifting to Deargh. "And you, old man. Yes? You have my word she will not be harmed or misused."

A young man who stood behind Deargh pushed closer. Dried blood darkened his nose. "What ye are saying is that she wilnae be misused as long as we obey you," he growled, his dark eyes flashing with hate. "That if we follow yer orders, and don't try tae escape, she wilnae be harmed, and we wilnae be killed. She's yer hostage and we're yer prisoners. We don't believe anything you say."

"Quiet, Nathan," Deargh muttered.

But Cull stared into the young man's eyes. "Believe whatever you wish."

He had no time for arguing with strangers over something that could not be changed. With a nod to the woman, and to Deargh, he turned and strode away.

To Graham, he said, "Bring them water, with which to wash, and allow them the same morning rations as the men. Then put them to work cutting timber. The woman will assist the baker."

"Aye, sir." Graham tilted his head in acquiescence, and turned on the heel of his boot to stride toward the temporary captives.

Robert appeared on horseback then, drawing Cull's destrier, with several other King's Guards following on their mounts. As they drew near, Cull swung into his saddle. Riding away from camp, they rode some two hours north, taking careful note of distance, the difficulty of the terrain, and landmarks. Once there, one step nearer to the Kincaid stronghold at Inverhaven, they scouted a location for their next encampment.

Specifically, they sought a position visually sheltered but also uninhabited, so that no warning of the army's approach would reach the Laird Kincaid's ears. They also wished to be close enough to Inverhaven that they might successfully launch a surprise assault on the castle. And yet there must be enough ground for all his men and livestock, as well as the almost equal force that would join them tomorrow. Men commanded by Buchan.

"These Highlands are beautiful, are they not?" Robert asked, as they paused atop a high hillock to look over the sweeping landscape. The other King's Guards had dismounted, and grazed their mounts nearby.

"Beautiful" seemed an insufficient description. As his eyes swept over the expansive landscape, Cull's chest tightened and his blood seemed to flow more quickly through his veins.

"If only we were not here to war," he replied.

Perhaps it was the high, magnificent sky, painted in the most vivid shades of blue and purple that he'd ever seen, that awakened a restlessness in his blood. And the endless expanses of rolling earth and stone, spreadiung out in all directions, as far as the eye could see, like a personal invitation from God.

There was something about this place that awakened his spirit. It made him want to ride, until he no longer felt the constraints of his life, with all its expectations. Something that made him wish to be free.

Free. The thought reverberated in his mind, unexpected . . . and more assertively than he liked.

For was he not already free? Certainly, he was no longer a slave, mired in fear and darkness. Aye, he was free, but there was duty, which bound him almost as strongly.

Here, in his saddle and flanked by these men, he could not forget that duty, to which he'd been sworn since he was a boy. A duty to Scotland—and, yes, to the man who had purchased his freedom, and who had asked little of him in all these years after delivering him to a gray, nameless fortification near Holyrood, where in the company of other young men, he had been immersed into a culture of discipline and warfare. It was there he'd learned to live, eat, breathe and *fight* for Scotland.

"Why was I brought here, Robert? Certainly there are other men who know this wild place, and these clans better, who would be better suited for fighting them."

Robert glanced at him, and smiled. "To be honest, I was surprised Father summoned you here as well, away from the border with England. Your authority is respected there, by both the Scots and English, and undeniably valuable. But he persuaded the king that it must be you." He exhaled, and his smile broadened. "It's because you are the best, Cull. Take pride in that. But watch Duncan, for he is envious of my father's admiration for you."

Aye, it had always been so with Duncan. Cull had trained for years, and soldiered for almost as many, before being named a King's Guard. It was at that time that Buchan again appeared in his life, introducing him to his sons. Robert had accepted him warmly, as a friend, whereas Duncan had always considered him with suspicion. But he would not speak ill of Duncan to Robert. They were brothers—a sacred bond, in the mind of one who had none. He would never seek to be a point of controversy between them. He diverted the conversation elsewhere.

"What have the Kincaids done to draw the ire of the Crown?"

Robert looked away again, to the north. "The conflict goes many years into the past, to a time before my grandfather was king. You know as well as I that many of the king's conflicts . . . my father and uncles' conflicts, are the result of personal and sometimes petty grievances."

"Which then become conflicts over land, and sovereignty," Cull murmured.

"Aye, Cull. You know the way of things. For men like you and me, destined to serve those more powerful, it's best not to ask too many questions." The smile fell from Robert's lips. "For we may find ourselves disappointed in the men we serve, and our consciences in conflict. You know as well as I do the best warriors do not question. They declare their loyalty to this power or that, and they follow orders, and for that, they are rewarded."

"Aye," answered Cull.

Unquestioning service to the Crown. It had been his salvation . . . his key to a life he'd only ever dreamt of as a boy, in the dark hold of that ship. He could not be anything less than grateful for the opportunities he'd been given, no matter how deeply stained in blood they might be.

He looked to the sky. "We'd best finish our task here, if we hope to return to camp before dark."

After a time, a suitable location was agreed upon. It was evening when he returned to the encampment.

"You'll sup with Duncan and me tonight?" Robert asked him, before blinking, and looking to the other guards. "All of you as well, of course."

"I would not miss it," Cull replied. "I hear Duncan employs a cook who rivals his father's, and has brought him to camp."

"Indeed he does." Robert grinned. "So let us take advantage of my brother's need to boast and impress, and enjoy a fine meal at his expense before we are mired in a siege!"

Cull lifted a gloved hand. "Until then."

Robert rode toward his tent at the edge of the encampment, and Cull continued into the center of all activity, toward his. Effric, his elderly, hunch-backed manservant, stood from where he perched beside a fire, wearing a heavy woolen tunic and a black snood, and came to take the reins when he dismounted.

"Welcome home, Sir Cull."

His "home," more often than not, had been a tent in some encampment, although on the border, he sometimes accepted invitations to reside in the castles of landed nobles, the expectation being that he would ensure their lands and hearth remained protected. There, he had seen lords and their families and vassals, and servants and peasants, banded together by something stronger than duty. By respect, honor, love.

It was in these places, where his dream had been born. He hoped one day for a land and hearth of his own. That, and a family . . . a wife and children . . . and a name.

Sometimes he wondered if he'd sell his soul to have them . . . or if perhaps he already had.

Pensive, Cull strode toward his tent, pulling his gloves from his hand.

"Sir Cull," Effric called after him.

"Aye?" He turned, looking over his shoulder.

Effric tied the horse to a long stake. "I gave the bairn something to eat. I hope 'at's all right wi' ye."

The bairn. Cull's shoulders tightened, and his mood soured. He'd momentarily forgotten her existence. He glowered at the flap of the tent, which remained closed against him.

"What has she been doing in there?" he asked darkly.

Had she caused any trouble?

"It's a *she*, then?" Effric's face bunched up.

"So I've been told," Cull replied dryly.

"I wasn't certain, with all the mud." He raised a wrinkled hand to his own face.

Indeed, he himself had taken the peasants' word that she—his temporary captive—was a girl, though earlier he had discerned nothing that would confirm her gender. Not even her voice, which had been thick with tears, and her words, nearly indiscernible.

In his mind, he imagined a waif of about twelve or thirteen, which some men considered a woman, but most certainly not he.

However, truth be told, he didn't know what was under all that dirt.

Cull scowled, thinking of *all that dirt*, drying on and likely littering his Persian carpet, for which he had paid handsomely to celebrate the day last year when he'd been knighted. "I suppose something must be done about that."

Effric shrugged. "She hasn't made a sound that I've heard. When I went in earlier, with the food, she was just sitting. Didn't look at me or move. Didn't speak a word. Should I bring warm water?"

He recalled the layers of garments on her. The wild, tangled thicket of hair atop her head.

"Nay," he answered, his lip curling with distaste. "She requires the bathhouse."

Effric nodded, his lips thinning into a fine line. "Aye, sir. I will take her there, then."

But Effric was old. A strong and willful child could easily overwhelm or outrun him.

"Nay, Effric," Cull said, in resignation. "I shall see it done."

Again, he proceeded toward his tent, a frown firmly etched on his lips. Effric followed close behind.

Aye, he wished to protect an innocent from harm . . . to provide the child with the protection and care he had not received as a boy—but it annoyed him to be deprived of his customary privacy. He was among men all day, forced at every moment to be a leader, his every word and action on display. At night, he preferred to be alone.

He could not return her to her kinsmen because once they had her they would no doubt attempt to flee, which would place him in the unpleasant position of having to capture them, and exact some sort of punishment or consequence. Curse his own momentary failing, he'd looked into the eyes of that old woman and that tattooed warrior and he liked them far more than he ought.

Absent giving her back to her kin, there was no one else in the camp whom he trusted to be the child's guardian. Aye, there were women. Camp followers and workers who existed, always, at the edge of camp, some of them wives, but most of them nothing more than prostitutes or beggars. He would not see an innocent young girl exposed to the depravities that occurred there at night, when soldiers sought out their pleasures.

Just before entering the tent, Effric knelt to pull off Cull's muddied boots, after which Cull thrust his feet into clean leather shoes that waited on a thick mat of reeds. Effric carried away his boots for cleaning. He paused a moment before pushing back the flap, bracing himself for whatever he might confront upon entering. He'd learned to expect the unexpected, which in this instance might be an attack by a shrieking banshee, wielding his own dagger. Or perhaps she'd torn his garments to shreds.

But inside, he found everything exactly as he'd left it, every weapon in its place, and the girl curled up on her side under the blanket he'd given her, sleeping like a dirty mongrel dog. And god, she stank like one too. The food and cup of ale Effric had left remained untouched on a small wooden trencher.

He reminded himself that her pitiful condition was not at all her fault, that she'd been a victim of his men, and for that reason, he owed her his care. It was, at the least, his knightly duty.

For a moment, his gaze settled on her face, and he

attempted to discern the line of her cheek, the shape of her mouth, but no, he could make nothing definitive out—nor should he wish to, he reminded himself. She must remain a blur at the edge of his consciousness. An indistinct presence, as all women and children must remain, as they were not the domain of a warrior in the field of conflict.

"Wake up little one." He toed her with his boot. She jerked up to sit, looking dazed—and instantly fearful. "You must come with me."

Chapter 4

He was handsome. The man, standing above her. A warrior, strong and beautiful, like something out of a fantasy, his blond hair shining with ethereal brightness in the light of the fire, framed about an angular face and jaw.

He nudged her again with the toe of his boot. "Up with you."

Then she remembered . . .

He wasn't handsome at all. Why had she thought it for a moment? He was a beast. The same beast who had confined her here, against her will, while the others . . .

Her heartbeat surged, rising on a sudden stab of anger and anxiety.

What had happened to the others? Were they even alive?

"My kinsmen . . ." she said, her voice thick and

unrecognizable even to her own ears, but when at last she'd been left alone, she'd cried so very hard.

"Alive and well," he replied, stepping back, looking bored and uninterested. As if she was an unpleasant duty to be dealt with. "But you must listen now, and come with me."

Derryth rubbed her face, seeking to calm the sudden, abominable itchiness of her skin, but her hands met the dried crust of filth on her face. Ugh, and she stank like a pigsty.

She glared at her captor, as she struggled to rein in her emotions and the torrent of words that filled her head, which she desired to unleash upon him for the outrage of her present condition. Never before had she been treated so poorly.

But he believed her to be a peasant, and she wished that to continue for now, until she knew better what to do. She would not have herself and the others used against Niall and Elspeth, as hostages or bait. For now, she must survive, and not needlessly inspire his anger or his violence by railing against him or making demands. Against her nature, she must be obedient.

Slowly, she stood. Her woolen kirtle unfolded to her ankles, half dry, but still damp and heavy and caked with muck.

"Are you taking me back to them?" she asked. "To the others?"

But he was already turned away from her. With a sweep of his muscular arm, he threw back the flap of the tent, and bent to pass through. She glimpsed the old man who'd brought her food. He hurried to bind the flap back, so it would remain open, and in the next moment, placed a pair of shining leather boots on the threshold. From outside, she heard voices. Heard the slosh and suck of countless feet striking into mud as soldiers moved about. Nearby, a hammer struck against a spike or some other piece of wood.

Thud. Thud. Thud.

Moving into the dim, gray daylight, she found Cull waiting for her beside a horse. He did not look at her, but directed his gaze off across the camp, as if judging . . . assessing everything. Beyond him, men were everywhere, some standing about fire pits warming their hands. Others emerged from tents. She stiffened, feeling a hundred interested eyes fix on her. Suddenly, she longed to retreat into the dim shelter of her prison again. But she must be braver than that. She must go with him, as he commanded, and keep her eyes open, with the expectation that she would successfully escape and make a swift return to Inverhaven. She must gather any knowledge that might be useful to the Kincaids, and note the location of any unattended horses that she and the others might use to flee.

"Come now," he said, his words clipped. "I have only so much patience, and you're testing it with each moment you delay."

She bristled at his tone. *She* tested *his* patience? Nay, his tone pricked her patience, as did his coldly issued orders and arrogant scowls. Derryth's hands curled into fists, and she counseled herself again to hold silent. To feign docility. Remaining invisible to this man was the only way she would be able to take in her surroundings, observe the weaknesses of her captors, and make a careful plan for escape.

She could not help but notice the destrier that stood proudly behind Cull. Enormous, black, and shining like glass, she'd never seen any animal so fine.

He climbed into the saddle, and extended a hand to her. "Up with you."

For a moment their eyes met, but again, he looked away. She took his hand, which she could not help but notice was strong, long-fingered, and fine, and allowed him to hoist her up, before him, into the saddle.

She flinched, as his arm came around her, too close for comfort. She bit down a gasp at the crush of his chest, hard and unyielding against her back . . . and the too-intimate flex of his thigh beneath her bottom. With a toss of its dark forelock, the animal started forward.

She'd ridden horses before, but riding with Cull, on top of his destrier, was a different experience. Everyone stepped aside, scrambled even, to make way for them . . . for *him*. She felt so high up off the ground, that she could have been perched on a treetop. From that vantage point she looked out over the camp, and counted some fifty tents, and what had to be at least two hundred men. Two hundred . . . it was a high number, but the Kincaids could fight them and win. A surge of pride rose up within her.

All too soon they rode free of the camp, and into a thicket of trees, and with each step her fear increased. Where was he taking her and for what purpose? Then she heard the ripple and splash of a river, and she could only assume he wanted her to bathe. Her heartbeat increased, and her cheeks burned. With him sitting atop his horse, watching? The idea filled her with dread.

Cull tugged the horse's reins, and they delved down

an embankment. The sound of water grew louder, and she saw a mud-colored, circular tent set upon the banks. In the distance, nearly obscured by the same trees, she saw men on horseback, and others standing, armed with spears. Guards protecting the furthest edges of the encampment.

At the riverside, two broad shouldered, middle-aged women scrubbed linens against stones, but paused in their work to eye them with interest. One stood and approached. Behind her, three large cauldrons steamed over fires and wooden buckets were stacked all around. Planks were laid to and fro across the earth, to make a path across the stones and mud.

"Go with her," Cull said, and urged her off his horse.

The woman reached up, helping her down, and kept hold of her arm afterward, making it clear she would not be allowed to wander away.

"Why?" she asked, looking back at him. "Am I to wash linens too?"

She prayed so. She prayed he would leave her here with these hard-faced women. She would wait until they weren't watching and she would run, and evade the guards and never see Cull again, until he lay dead and defeated by her brother-in-law's sword. A stab went through her heart at the thought, but she did not question why.

"Nay, little one," he replied with a mirthless chuckle. "You're going to have a bath, and clean garments."

The other woman drew back the panel of the tent. Inside she saw a large wooden tub, a stool, and folded linens all about.

"I don't want a bath," she retorted.

It was a lie. She wanted nothing more than a bath, but not like this. Not with him standing here, and those strange women assisting her.

"There's no refusing," he climbed down, dwarfing her and the woman. "Consider yourself fortunate that I feel inclined to share my bath with you at all."

Derryth's pulse surged high.

"I will *not* bathe with you!" she choked out, horrified.

His eyes flared with annoyance. "You misunderstand. I don't wish to bathe with you either, *peasant*." He spoke through clenched teeth. "I simply meant that I am sharing a luxury that a fortunate few here in this camp may enjoy." He raised his hand toward the structure and gestured with impatience. "So please go, and be done with it."

That was different. If he would not join her . . .

She turned, yanking her arm free of the woman's grip. Both wash maids followed her, but she turned and pulled the flap down against them before they could step inside. She backed away, over wooden planks that moved beneath her feet. And yet in the next moment one passed through, and then the other, their expressions amused and determined.

"Behave yerself, child." Roughly, one divested her of her sodden kirtle, yanking it over her head, which left her in just her *léine*, hose, and shoes. The other shuttled in buckets of steaming water, which swung and sloshed from a bar lain across her shoulders. Her companion paused in undressing Derryth, to dump the water into the tub. When the tub was filled, and the tent thick with warm steam, they both turned to her again, reaching, but she'd had enough of their handling.

"I will tend to myself." She pushed the flats of her hands against their shoulders, directing them to the door. "Leave me."

Thankfully, they did as she commanded, snickering and shrugging and pushing through the canvas, leaving her alone.

"'Er ladyship wants nane o' our help," she heard one declare, her words thick with sarcasm.

Heavy bootfalls approached, crunching against the earth, coming nearer. Derryth drew in her breath, fearful that he would burst inside and force her into the water himself—

But he did not.

"You there, peasant," he said in a low, yet commanding voice. "Are you listening? Do not tarry overlong. I do not have all day to tend to you."

She imagined his blue eyes flashing with annoyance.

"I will *hurry* as best I can," she answered, as subserviently as she could manage, so that he would not recognize the rebellion she intended.

Aye, she'd be done with this bath faster than he knew. Heart pounding, she crossed through the thick steam to the back of the tent. If she were to escape, she did not have long.

Soon enough, he would discover her gone, and follow. But if she disappeared into the forest, and took an erratic path away from the river and the guards, she prayed he would not find her quickly enough to intercept her. This moment might be her only chance of ever escaping, and making her way back to Inverhaven to warn the Kincaids of the impending attack, and she must take it, without overthinking every detail . . . or of the consequences of failure.

Escape was likely the most foolish and dangerous thing she had ever considered doing—given the distance, and that she had no mount to carry her—but she had to try. She could not simply remain here helpless, doing nothing. Elspeth, and the rest of them, meant more to her than any fear she might experience, or any hardship she might suffer. Oh, she wasted time just thinking now . . . pondering everything.

She had to *move*. They'd taken her kirtle, and outside the tent the air would be cold. She plucked a large swath of linen from a nearby stand. After doubling it, she wrapped it around her shoulders. She threw one last, longing glance at the steaming bath, for her skin still itched from the dried mud caked there. 'Twould be paradise to indulge, but no. She must go and go now.

Kneeling, she lifted the thick wall of the tent and slipped under. Cold water and mud soaked her legs, chilling her skin. She winced, as stones jabbed into her knees. She scrambled up. Standing in the wane, gray light, she assessed her best path of escape, and deemed it to be away from the river, into the forest just behind, where the trees were the thickest. She let out a small, anxious moan, seeing little other choice. Unless he was a complete dullard, which she knew he was not, he would easily discern her path of escape and know exactly where to pursue her.

Still, she hurried in that direction, racing over the uneven ground, her terror rising with each step, doing her best to make no sound.

The more distance she could put between them, and quickly, the better. The moment she stepped into the protection of the trees, she veered southward, breathless from fear, toward the camp, thinking to continue on for a short while before cutting northward toward Inverhaven—

Only to be *yanked* to a sudden stop.

She let out a panicked cry, and glanced over her shoulder to see him, huge and terrifying, behind her, lunging—his hand gripping her makeshift cloak.

Ducking, she frantically pushed at the cloth and slipped free. She ran a few feet more before the full weight of him barreled into her—

"No!" she shouted.

She fell hard—but somehow landed sprawled on him, as if he'd turned to protect her from the punishing impact. Cold air swept up her calves and thighs, laid bare in the fall, her *léine* now bunched just below her bottom, across which one of his large hands was splayed. He gripped her arm, and though she wriggled and pushed and pulled with all her strength, desperate to be free, he held her rigidly still.

"Stop that," he growled, peering up at her with burning blue eyes, from a pillow of fallen leaves.

When she did not, he gave her a yank that made her teeth click.

She stared at him, her heart beating, the knowledge she couldn't escape him ripping through her like a storm.

"Kill me then!" she cried, feeling like a failure. Useless to those she loved.

"Kill you?" he said, sitting up . . . turning her, bringing her upright beside him. In doing so, she felt the movement of his muscles against her, his stomach and chest . . . his arms where they touched against her. His heat.

"Who said anything about killing you?" he growled, his cheeks and jaw tight with anger. "I just want ye to take a damn bath."

With another growl, he stood, dragging her up onto her feet, his hand now clenched in the back of her *léine*. The cold claimed her quickly, and sent her teeth to chattering.

"Ye're cold, are y'?" He released her, and she spun around to look back into his eyes, as her chest rose and fell with her labored breath. "Serves ye right."

He jabbed a finger at her.

"The sooner ye do as I say, the sooner ye'll be warm." He rested his hands on his hips, breathing hard, and rolled his eyes.

She said nothing. She only stared back at him.

"Why are ye fighting me on this?" he demanded, exasperated.

She wasn't fighting at the moment, as she ought to be. Instead, she was staring at him. *Handsome*. Oh, he was *indeed* handsome, with his loch-blue eyes, and the scar at the corner of his mouth that she hadn't seen before.

And he didn't seem to want to kill her.

But he was her enemy, because he intended harm those she loved. For that, she hated him. She had to.

"Just let me go," Derryth whispered, still breathing hard from their tussle—her body frozen, but strangely *burning* from the shock of sprawling across his, back there on the ground. "I'll never be anything but trouble to you."

"I don't doubt that, but nay, I won't let y' go," he gritted out. "Not yet."

"I won't tell the Kincaids—"

"That's right," he replied coldly, his eyes flashing brighter and more dangerously with each step he took toward her. "Y' *won't*. Because ye'll stay here. In my camp. Where I know exactly where y' are, until I decide to let you go. Do y' understand?"

"Aye," she whispered. "I understand."

"Then come with me." He pushed past her, striding in the direction of the river.

She turned and ran in the opposite direction.

Only to hear his curse, and the thud of his boots behind her.

The world spun as he hoisted her up from behind, and spun her midair, stomach down, tossing her headfirst over his shoulder.

"No!" she cried, kicking.

"I see y' are not to be reasoned with in any sort of rational way," he muttered.

"Aaarrggh!" she shouted, kicking—but his arms banded her legs like an iron vise.

The world passed by, upside down. Tree trunks. Gray sky. Fallen leaves. Mossy stones.

The women cackled when he stormed past them, carrying her, apparently delighted and amused by her capture and distress. He bent—and she heard the sound of canvas slapping against canvas. Steam enveloped them both.

Abruptly, he set her down.

She met his gaze, and found it shimmering with an anger so intense, she gasped from it. All she could think is that she wanted him gone. The thought of his hands on her . . . oh, she couldn't allow it!

"I'll take their help now," she squeaked.

"Nay, ye already made clear ye didn't wish it, lass." One brow slanted, and his nostrils flared. "So that leaves me. Yer choice, do y' see?"

"No, that's not what I want—" She shook her head.

He flashed a lecherous smile at her before seizing her by the shoulders, and spinning her toward the tub. Unsteadied she grabbed the edge—

Suddenly, her *léine* flew upward, over her head.

She grabbed—trying to keep it, to cover herself, but he was too fast and she, suddenly naked, save for her hose, her shoes, and the steam.

"Devil!" she exclaimed—humiliated and fearful of what he would do to her now. Hands clenched her ankles. Just as she stiffened in surprise, he wrenched her up and tipped her forward.

She splashed face-first into the tub—as she felt her shoes and hose unceremoniously tugged from her legs. Twisting, she slid through the water . . . floundering . . . splashing and sputtering to the opposite side, turning to glare at him.

But she only glimpsed his broad back, covered by a smudged tunic, and his shining hair as he passed through the tent opening. In came the wash women, chuckling gleefully over her humiliation.

Both took up rough bars of soap. Approaching, one grabbed an arm, the other, the length of her hair, and they began scrubbing.

Cull stood beside his horse, adjusting its saddle . . . its bridle . . . and stirrups, though there was nothing at all to adjust.

Stilling, he stared toward the trees, his teeth clenched. He closed his eyes.

Damn.

All he saw in his mind was pale skin. A slender back. A beautifully rounded bottom.

He hadn't intended to see. He hadn't looked on purpose. There'd been no curiosity in him about her. But then . . . he *had* seen her . . . naked through the steam, save for the woolen hose that darkened her slender thighs.

And now he couldn't stop seeing.

Of course, he wasn't blind, and he had not been blind before. Not completely.

He'd realized the "child" in his care wasn't a child at all when he'd chased her down in the forest. When she'd fallen on him, and her wiggling and struggling had revealed her full breasts and the womanly curve of her hips. Even so, he'd told himself she was young. Just a girl. He hadn't felt the slightest attraction, being that her features were still painted with mud. Only anger and annoyance at her attempts to escape, and the inconvenience she was proving to be. But seeing her there in the haze of steam, with her dirtied, bright golden hair, tangled and full of leaves, falling down her back . . .

He'd continued on, pitching her into the water and sending the women in to finish the job, just as if nothing had changed. As if she was the child he'd believed her to be. But something *had* changed. He exhaled through his nose, his teeth clenched.

Something felt . . . imminent.

He prayed he was wrong, but even now an attraction that hadn't existed before simmered up inside him, its delicious, teasing warmth licking at his insides . . . along with a powerful anticipation that rarely ever occurred in one whose every decision was purposefully and intentionally made. That included the seduction of women. He did not seduce recklessly, without thought, without gaining something. He most certainly did not seduce peasants, who had nothing to offer him in his quest to claim a name.

The wind moved through the trees, making a restless sound in the boughs and the fallen leaves.

There came a sound from behind him. A rustling of the canvas and soft footsteps.

He breathed out through his nose, bracing himself, and turned, opening his eyes . . .

Chapter 5

It was worse than he'd expected.

He felt deceived. Tricked. As if the world had momentarily upended.

She stood on the wooden platform outside the bath tent, staring at him, her blue eyes stormy, her damp hair gleaming like liquid gold on her shoulders.

She had the face of an angel. An ill-tempered angel. Delicate-featured, with a pretty, slender nose and frowning, rose-petal lips. His groin twisted with a sudden spasm of desire.

"I can't wear this," she announced sharply, with the impudence of a queen.

"This" being a man's long-sleeved tunic, the only thing the women had found for her to wear. The neck gaped, allowing him the sight of her throat and a smooth collarbone. The garment left her legs bare, from her knees down. A gust of wind rustled through

the trees, plastering the linen against her body—revealing the shape of her breasts, and her hips. Her thighs. She shivered, her nipples sharpening to points. Scowling, she crossed her arms over herself. A tantalizing blush stained her cheeks.

"My apologies," he said, not feeling sorry at all, and wishing the wind would blow some more, and perhaps sweep the tunic right off her body—a reaction that annoyed him, because what in the *hell* was he supposed to do with her now?

He needed no distraction. No temptations. Not when so much depended on his remaining absolutely focused in the coming days.

He stated, "It's not as if we keep a whole wardrobe of readymade garments for ladies at the ready. You'll have to wait until your clothes are cleaned and dry. Now come with me."

She glanced down at the mud. Her nostrils flared.

He strode toward her. Not because he had a chivalrous bone in his body where she was concerned but because he *needed* to touch her, to prove to himself that she was just a woman, and nothing more than that.

"No," she said, looking up—her gaze flaring, because she realized what he intended. "I don't mind the mud. I can walk."

He took her hands and placed them on his shoulders, before touching her side . . . her waist . . . and lifting her off the platform. He stared into her eyes as he pulled her against his chest, slowly bringing her legs around his waist. The muscles of his shoulders . . . his abdomen and his groin, seized tight.

He held her there, his hands on the bare, smooth bottoms of her thighs. She stiffened and her cheeks flushed dark pink, but she did not rebuke him with words. She merely stared into his eyes, as if daring him . . . expecting him to prove he was the monster she believed him to be.

Even the two wash maids watched from the tent, riveted, as if he might force himself on her there, in the mud, for anyone to see.

He would disappoint them all then. He was not, and had never been, that sort of man. His willpower, and his logic, had always been stronger than his desires.

Turning, he strode through the mud, back to his destrier. Hoisting her by the waist, he set her atop the saddle. She was a fine, delicate thing, compared to his own height and bulk, and required only the slightest exertion of his strength to maneuver about, which he tried not to ponder overmuch, but *damn his rampant thoughts, he imagined her in his bed, her naked body turning this way and that, while he—*

"You can stop looking at me like that," she ordered haughtily.

"Like what?" he replied darkly, as if she was ridiculous and vain . . . but he feared she saw straight into his mind.

"You thought I was ugly and dirty before, and now that you see that I'm not, you're looking at me like"— she swallowed, and glared at him with bright, accusing eyes—"like a—

Her voice cut off and she swallowed, her eyes bright and her cheeks burning.

"You're wrong," he lied, climbing up behind her.

She said nothing more. Because she was too innocent, or because she feared provoking him, or both? Damn, but his blood hummed in his veins, being this close to her. His attention dropped to her hair . . . and inadvertently, to the shadowed valley between her breasts, visible from his higher perspective.

He tore his gaze away. "Nothing has changed, peasant. As I told you before, I have far finer tastes than someone like you."

He did not speak the words in a cruel or taunting tone. They were not issued with an attitude of derision. Nay, the words were truth, simply spoken. Just as his every move in battle or conflict was carefully plotted, so were the decisions he made about sharing his affections and his bed.

Cull the Nameless.

He had been known by that name from the moment he had come to the king's court. In the years following, that name itself had become known. Remembered. Celebrated. He had gained favor among Scotland's most powerful, and understood that with care he could become something more.

If there was a chance he could gain property, estates, and title through marriage—a life for himself—a *name* for himself and the sons he wanted more than anything, then he would do whatever he must to take it.

She sat stiffly, with her shoulders rigid. Holding her like this, he felt the chill on her skin. Her hair was still wet and she shivered. His heels jabbed the horse's side, and he directed the animal toward the tent, where he ordered the women to fetch him a dry blanket, from those beside the fire. This he tucked around the girl for warmth, also covering her hair, because hell, if he hadn't wanted the men to see her before, he certainly didn't want them getting a look at her now.

"What is your name?" he demanded, as he turned them toward camp.

"What does it matter?" answered the mystery, now hidden beneath the blanket.

"Because I'm tired of calling you 'peasant.'"

"You seem to take pleasure in it." Her voice was like silk. How could he have been deaf to it before? How had he *ever* imagined her to be a child?

Already he prayed that he'd been momentarily dazzled by the color of her hair, and that the rest of her wasn't as lovely as he recalled. Mayhap, he thought hopefully, she had yellow, rotten teeth that he'd not observed at first glance.

"*Your name*," he repeated impatiently.

She turned to look at him then, and her blue eyes struck him through. Eyes rimmed with dark lashes.

"Derryth. My name is Derryth," she bit out.

And of course, her teeth were fine, white and straight, and she was just as damningly pretty as before. She looked away again, but even absent her hair and her face and her teeth, there was her body, settled across his thighs, and her hands, with their slender fingers wrapped round the pommel of the saddle. His scowl and his mood darkened further—and at the same moment his sex stiffened in the confines of his trousers, making a clear declaration of its interest. He shifted, doing his best to conceal the apparent.

It was a hell of his own making, he knew. It was he who had insisted she be ensconced in his quarters.

In silence, they traveled back to his tent, much the same way they'd come. The wind increased, and leaves swirled. Above them, the sky darkened. He could not deny that something felt different now. That every inch of his body felt painfully alive, and honed toward hers. Now, he felt the desire to shelter her from the ugliness of the camp. To make sure that any man they passed along the way knew that she was under his protection.

As promised, he would keep her . . . *Derryth*, and the others of her traveling party, only long enough to ensure they would not reveal the presence of his army to the Kincaids.

Until then, he would protect her, then release her and never see her again.

Cull drew the warhorse close to the tent, and with a nudge of his hand against her back, urged her off the saddle onto the carpet. Turning on bare feet, Derryth peered up at him, to see if he would join her. Behind him, the sky had darkened to clouded violet, and she knew the coming night would also bring rain.

How she wished it were summer, with its long days and no long, dark hours to pass. She could not help but wonder, with a mixture of curiosity and dread, how the night, in his quarters, would pass.

"Find some way to make yourself useful," he ordered distantly, his eyes devoid of the fire she'd glimpsed in them before. "Make my bed. Tend the fire. There are garments to be repaired. Effric can give you whatever supplies you need."

Effric, she supposed, was the bent old man stationed outside the tent beside a small fire. She peered up at Cull, clutching the blanket at her chest, for already, with the coming of night, a deeper chill claimed the air. Cull made no move to dismount from his horse, and she could only assume he intended to leave her.

She ought to be relieved by his renewed detachment. His intention to go. Certainly, she did *not* want him to stay. Certainly she did *not* wish his eyes to fix on her with heated interest, as they had beside the river.

"You command me to be your personal servant, then?" she said sullenly, before she could stop the words.

It was just that she did not like the idea of serving him! Of repairing his clothes or making his bed. Of doing anything that might improve his comfort. Indeed, she did not embrace the idea of her remaining in his quarters at all, when the others of her party would likely spend the night in much more unpleasant conditions.

"Command?" Cull replied, his voice like a blade. The destrier stamped, as if he sensed the displeasure of his rider. "Aye, yes I do command you. This is an army camp—and I am its commander. If you want to eat, then you work. If you wish to sleep, then you work. If you want my protection . . . then you work. Everyone does their part. Have you any difficulty understanding that?"

His blue eyes raked over her, and seemed to find her lacking, as if she were a spoiled child complaining of chores. It was an expression she knew well. She'd seen it in faces all her life when her mother, or her stepmother, or her stepmother after that (yes, there'd been two of them) had insisted she assist the maids in cleaning the solar or learn how to cook, so she would understand firsthand, one day when she had her own castle to oversee, the work that must be done. But it was not the chores of which she now complained, but him.

She fixed her lips into a firm line. "You'll find I'm not very skilled at any of the tasks you've given me, and will most certainly be displeased with the outcome. You should return me to the company of my kinsmen. I'm certain I could be more helpful there."

His nostrils flared in response and his eyes narrowed on her so sharply she almost took a step backward in response—but she forced herself to remain fixed to the carpet, exactly where she stood.

He uttered, "You would do well to recall that you don't make the decisions here. I do. You'll be returned to your companions in a matter of days. You are not my prisoners. You will all be released. In the meantime, just do as you are told."

"I *am* a prisoner if I have no choice but to serve you," she retorted.

"There are always choices, little one," he replied, his voice low and cutting. "If you prefer, I will give you over to another warrior . . . one of my captains, or Duncan perhaps. They would most certainly find different *tasks* for you than those I've suggested, with which to earn your keep."

The blood drained from her face, because she understood the implication of his words.

"No," she whispered, dourly. "I do not prefer that."

"Good." He straightened in the saddle. "Then we understand each other."

"I wouldn't say that," she replied beneath her breath.

He'd heard. She knew that from the way his gaze darkened on her.

He gathered the reins in his hands. "I will return late."

"And I suppose I will be here waiting," she replied—her final farewell to him a scowl.

Derryth paced the uneven yet lushly carpeted floor of the tent, back and forth, more times than she could count. Eventually, the light that crept beneath the doorway of the tent faded to darkness—as did the voices she'd heard all evening on the other side of the tent walls. She moved toward the portal, touched a hand to the canvas, pushed it aside to peek out.

She was immediately disappointed by what she saw.

Effric looked up from where he sat beside a fire, his aged face, traced with lines, illuminated by flames. He oiled a pair of boots. No doubt his master's. Several garments lay spread on wooden racks beside the fire. A tunic, a snood, and a pair of hose. Beyond him, shadows occupied the darkness. Soldiers moving about, or sitting outside their tents.

"Get ye back inside there, lass. There's nothin' out 'ere for ye." He looked at her sternly, but his demeanor was no more threatening than a kindly old grandfather's.

Still, he'd caught her looking, and her mind scrambled to supply some reasonable explanation in order to gain his trust. "I was only hoping to ask you if you might have thread and a needle, so that I might repair your master's garments, which he has *ordered* me to do as a means to earn my keep."

"Oh, aye. I've needle and thread, though they've gone unused for some time." He nodded, coming to his feet.

His gait unsteady, he went to the wagon behind him and returned with a basket, which he handed over to her. Beneath his dark snood, she saw the gleam of his silvery hair.

She glanced into the basket, and found everything she might need—threads and yarns of various thicknesses and colors, along with a folded pouch she knew would hold needles.

"Unused, why?" she asked.

His lips thinned, and stated plainly, "He's been keeping 'is mending from me, y' see, because he knows me old 'ands can't manage a needle anymore, and me poor eyes can't see the stitches or the thread."

Despite her situation, she could not help but feel sympathy for the man. When he could no longer travel and work to the degree a young and important warrior required, where would he go? Did he have family? They were questions she had no right to ask. For now, she must limit her sympathies and concerns to herself and those whom she loved.

"Thank you," she said.

He smiled back, his eyes sparkling warmly. "'Tis no trouble at all."

He seemed friendly enough. Perhaps . . . perhaps she could win him over, and persuade him to go off on some task. Once he was gone, she could briskly gather the garments drying beside the fire, and once inside the tent, dress in the snood, which would conceal her features so that she could flee.

"Have you served Sir Cull for very long?" she asked . . . giving him her most winning smile.

He looked at her a long time without answering, then lowered his head.

"I may be a doddering old man," he said. "But ye can stop right there. I know exactly what you're trying to do."

Her smile faltered. "I . . . don't know what you mean."

"Oh, aye, yes you do." His smile faded then too. "You're a pretty girl. A beauty, that's for sure. And I'm certain you've won many a swain's heart with that smile. But I know there's only one reason you're smiling at an old hunchback servant like that." He peered into her eyes, his gaze striking straight into her heart. In that moment she felt ashamed and sorry, because what he alleged was true.

He backed away, and made his way back to his stool beside the fire, where he sat and took up the boot again. "And I'll tell ye now, no matter how sweetly you smile at me, no matter how gently you talk, my loyalty is to Sir Cull. If ye step one pretty little foot off his Persian carpet, I'll know, and I'll sound the alarm."

Holding a cloth, he buffed at the toe of the boot.

"I shall remember that," she answered softly.

He nodded curtly, without looking up again. She stepped back, taking the basket with her. There, in the shadows of her captor's tent, her chest and shoulders tightened and tears welled in her eyes. Putting the basket down straightaway, she turned toward the shadows, and covered her face with her hands.

She had never felt so helpless. So alone. She wasn't going to be able to escape, especially if all it took to destroy her efforts were a few words of rebuke from a sweet old man. And if she could not escape, how would she warn those she loved of the impending attack against them?

She wanted nothing more than to speak to Deargh, and to have his counsel. To ask him what she must do. She wanted nothing more than to see Fiona's face, and to know the elderly woman was all right, and had not been mistreated. Even if they could not escape, she ached for the comfort of their presence, almost beyond bearing. They both must be equally distraught and worried for her.

She paced again, her gaze settling on his armor, proof of Cull's status among men. Of his formidable strength. His gleaming helmet, mail, and shield. Shivering against the chill, she moved toward the brazier and sank down inside the circle of its warmth. How could she, a mere *peasant*, get the commander of this army to do what she wanted him to do?

At the river, she'd glimpsed something in his eyes. *Desire?* Perhaps yes, tangled up with disdain for her, and displeasure.

The idea of touching him . . . kissing him . . .

She closed her eyes, as heat scalded her cheeks. No. She would not attempt to gain her freedom in that manner.

There had to be some other way.

Chapter 6

It was some two hours later when the flap of the tent swept aside. Startled, Derryth put down Cull's tunic, the torn sleeve of which she'd been carefully repairing, and stood. For a moment she'd thought it was Cull returning, but no, it was Effric, who carried one large, rolled bundle and another bundle that hung from a rope on his arm.

He looked at her steadily, the gentle sparkle in his eyes all but nullifying his stern expression. "Just so ye know there are no sour feelings between us, I brought ye a pallet and a bit of warm wine, and some other things. I hope 'twill will make your night pass more comfortably."

Derryth exhaled, her heart swelling in her chest. She stood, and smiled.

"Thank you, Effric. I have been sitting here alone . . . in this tent, feeling so lonely for my kinsmen, and downcast over being separated from them." They were honest words, without alternative intentions. "Your kindness means more to me than I can express."

He grinned, displaying several missing teeth, and passed the pallet into her open arms. He set the bundle near her feet. "Well there ye go then."

She crossed the room and spread the pallet on the ground in the same spot where Cull had insisted earlier that day that she sit with her blanket with the warning that she not touch anything.

Only this time, during his absence, she'd dared touched quite a bit. Her pulse jumped nervously in her veins, as her glance fell upon Cull's bed—its thick mattress, fine linens, and furs set upon a sturdy wooden frame. As the hours had passed and weariness had begun to claim her . . . she wondered if she'd made a terrible mistake.

Aye. She felt quite certain that she had.

"I'll leave ye tae yer sleep," said Effric.

With a nod, the servant returned to the door.

"Effric?" she called after him.

He turned on the threshold, his eyebrows raised. "Aye lass?"

"Should I fear your master?" she asked pensively.

His expression became grave. "Oh, aye, lass, you should indeed fear him. He is the commander here, and command he does. Do not mistake his fairmindedness for weakness. He would punish any who threaten his mission most harshly. You mustn't even think of displeasing him. Those who do, regret their mistakes most severely."

His words echoed in her ears after he was gone.

Nervously, she opened the bundle he'd left, and with the wine flask, found several soft washing cloths, a chunk of fragrant soap, and a comb, its spine carved into the figure of a long-tailed fox. There was also a small wooden box filled with a mint-and-rock-salt paste and wooden picks with which to clean her teeth. Such kind and generous luxuries!

What if Cull reprimanded Effric for not watching her closely enough? She prayed he would in no way be punished for what she'd done. Why had she not thought of that possibility before?

She uncorked the flask, and after giving it a sniff, drank deeply. The wine, which was dark red, warm and spiced with herbs, seemed to spread through her veins, dulling the chill that permeated the tunic she wore. It did nothing to calm the dread she felt, for now there was no way to correct the damage she'd done. No way to retreat from the challenge she'd set forth.

With agitated hands, she finished stitching Cull's tunic, and set it and the basket aside. Quickly, she washed with the soap Effric had brought to her, and cleaned her teeth. It would be best if she were asleep when he returned, if only to spare herself the trepidation of his response.

She'd just started to braid her hair when the sound of a horse's hooves met her ears, and she heard Effric's voice calling out in greeting to his master. Her pulse racing, she snuffed the candle and fled to her pallet, pulling her solitary blanket over her head. She shivered, the thin wool providing her with little warmth against the colder air that occupied this furthest edge of the tent, so far away from the brazier.

Cull entered. She furtively peeked out, knowing the darkness concealed her. A tall, imposing shadow in the night, he glanced in her direction, his expression inscrutable other than the unyielding line of his jaw.

Every muscle in her body drew tight. She did not move. She did not breathe.

He turned away then, and set about removing his leather hauberk . . . and his tunic beneath. Her tension only increased, for soon his wrath would turn on her. But was that not what she'd intended? Cull's hands moved near his waist and his trousers fell to the floor.

Derryth's breath caught in her throat—

She did not know what she expected, but not that he would be *naked*, so suddenly. And yet as another moment passed, it was not her fear that transfixed her, but the sight of his body in the wavering light of the brazier, the fascinating cut of the muscles of his shoulders and arms traced by shadows. The scars, which had no doubt been inflicted by a whip. His buttocks, taut and smooth, flexing above muscled thighs.

It was not that she admired him or wanted him. Nay, that would be a betrayal of all those she loved. It was just that she had lived a protected life, and while she'd seen men's bodies as they practiced at weapons and bathed in the courtyard, she had never seen one fully naked.

Cull half turned, reaching to raise the lid of his trunk.

Her breath caught in her throat—

She averted her gaze, but too late. She'd glimpsed *that* part of him—the one that defined him as a *man*—and though the moment had passed, the image of what she'd seen remained etched into her mind. Her cheeks burned and her mouth went dry, remembering his male sex, so . . . *substantial* and intriguingly formed. She felt ashamed for having observed him with such secrecy, and guilty for being more curious about him than she ought to be.

With a start, she realized he moved toward his bed, now wearing linen *braies*, noticeably tented by the same part of him she'd glimpsed just moments before. And yet the moment had come, one she'd put into motion. She closed her eyes and clenched her teeth, fearful anticipation replacing all else.

Bending, he lifted the furs and the coverlet beneath and climbed in. She burrowed further into her bed, breathless . . . dreading the explosion of anger to come.

He stretched out—and *cursed*, springing up, having discovered the ice-cold water she'd dumped from the basin, across his bed.

Blood pounded inside her head, as she waited to see what he would do next.

He stood for a long moment, his shoulders bunched, his hands clenched into fists. Then . . . taking up a pillow and a fur . . . he strode toward her.

"I know you are awake," he muttered darkly.

"I assure you I am not," she whispered.

"Move over."

"What?" She sat up, her eyes widening upon him. Panic shattered her thoughts. "*No.*"

"You've destroyed the comfort of my bed," he said, his brows gathered. "It is only right that you share yours." Scowling, he dropped the pillow and lowered himself to sit on the pallet, he a long-limbed giant beside her, flinging the fur over them both.

This close, he was too large. Too powerful. Too real. She could smell the scent of soap and spice on his skin. He was not simply an enemy to despise, but a man who had every right to be outraged with her. She could feel the blaze of heat from not only his eyes, but his body.

"I will sleep on the floor," she choked out, scrambling away.

He caught her arm.

"Lie down," he gritted through his teeth. "And go to sleep."

But the pallet was far too narrow. Their legs . . . their hips touched even now, separated only by thin cloth. She stared into his eyes.

"I can't sleep beside you," she said, her voice trembling.

Annoyance tightened his jaw.

"Then you shouldn't behave like a child." His gaze narrowed on her. "What were you thinking with such mischief?"

Words tumbled from her lips, plain and true. "I'd hoped you would be so angry with me, that you would let me go back to my kinsmen."

He breathed out through his nose, as if he heard the reasoning behind her words, and attempted to calm himself . . . yet he did not release her.

"*Look* at me, *Derryth*, and *listen* this time," he said, his hand large and unyielding on her arm. He pulled her closer. Not roughly, but slowly . . . purposefully, and he stared into her eyes. "It will not happen. I will not return you to your kin. Not tonight. Not tomorrow. But *perhaps* the next day. I cannot yet say for certain."

Freedom. He all but promised it, but could she believe him? An anxious breath left her lips.

His gaze fell to her lips. Heat rose up from her breasts, into her neck and cheeks.

He closed his eyes, and returned his gaze to hers, hard and cold, before speaking again. "*Why* must you remain here in my tent? Is it because I prefer the company of peasants? *No.* Is it because I want *you* in my bed? God, no."

She flinched, hearing the derision in his words— seeing the terse line of his lips.

"Here is the answer. So again . . . listen carefully. I only have their cooperation as long as I have you. If I return you to them, it is very possible they will attempt an escape. Why? Is it because they are Kincaids and wish to warn their kinsmen of my presence here? I don't know." He tilted his head, biting out the words. "Most likely, it is simply because they are *Highlanders*, and it seems that is what *all* Highlanders do." His gaze intensified, and his nostrils flared. "They cause trouble, one and all. They defy the orders of any Lowlander, for the simple purpose of being defiant. *They. Waste. My. Time.*"

Hearing him speak such words against Highlanders sent Derryth's temper flaring. She attempted to yank her arm free, but he held her fast.

"If they escaped, *Derryth*, then I will be forced to capture each and every one of you, and because every warrior in this camp is watching, I would be forced to punish you. Perhaps, even kill someone you love." His eyes held hers. "Is that what you want?"

"No," she replied, trembling. Hating him and his threats.

"Neither do I," he said, through his teeth. In his eyes she glimpsed something different than she expected . . . something honorable, and good.

The observation surprised her, momentarily pulling the rug of hatred out from under her.

"And neither do I wish to sleep with you," he said gruffly, releasing her arm. "But these are *my* quarters, and I prefer you and this pallet to Effric's snores and the wagon. So lay down, Highlander, and close your eyes." His voice was hard, and the words, an order. "If you cannot sleep, then at least be still and do not move, so that I may have my rest."

She had no choice. If she did not comply, she feared he would force her, by laying hands on her again, which she must not allow if at all possible. She shifted so that no part of them touched, and lay down, turning away from him, perched at the furthest edge of the narrow pallet. And yet still, she felt him beside her. His presence. His warmth along her back. She clenched her eyes shut, bracing herself for a miserable night.

Not because he frightened or repulsed her. Nay . . . to her shame, it was the opposite. She did not abhor his nearness at all.

Cull lay staring up into darkness, his teeth clenched and his muscles tense, all too aware of the young woman beside him. They did not touch now, but his heart thudded hard still, pumping hot blood through his veins. One question filled his mind.

What made her so different?

She was not the only woman ever to lay beside him, and certainly, those who'd come before her had arrived there in much more pleasurable circumstances. So why this pressure in his chest . . . why this fever in his blood?

He had been angry at finding his bed ruined, and had thought to startle her by insisting on sleeping with her, yes. To teach her a lesson so she wouldn't cross him again. It was just that as soon as he'd seen her, looking up at him from the darkness, her eyes wide, her bright hair shimmering over her shoulders, he'd wanted her, and as soon as he'd touched her . . . his hand on her arm, it hadn't seemed enough. Even now his hands ached to touch her. He struggled against the urge to pull her close, to make some excuse about the necessity of sharing their body heat even though he was already on fire, simply to see how she would feel there, in the crook of his arm, against him. God, she smelled heavenly, like nutmeg and cloves.

The power of his reaction to her startled him. Aye, he had felt a startling attraction to her that afternoon. He had been attracted to plenty of women, and this felt different. Somehow *profound*, although he chided himself for thinking it. Perhaps it was just that he was here, in this wild, beautiful place that affected him so greatly, about to engage in what might be a long and vicious siege.

Perhaps this Highland beauty represented the freedom his heart longed for, despite the rational warnings of his mind that he *must* be satisfied with a life spent in service to the king.

He reminded himself that he might achieve both, but only if he was disciplined and careful, as he had always been before. He could risk no missteps. No distractions.

Beside him, Derryth exhaled unevenly, no doubt hating him. Cursing him. Wishing for his death. Perhaps shedding tears.

Why should he care? She was nothing to him. The little peasant could never be *anything* to him, no matter how lovely or engaging she might be. Eventually, and only through the utmost care and discipline, he would marry a woman who could give him what he wanted most—land and a name. It would not matter what that woman felt like in his arms, or whether she made his heart come alive with passion and fire.

Eventually . . . after a long while, her breathing slowed, and her body went lax. She emitted the softest snore.

Amused, he let out a silent breath. Almost a chuckle. She . . . Derryth . . . *snored.* For some reason that amused him . . . and warmed his heart.

Eventually, he too dozed, but he awakened with a start, the tent still in utter darkness, to find her nestled against his side like a kitten, her cheek resting on his shoulder, her hand flat on the bare skin of his waist. He lay awake and aware, his body almost painfully alive, savoring how perfect she felt against him, so soft and sweetly feminine. How he would ever sleep again as long as she was here beside him?

And yet his eyes opened hours later to the dim light

of early morn to find her narrow back against his chest, and him wrapped around her, his bare legs aligned with hers, his arm across her waist. The rich, shining tumble of her hair lay on his shoulder, fragrant and silky soft.

Heart pounding, and his body already sleepily aroused, he lifted his head to peer down at her face, her cheeks flushed with warmth and sleep. He liked her here, in his arms, like this. He liked it too much.

He dared touch the pad of his thumb to her cheek and let out a low breath. Carefully, he removed himself, and left her sleeping beneath her fur. After quietly dressing, he made his way outside.

Derryth wakened alone, to the sounds of the camp outside the tent, and wondered whether Cull had gone to sleep outside with Effric after all. Perhaps she had snored. Her younger sister Mairi, who'd slept with her often through the years, had sometimes complained of it, and Derryth hadn't minded at all, because sometimes it got her a bed to herself. But if Cull had heard . . .

Well, then so be it. It wasn't as if she wanted him to find her attractive.

She pushed up, and touched a hand to her tousled hair, remembering the events of the night before. Her cheeks burned, remembering how he'd looked in the night, so immense and muscular, laying beside her, beneath the fur that still covered and warmed her body now.

It was a miracle that she'd fallen asleep beside him at all. But she'd been so exhausted by all that had occurred the day before, and concern for her companions weighed heavily on her mind as it still did, along with fear for everyone at Inverhaven.

Her fears had only increased with the passing of night. Though she sat utterly still on the pallet, her mind swirled, crowded with thoughts, and her heart beat heavily in her chest. Buchan's army was one day closer to striking against all she loved. She remained in a quandary over what to do to help. Should she make every attempt to escape, or was it better to remain here in the commander's tent, docile and silent, watching and listening for any bit of knowledge that would help the Kincaids?

"Good morn, lazy bee," said a voice at the door.

Effric entered with a trencher and cup, and a bundle under his arm. Derryth remained on the pallet, the fur pulled to her chin, watching him. She had never see him without his dark snood. For the first time she saw his bald pate, encircled with short-shorn silver hair, which looked very much like a dignified crown.

"I've brought something to break your fast," he said. "And your garments, clean and dry from the washer women. When yer ready, come outside to me."

"Outside?" she said, sitting up. "Oh, no. I won't be tricked." She only half teased. "You already told me what would happen if I stepped foot off this Persian carpet."

"Ye won't be followin' my orders in doing so. Ye'll be followin' Sir Cull's. Just as I will be, once ye get yourself tidied and come out 'ere."

Orders. Cull had issued orders for her?

"What kind of orders?" she asked, uncertain if she should be happy or afraid.

Effric did not reply. Instead, he threw back the furs and blankets that remained on the bed and, touching his hands to the linens, threw a scowl over his shoulder at her, and quickly gathered them up. "I hope they'll be no more such mischief from ye, lass, such as this."

He limped toward the door, and was gone.

She lay back down and pulled the fur high, feeling rebuked. Aye, she regretted dousing Cull's bed. In the light of day it seemed a foolish thing to have done, and made more work for poor Effric, but she'd been so desperate to do something to change her circumstances.

Curious about what awaited her outside, she ate the chunk of brown bread and cheese quickly and drank the ale, before dressing in the same shapeless garments she'd worn when she'd come to this place. They were still very ugly—though she would not complain, given her surroundings. Unfortunately, they were even scratchier after being washed with whatever inferior soap the women used on the soldier's garments. Taking the comb Effric had given her from her pouch, she worked the snags out of her hair before tightly braiding the long tresses into a neat crown, in what she hoped was the plainest style possible. Her garments had been returned to her in her cloak, which, she recalled with a pensive frown, had been torn from her in the attack, a reminder of the threat of danger that awaited her outside the tent. Finding the fastenings repaired, she secured the garment at her neck and pulled the hood over her hair, then passed outside. Her breath turned to vapor in the cold air.

Though she held her cloak closed at the throat and bowed her head low, already men paused in their work to stare at her. While she knew all men were certainly not evil, after yesterday she could muster very little trust for any man who walked this camp. It made her nervous to be here with only Effric to protect her, and not Cull, for what could the frail older man do to protect her, if protection became necessary?

Effric waited a few steps away with a gray palfrey, much smaller than Cull's magnificent destrier, its reins wrapped round his palm. "Up with ye."

She frowned, immediately suspicious. "Where are we going?"

"Not far. Over there—just beyond the trees."

Beyond the trees. He pointed in the opposite direction of the river and the bathhouse. She squinted, but saw nothing there that relieved her curiosity.

"Why?" she asked, her heartbeat increasing.

"I don't know, lass," he answered patiently. He blinked at her, looking very much like a wise old owl in his snood, which he'd returned to his head. "I am only a lowly servant and I wasn't told. I was just told to bring ye."

"Well why?" her voice cracked. "Am I going to be flogged for ruining Sir Cull's bed—or will I be set free? Effric, I want to know!"

Effric's eyes widened. "I would not expect anything so dramatic as that, but who am I to say?" he replied with a shrug.

She stood looking at the horse, a scowl on her face, pensive and unwilling to move. How strange that after wanting to escape Cull's tent so desperately, she wanted nothing more than to return there.

Effric lifted his hands in exasperation, and grumpily implored, "Either ye can get on the horse, or I can tell Sir Cull ye decline to comply with 'is orders. Your decision. But I'm not going to stand 'ere all day waiting."

"Very well," she exclaimed, with a toss of her head. "I'm coming."

Moving near, she grasped the saddle horn and thrust her foot into the leather stirrup. Pushing up, she swung her leg over. She adjusted her kirtle for modesty. "Take me to my doom."

Effric nodded, and bent in a courtly fashion, giving a flourish of his old hand. "'Twill be my pleasure, m'lady."

The old man trundled forth, in the direction of the trees, guiding the horse along behind him. From behind them, a man's voice shouted out a vulgar compliment to her.

Heat scalded her cheeks, and fear simmered up from inside her, a terrifying remnant of the day before. She stiffened, but did not look back, though Effric made a point to stop, and step aside to cast a darkly reproachful glance behind them. A moment later, he again led her forward. Around them, the camp went on as normally as before. Still, she did not relax.

"Effric, have I any cause to fear the soldiers?" she asked, her voice a whisper.

"The soldiers?" He scowled. "Nay, words are one thing, when our backs are turned and men are brave, but none would dare touch ye when all know ye belong to Cull the Nameless."

"I do not *belong* to Cull!" she cried, her cheeks hot at just the mere insinuation that she was his possession.

But it was the other words he'd spoken that rang in her ears, darkly ominous. *The Nameless*. It was the first time she had heard Cull referred to as such. Had he no name? It reminded her how little she knew of him. That he was all but a stranger. She had assumed from his bearing and his position of importance among the King's Guard that he was the son of a noble or powerful family. Mayhap he was a powerful lord's bastard.

"But ye are under his protection." Effric cast her a sideways glance. "At least for these few days. Unless he decides tae keep ye longer."

She scowled, but realized he was only attempting to tease her.

"In this camp 'tis not Cull's warriors ye must concern yerself with, but the Highlanders. They are fearsome fighters. Mercenaries for the king. But little more than savages!"

"Savages," she repeated sharply. "Effric, I am a Highlander, and I am no savage."

"Nay, girl," he replied softly, looking at her with what she might almost call affection. "Ye most certainly are not."

And yet she felt the need to offer those men some defense, though she would never defend the men who had attacked her yesterday morn. She did not consider them Highlanders, but criminals. A different breed from the honorable, brave men she knew. But she looked beyond that, as she felt she must.

"The Highlanders you call savages most likely have been deprived of their homes by your king, or by men he has empowered. Is that not what this army is here to do again? To lay siege against some unsuspecting clan, for daring to prick some nobleman's ire?"

She could not name the nobleman—Buchan— without revealing she knew more than she ought.

"Aye, lass. That is likely true, but who is this old man to pick one side or the other? In this life, we must all decide what path to travel, and I have chosen to follow Sir Cull. He is here, and thus, so am I."

What about Cull inspired such devotion? She found herself more intrigued by the mystery of him, as each moment passed.

"You called him 'the Nameless,'" she murmured. "Why is he called that?"

"Because he had no father, and he had no name, and when he was knighted, they had to call him something." He tilted his head toward her, and grinned. "The ladies seem to like it. The ladies seem to like everything about him."

At hearing those words, her cloak seemed to grow heavier. Her mood, sour.

"Does he boast conquests of many ladies then?" she asked, wanting to hear everything shameful about the man who held her captive, so she could dislike him more.

"Why do you ask?" he inquired, smiling, his eyes twinkling.

"Because I love to gossip, Effric," she exclaimed, eyes wide, her cheeks blushing that he insinuated that she had any interest in Cull at all, of a romantic sort—which she did not. "That is all."

"Then I would tell you, I do not gossip about Sir Cull." He winked at her, and she scowled back at him. "I would protect his every secret to my death."

Despite his very annoying personal code of honor where Cull was concerned, Derryth was glad to have Effric with her, and even more glad he seemed to enjoy talking. The flow of words helped calm her nerves over what was to come, as she still did not know where she was being taken.

But then, as they broke past the line of trees, she knew. Unfettered joy rose up inside her—an emotion she feared she'd never get to experience again. Two familiar figures waited there—Deargh, and Fiona, whose faces broke into relieved smiles at seeing her.

Chapter 7

Without thought, she leapt from the horse and ran, throwing her arms around them. They both smelled of earth and rain, and looked very weary, but they were warm and alive.

In the next moment, she recalled what Effric had said. That he only followed Cull's orders.

Cull had arranged this meeting, because she'd explained to him what she'd hoped to accomplish in ruining his bed.

Her emotions wavered, and in her mind she remembered his face the night before, and the moment when he'd told her he had no wish to harm any of them. Was it possible there was kindness behind those cold blue eyes? And an honorable heart that sought to do what was right?

"I am so happy to see you," she exclaimed, tears blurring her eyes. "Are you well?"

Effric led the palfrey some distance away, where he seated himself beneath a tree to wait.

"Aye lass," said Deargh, the tattooed patterns that covered his bald head and face stark in the clouded daylight. "Better now, seeing you."

"What of *you*, child?" Fiona cried, tears rolling over her cheeks. Her former nursemaid wore a head covering and an apron over her kirtle, all of which were heavily dusted with flour and dried bits of dough. Her hands squeezed Derryth's shoulders, and pushed her hood back from her face, as if looking for marks or bruises. "Have ye been harmed? Don't spare my old heart. Tell me the truth."

"I am well," Derryth replied, eyes wide and hiding nothing. She pressed a fervent kiss to the woman's cheek. "I have been protected, and no harm has come to me."

Just then, she spied a shadow in the distance . . . three riders on horseback, watching them. All three were warriors, but it was Cull at the center, tall and broad shouldered, sitting atop his black destrier, who commanded her attention. He wore a hauberk, leather trews, and boots. Cull held her gaze a long moment before looking away.

Even in the cold, her cheeks flushed. Indeed, everything inside her warmed, as if a fire had suddenly come to life at the center of her belly.

He remained there, a witness to their reunion—but making no move to approach. The meeting was a gift from him to her, she realized, one that implied some degree of goodwill and trust, because she, Deargh, and Fiona could be plotting escape or even harm to Cull, and from that distance, he would not overhear. Despite herself, her heart opened to him in that moment a fragment more.

"How are the others?" asked Derryth.

"All are well," Deargh growled, looking down at his calloused hands. "Working dawn until dark, cutting and stacking timber for our enemy's fortification, but we will do what we must for the time being, in order to survive—and to gain their trust."

They huddled together in the cold. She clasped his hand, and spoke in a hushed voice—afraid that the wind might carry her words to Cull's ears. "Someone must escape and warn Niall of the attack to come."

"Nay, child," he said gruffly. "To attempt an escape now, when we are watched at every moment, would be foolhardy, and most certainly lead to all our deaths. He has promised to release us, and we must bide our time until then. For now, we must keep our eyes and ears open, so that when we are released and make our return to our Kincaid brethren, we will take whatever knowledge we can, to give our side the advantage. And if ye are not in danger, lass, and merely keeping his quarters clean and neat as he says ye are, then ye are in the best position to overhear or observe something of value."

Derryth's heart sank. She wanted nothing more than to convince Cull to release her . . . but she knew Deargh was right. If she could gain some advantage for the Kincaids by remaining in Cull's quarters than she must do so.

"Does he hold meetings there in his tent, with his captains?"

"Nay," she replied. "Not yet, at least."

"Does he keep maps there?"

"Perhaps," she said. "If so, they are stored away with his things."

He touched her arm, and pulled her close, pressing a kiss to her hair. "I don't want ye to take any chances. Stay safe. Do not place yourself in danger. But learn what you can. I vow to ye, our laird will send the Wolf a message that the Kincaids are no' to be threatened without consequence and see this army and their leader—this Cull the Nameless—cold and dead in the ground."

The words struck Derryth like an unexpected blow to the chest.

Cull . . . dead? The same man who had spread a fur across them both the night before, rather than punishing her for what she had done? The same man who had told her he had no wish to harm them?

A cold chill settled in the pit of her stomach.

But it *was* true. If this march upon Inverhaven continued, someone would die, and it would not be . . . it *could not* be Niall. Her sister's husband! The father of Elspeth's unborn child. The man who had protected her as if she were his own sister, in the years since he had returned to Inverhaven.

But . . . Cull.

Why did she feel the slightest bit regretful over the prospect of his defeat? Of his death . . .

He was so cold, so distant. How could her heart have found anything at all within him for which to care?

She looked over Deargh's shoulder, to the hillside where he remained watching them. Watching *her*. Aye, she felt his eyes on her, just as real as a touch. A frisson of heat warmed her spine.

"I know you are right," she said quietly. "As you say, the Kincaids will carry the day."

But she knew very well that just saying the words did not make them true. The Kincaids had prevailed once before, but there had also been an intervention by Niall's ally, the Earl of Carrick, the Earl of Buchan's older brother, who had since been grievously injured by a horse, and as a result, been left weaker in both body and power. Who could be relied upon to intervene for the Kincaids now?

If the attack was stopped then everyone would be spared. *Including Cull.*

Deargh bared his teeth. "Do not fear, dear girl. Just be ready, for when the moment is right, we will rejoin our kinsmen behind Inverhaven's castle walls, to fight anyone who thinks to take her from us."

"What if he does not let us go?" she whispered.

Deargh muttered under his breath. "Then I've another plan. One the men and I are already working to put in place."

"Another plan?"

"Aye, lass." His eyes gleamed with mischief. "We're all doing our best tae convince them all that we truly are MacClellans, and that we'd much rather fight the Kincaids then farm."

"Why would ye do such a thing?" Fiona demanded with a frown.

He leaned nearer. "If we can convince them to let us take up arms, and occupy a place in the line outside Inverhaven . . . well don't ye see? By doing so, we could ensure a safe path for all of us to get inside the castle . . . or even better—provide the perfect weak spot for the Kincaids to break through the line, and make their own surprise attack."

Fiona exhaled, and covered her mouth. "Oh, Deargh."

Derryth's chest seized tight. The plot he proposed seemed so dangerous. She hated to think of what would happen to him and the other warriors if their true loyalties were discovered.

But Deargh was a Kincaid warrior. If his kinsmen were in danger, he would never stop thinking of how he could help them in whatever way. Derryth summoned her pride and her courage. She was a Kincaid too, by marriage and through the love she felt in her heart for all those at Inverhaven. She must do all she could as well, and not be afraid.

More would have been said but Effric walked toward them, leading the palfrey.

"Time to go, lass," he said, earning him a glare from the tattooed warrior.

He glared back.

She would not refuse to go with him. To do so would ensure she would not be allowed to meet with Deargh and Fiona again.

Derryth embraced them both once more, and said her good-byes. A moment later she was riding away, fighting tears at being alone again, but heartened by Deargh's valiant words . . . all but the ones where he'd spoken of Cull's death, and which now hung over her like a dark cloud.

"Child!" Fiona called. Turning back, she saw the old

woman hurrying toward her with something—her small wooden trunk, which had been on the wagon when they were attacked. "Your things. They aren't much, but they are clean still, and yours."

Derryth lifted the trunk, and perched it before her on the saddle, grateful for any fragment of her life before, no matter how simple the garments. They belonged to her. They were a reminder of who she was. Derryth MacClaren, whose heart belonged with the Kincaids.

Some hours later, after spending the afternoon training with the elite warriors of his company and reviewing preparations for the next stage of advancement toward Inverhaven with his captains, Cull returned to his tent, his boots and garments spattered with mud, intending to quickly wash and change.

He encountered Robert along the way, who held a missive in his gloved hand—one bearing a familiar black and gold seal, and tied with silken cords of the same color. In the distance, Cull saw a courier riding fast away.

Robert handed the folded parchment to him.

"Why didn't you open it?" Cull inquired.

"Because it's addressed to you," Robert replied with raised eyebrows and a smile.

Cull broke the seal, drew aside the cords, and read the words within. Buchan, and the two companies of men he brought with him, would arrive that night.

"We are ready," he said, without a qualm of doubt.

"I pray so, else we'll not hear the end of it," Robert teased.

Cull removed his hauberk, and stepped back. "I'm going to my quarters to change."

Robert's gaze narrowed at the front of his chest.

"Oh I wouldn't change, if I were you. I would wear that tunic always, every day and forevermore." He spoke through laughter, his gaze fixed on Cull's chest. "Good lord, are those *kittens*?"

Cull looked downward, and with his gloved hand, pulled the tunic out where he could see it better. Though upside down, he could clearly make out the pattern of embroidery at the collar, formed of kittens' faces. Some laughed. Some bared their teeth. Some stuck out their tongues.

His cheeks warmed. His eyes narrowed and he growled. It was one thing for Robert to have seen, but if his men had, he'd have been a laughing stock.

"*Peasant*," he bit out.

"Who?" said Robert, mirth bright in his eyes.

"That Highland girl," he replied darkly. "Effric put her to work with my mending, but I dressed in the dark and did not see."

"I like her humor—and her daring." Robert laughed outright, shaking his head in delight. "I think you should keep her."

"I won't be doing that," Cull muttered, scowling. "That much is certain."

"I hear she is lovely," said Robert, his gaze growing sharper, more examining.

Aye, she was that. But he didn't like Robert saying it. He didn't like that anyone else had seen her or formed an opinion as to her beauty, though he could not precisely understand why.

"I had not noticed," he said, keeping all expression from his face.

"You *would* say that," Robert retorted. "Really, Cull, I do believe you would have been better suited for the priesthood than for fighting." He laughed and held up his hands. "I jest. I jest! Please do not leave us to take the vows. Until later. And please, don't kill the girl. I may wish for her to do some of *my* mending. Do you think she could do as well with puppies? I do prefer them to kittens."

He turned, laughing, and strode the other way over the muddied, rutted ground.

Cull continued on to his quarters. He found Effric there, dozing beside the fire. The old man had grown even older of late, it seemed. Though he had thought to mildly chastise the old man for not better overseeing Derryth in her embroidery, he would not disturb his rest, not when the coming days would require all his strength to keep up with the moving army.

He paused, looking at the tent . . . allowing his annoyance to burn deeper, into something more like anger. To think that he'd been wearing those ridiculous kittens on his tunic all day, even as he did her a kindness in allowing her to reunite with her kinsmen. Why had he even undertaken to do that? Why was he concerning himself over the wishes of a peasant girl when he should be entirely focused on his men, and the strategy for the conflict that would occupy the days to come? One thing was sure. He wouldn't make that mistake again.

With words of confrontation on his lips, he pushed open the flap of the tent, and stepped inside—

Only to be stopped in his tracks.

Derryth stood beside the brazier, her back to him, naked to her waist, in the midst of pulling a blue *léine* up her arms. The brief moment before she realized he had entered was long enough to burn the image into his mind forever.

Aye, by then, it was too late. He'd seen the smooth, pale skin of her back sweeping down to her pinched waist. Aye, and he'd seen the alluring profile of one full breast.

She let out a sound of distress, and crushed the garment against her bosom. Clearly afraid of him, and what he might do.

He did not begrudge her that. She did not know him, and he did not know what had occurred in her life before this moment to make her mistrust a man. Perhaps it was only that he was a stranger. Perhaps she thought he would expect some wicked favor in exchange for the generosity he had shown in arranging the meeting with her kin.

Her hair was braided still, and offered her no curtain, no shield. He released his hauberk to the floor, and moved forward, his gaze fixed on the delicate line of her spine—aye, wanting nothing more than to touch her there . . . to trace the path of it with his fingertips. Wanting nothing more than to push the garment away until it fell to the floor. But there was no pleasure in such things if the woman was not willing, and this one considered him her captor. Her enemy.

Coming to stand just behind her, he reached over her shoulders, ignoring her visible flinch. Taking care not to touch her naked skin, he drew the *léine* up her arms, covering her.

"There," he murmured.

She expelled a quavering breath. One of relief?

But he felt no relief at all . . . for it seemed he did not need to touch her skin, or kiss her, to be seduced. Just being close to her . . . touching the garment that concealed her nakedness was enough to command a forceful reaction from his body. His hands throbbed, demanding more satisfaction than cloth. His sex stirred.

Cull closed his eyes for a moment, and exhaled evenly. He had never been a man ruled by temptations. Indeed, he took a certain kind of pleasure in resisting them, in proving the strength of his self-discipline. And now, it took all his strength to resist the lure of her body . . . her hair . . . her lips. Her lovely shoulders, and bare nape.

Carefully . . . purposefully, he tightened the lacings of the garment from the small of her back, upward, to the nape of her neck, drinking in every inch of her bare skin as it disappeared from his view.

"All done," he said in a low voice, taking her by the shoulders, and turning her toward him. Dark lashes lowered, as she averted her gaze. "Do you see? I am no threat to you, peasant."

Yet his voice was tight and overly husky, even to his own ears, and his hands did not want to break free of where they touched her. For the first time, the word "peasant" had sounded more like an endearment than a slight. An unintended mistake of inflection he must not make again.

Yet . . . the magnetism between them seemed so powerful, and hot. Was he the only one to feel it?

"Oh, but you *are* a threat to me," she whispered so softly he could barely hear the words, her chin down, her gaze held low.

Everything inside him halted. His heartbeat. The flow of blood in his veins. Time stopped, and there was only him standing here with her. Her pink lips, and flushed cheeks. Her perfect skin.

She exhaled shallowly, her breath coming in small gasps. The *léine*, which he had thought would conceal her and make her less tempting, skimmed her narrow waist and cradled her temptingly rounded breasts, which rose and fell with her distress.

The words she'd spoken. What had they meant?

Suddenly, she lifted a hand, and with her pointed finger touched the front of his chest, near his throat. At that single touch, every muscle in his body drew tight.

"The kittens," she said, backing away abruptly, her cheeks flushed, and her gaze shuttered, even more so than before . . . as if she regretted the words she'd spoken just moments before. Words he would not forget. She inhaled, as if for courage.

"You're very talented," he said quietly. "Such detail. Robert Stewart found them very amusing."

She closed her eyes and clasped her hands, appearing mortified. "I . . . stitched them . . . last night when I was trying to think of ways to make you angry. And then this morning you were gone before I could remove the tunic from among your garments." She opened them again. "I ask for your forgiveness."

Her eyes pleaded—and he found that he did not like that. He did not want her to be afraid, though he was well aware of the contradiction there, for it was he who had intentionally made her fear him, to gain her obedience. That was before. This was now. He preferred things to be easier between them.

He nodded. "Is there anything else of which I should be aware?" He looked off, across the room. "A broken leg on the chair? Vinegar in my wine?"

"*No*," she answered firmly. "Although those are very good ideas, and I shall have to remember them."

Her lips took on the smallest smile, and her eyes shone.

The muscles of his lower belly tightened. She wasn't just pretty, he realized then. She was beautiful, with her dark-lashed blue eyes and her delicate nose and mouth. Her neck and shoulders . . . her limbs, were graceful, and finely formed as any noble lady's. But it wasn't just that. It was the way she moved, that drew his eye. The way she spoke—his ears craved the sound.

"Sit," she said, turning from him. He watched her move toward the far side of his quarters where his garments were kept, her lovely swan's neck exposed by her high crown of braids. She returned with a linen cloth.

"Cull, I said sit," she ordered gently.

Her hands on his forearms, she urged him into the chair, and knelt at his feet.

He tensed, his gaze fixed on the shining crown of her head, not understanding what she intended. Never before had she spoken his name. He felt dazed by the moment. Bewildered.

"Your boots," she said. "You forgot to take them off."

Indeed he had. He'd seen her nakedness, and had forgotten all else except getting close to her. In the process he had tracked mud onto his precious carpet. In this moment, he did not care. He only wanted her hands to touch him again. For her lips to speak his name.

With the linen in hand, she grasped his boot by the shank and heel, and pulled it from his foot. Only Effric had ever served him in such a way, though he had at times wondered what it would be like to be tended to by a wife.

A sudden realization came to him. One that struck him through with darkness. The realization that she might belong to another.

Chapter 8

"You seem as if you have done this before," he said, his manner cold again.

He felt suddenly very surly at the idea that her next words might forbid her to him forever. Was she married? Was her husband among the men he'd captured? Why had he not considered that possibility before?

Derryth paused, before taking hold of the second boot. God help him. She blushed each time he looked at her. It made him want to kiss her cheeks. Her lips. Her throat. And every bit of her skin, underneath her clothes.

"I have indeed," she answered softly. "For my father."

Now it was he who blushed, in relief. Thankfully, her head remained bowed, so she did not see.

"At first, I thought Deargh might be your father," he said in a quiet voice.

"My father is dead," she replied, setting the second boot beside its mate. "For two years now."

"And your mother?"

A warning sounded in his head. He'd broken his own rules now, pressing to know more about her.

She stilled. "She died years before him, when I was very young. I have only a child's memories of her."

"You are alone, then?" he murmured.

Alone . . . like him.

"No," she replied, unsmiling, her gaze on her lap. "I have never been alone. Not until now. Here in your tent." The words gouged him softly. "There are many whom I love. I have three half-sisters. A stepmother, and many friends and kinsmen. They are my family."

Aye, he'd known that somehow. That she was well loved, and protected. Deargh and the older woman, Fiona, cared for her deeply, that much was clear. Others would as well. And certainly, she would have suitors. Men who wished to be near her. Men who would want to claim her for their own. Even if she had no lands or riches to offer. What man in his right mind would not?

He wanted to ask more questions, such as why she traveled with the others. Her delicate hands with their slender fingers and oval nails, did not appear to be the hands of a farm laborer. Her speech was careful and refined. He could not help but wonder what her life had been like before now . . . and who waited for her at the end of this journey. He held silent, knowing he must not ask those questions. He had already dared too much. Allowed himself to feel too much.

Still, he could not deny there was something very pleasing . . . almost sexual about her kneeling at his feet, that kindled the flame already burning in his chest.

In the same moment, his conscience declared his assessment as *wrong*, because certainly in her mind, she had no other choice but to serve him. He knew if she was given any choice at all, she would not be here in his quarters with him.

She stood and carried his boots to the door, where she placed them on the mat just outside. She returned with clean leather slippers left there by Effric earlier, which had been forgotten the moment Cull entered the tent.

She moved to kneel again—her intentions, he realized, to place the shoes on his feet. But somehow that was too much. There was something wrong in allowing her to do something so personal for him. Aye, he'd ordered her to tend to his quarters, but he was not her master, and she was *not* his servant.

He leaned forward in the chair.

His sudden movement startled her, and she froze. A small breath came from between her parted lips.

"I will do that," he said.

He took the shoes from her, his fingertips unintentionally grazing her hands. His gut seized in response to that barest touch.

She stepped back, balling both of her hands tight, against her sides. Bright spots of color warmed her cheeks . . . as if she too experienced the same effect.

She was the most fetching thing he'd ever seen. Each

moment made him more and more attuned to her. Her every word, her every breath, demanded his notice.

"There is wine warming on the brazier," she said, turning to move in that direction. He watched her movements, as she took up a simple goblet from his table, and poured from a long-handled carafe. Though clearly not at ease, she moved with grace. He could easily imagine her in a castle hall filled with tapestries and carved furniture. Her simple *léine* replaced by an elegant kirtle, her golden hair falling free down her back.

Carrying the goblet, she returned.

"No vinegar, I promise," she said, with a flash of a smile, lowering the cup into his hand.

Having her here . . . caring for him . . . he liked it too much. It pleased him. It made him grumpy. Damn . . . he did not know what he felt.

"Sit, and rest," she urged. "There is also warm water, and I will pour it into the basin for you to wash, when you are ready."

Once more she turned, going to the basin. He couldn't stand it one moment more. This pretense between them. Not touching her.

He stood from the chair and followed, his pulse pounding, coming to stand behind her. It was all it took—to be near her—for his body to come alive. Her shoulders straightened and she set the pitcher down, only half emptied. She'd heard him . . . she knew he was there.

Taking her by the arms, he turned her round to face him.

"Why are you doing this?" he said.

She blinked rapidly, and looked down at the carpet between them.

"I am . . . grateful to you for what you did for me today, in letting me see Deargh and Fiona. And because Deargh told me I must."

Slowly . . . knowing he played with fire, he touched his fingertips to the underside of her chin, and lifted her face, directing her gaze to his.

Emotion gleamed in her eyes, but not fear. No, not fear. To his surprise, he saw a glint of anger there. Of challenge. She lifted her chin higher, but did not look away.

"You are angry at me," he said, his heart beating faster, feeling as if he peeled away another layer of her, and somehow saw beneath to something that was even more beautiful . . . more complex and intriguing.

"Nay, Sir Cull," she whispered, her breasts rising and falling with each breath she took, drawing his glance to the deep shadow between. "You are who you are. You do what you must do. I am angry at myself."

His heart seemed to stop then.

"Tell me why," he said, fixing his gaze on hers.

He felt her tremble then, and a sudden rush of tears gathered against her lashes.

"Derryth . . ." He held her gaze, feeling as if he were falling . . . and being tangled up in her.

"Because I do not hate you as I should," she blurted.

Her words sparked a fire in his chest, and a powerful rush of need swept through him. He shifted nearer, his hands sliding to her back. He wanted to gather her into his arms, and hold her tight against him. He wanted to lose himself in her.

Her hands flattened against his chest, as if she would push him away, but she did not. Instead she seized fistfuls of his tunic, her lips emitting a frustrated sound.

He stared down into her eyes, tempted. Intoxicated. Beguiled. And yet some part of him held back, warning there would be consequences if he gave in to this temptation.

One kiss, his desire demanded.

One kiss, to clear the tempting haze of her from his mind.

He bent his head slowly, his fingers spearing into the silken hair at the nape of her neck, below the braid.

Her breath caught in her throat, and her eyes flared wide. He held himself rigid, his mouth a fraction from touching hers . . . giving her the chance to break free, but again, she did not.

Nor did he.

He pressed his lips to hers . . . gently grazing his mouth against hers, testing her softness, her sweetness.

Something roared inside his head, a raging river of passion, tearing his discipline to shreds, and sweeping him away.

Vaguely, he knew that she moved toward him, her hands clinging to his shoulders, and that he seized her closer, so that her breasts crushed into his chest, but above all, there was the continued, dizzy headiness of the kiss, as he angled his face and pressed his mouth to hers in deepening fervor, inhaling her sweet, rapid breath into his lungs, and tasting the paradise of her mouth with his tongue.

Oh, but no.

How wrong he'd been to think it.

Hers was not a kiss to be done with, and forgotten.

"Pardon my untimely interruption," said a man's voice, amused, from behind him.

Hearing the voice, Derryth jerked away from Cull, her pulse instantly frantic. It was as if a spell had been broken. That which had been so wonderful just moments before now seemed overwhelmingly shameful. Cull moved quickly, shielding her with his body, his arm coming back to protect her further, his hand splayed against her hip.

She covered her mouth with her hand, as if that would erase the proof of her betrayal. For she *had* betrayed the Kincaids, had she not? Not only had she allowed Cull to kiss her, but she had kissed him back. Even now her lips burned, and her body seemed overtaken by fire.

It was disgraceful enough that the moment had taken place, but even more so that someone had seen. Without thought, she clenched his forearm, taking comfort in his strength, wishing to remain in his shadow, invisible to whomever had entered.

Cull stood strong and sure, and issued no words of rebuke to the man who'd entered. And why would he? Was she not merely a conquest? A peasant to be taken? Did not men congratulate each other for such things? But even now, in her shame, her heart could not grasp hold of such accusations.

Cull was different. She sensed that beneath his guarded, rigidly controlled exterior. However, that belief did nothing to lessen her regret.

The man spoke again, his voice deep and smooth. "Duncan said you had a woman here. To think, I did not believe him."

"My lord Buchan," said Cull, his voice deep and rich. "Welcome. I did not expect you for some hours yet."

A ripple of shock coursed through Derryth's limbs, as Cull spoke the reviled name.

The Wolf, here. Standing just feet away.

The man who threatened everything she loved . . . and who made Cull her enemy.

Fear and panic thundered in her chest and inside her head.

Her gaze fixed on Cull's sword where it gleamed on its stand beside his armor. The weapon was nearly as tall as she was, and likely heavier. Even if she lunged, and took hold of it by the hilt, it was unlikely she'd even be able to lift it, let alone manage to slay the man. And yet she thought it. She wished it.

She kept her gaze lowered, but saw the earl's rich leather boots take several steps inward, tracking mud on the carpet. She noticed that Cull shifted, turning by the slightest degree—shielding her still.

The earl chuckled. "Traveling with catapults is tediously slow. After I sent the courier with word I would arrive, I grew impatient. I and my personal retinue rode ahead."

Catapults! Her stomach clenched with anxiety. If he had come with catapults, no doubt he had also brought more men, which meant more than Cull's two hundred would move against the Kincaids. Her stomach pitched and roiled, and she felt nearly sick with trepidation.

"Sit here, where it is warm." Cull extended a hand toward the brazier, and the pair of chairs beside it. He spoke in a low, even tone. Rather than sounding in awe of his visitor, he sounded at ease. "There is wine warming over the fire. May I pour you some?"

Unexpectedly, he did not order her to tend to the earl.

"I only came to greet you," replied the earl. "To inform you I was here, and to extend an invitation for you to sup with me this night."

"Of course. Yes. I will join you," answered Cull.

"Until then." She heard the brush of Buchan's boots on the carpet as he turned to go. "Oh and Cull . . ."

"Yes, my lord?"

"Bring that lovely girl as well." He laughed, low in his throat, amused. "The one you are trying so gallantly to hide from me. I do insist."

Her heart stopped, hearing the words. *No.* She clasped her eyes shut, and clenched her teeth against the wave of terror that rose up inside her. At the same time . . . she felt the slightest change in Cull. The muscle in his arm, where she held it, grew hard and tight.

"Aye, Earl. I will."

Of course he would agree. His loyalty was to Buchan. Not her. Not the Kincaids. Nothing was more clear to her in that moment.

The moment they were alone again, she broke away from him.

"Buchan," she spat, feeling as if the name were a sour taste she had to expel from her mouth.

Aye, she'd known the earl's sons were here in the camp, and that Cull was acting on orders that the Wolf had put into motion—but it had not occurred to her that Cull knew the hated nobleman on such intimate terms as to greet him as a friend, rather than with a subservient bow.

The realization made her feel sick. Sick to her soul.

"You know of him?" he asked, casting her a narrowed glance.

For a moment she feared he would see straight into her soul, and know she was a Kincaid. She banished all emotion from her face.

"Everyone in the Highlands knows him—and reviles him," she hissed. "He has sown much havoc and unhappiness here, misusing his authority when he was Justiciar of the North. Now, surely he seeks to do the same again."

He replied in a tight voice, "And everyone in Scotland knows the Highland clans despise royal interference in their affairs. They can't even get along with one another. Someone must exert the law of the land over them, for they are plainly incapable of imposing order upon themselves."

"'Tis not just that!" she countered, her anger rising. "He plots and kills those who displease him, without conscience."

"Aye, name one noble in this land, one laird or chieftain, who does not. No man is a saint, Derryth," he retorted, his voice deep and silencing. "In fact, I know not one."

"There are good men still." Niall and Faelan Braewick, to name two, but she could not declare them without revealing her loyalties. And yet she would not be silenced. "Buchan is the devil."

Cull looked at her coldly, his nostrils flared, a stranger again. Clearly she had offended him, by offending his lord. "Then it seems you must sup with the devil tonight. He would not take kindly if his invitation was denied."

"Even by a *peasant*?"

"Aye, peasant," he growled. "Even by you."

She had thought to strike a blow against him with her words, but he struck back in equal measure, and the words stung.

He stalked toward the water basin and almost angrily wrenched his tunic over his shoulders. Thrusting a cloth into the water, he washed his face, his neck, and his chest.

She stood silent, watching, her mouth gone dry at the sight of his bare skin and muscles, honed from years of warrioring. The scars . . . that, aye, most certainly looked like lashes, rather than battle scars.

Despite her anger . . . her understanding that he could only ever be her adversary, she wanted to know him. His secrets, and his past. How his life had brought him to this place. More than anything, she wanted him to turn around, and stride toward her and take her in his arms again, and kiss her with the same thrilling passion as before, and tell her he knew she was right about Buchan, but that he had no choice, that he was a warrior sworn to follow the orders of the monarchy, thereby making him almost as much a victim of Buchan's plotting as she.

Instead, he stilled and spoke over his shoulder.

"You will stay by my side tonight, do you understand?" Gone was the warmth in his voice. Once again, he spoke to her as an inferior. "Do nothing to draw attention to yourself."

Inside, she went cold. Perhaps he had desired her for a moment, here in the confines of his lonely warrior's tent. But clearly his interest in her did not extend beyond that. Indeed, all the emotion that had so thickly filled the quarters before Buchan's interruption was gone, only to be replaced by stark, cold emptiness.

Cull's displeasure at being forced to take her to his lord's table could not be more obvious. No doubt he was accustomed to sharing a trencher with much nobler and finer ladies. No doubt that was also where he had learned to kiss with such confidence and skill.

"You needn't worry," she responded, feeling as if her eyes had been opened once again, to the man who held her against her will, and who threatened everything she must protect. "This peasant understands her place. I will not speak a word."

"Good. I hope you mean to start now," he muttered.

She moved to the other side of the tent, and lowered herself onto her pallet where she pretended to organize the contents of her trunk, but the words and his manner stung. Though she kept her face averted, she knew he pulled on a clean tunic, and then a fitted leather jerkin that displayed his warrior's physique to its finest. Without another word, he left her alone in the tent.

Tears blurred her eyes, but she dashed them away. She would not sit here, feeling defeated and inferior. Perhaps she was a woman, and did not have armor to wear or a sword to hold, but she must be a warrior no less. She had her own strengths. Her own talents. She would gather herself and proceed into battle, as any warrior would.

Though she dreaded the thought of seeing Buchan again, she knew she must forget what had happened between herself and Cull. Their kiss. Her only thought must be of the Kincaids, and how she could help them. Mayhap tonight she might overhear something useful to their cause.

She was grateful for her plain, unadorned garments, and she spent extra time painstakingly sectioning and plaiting her hair. Her brilliant, almost white, unbound hair, had always been her greatest pride, and the feature that most often drew a man's admiration. Perhaps if she presented herself as neat and dull, she would remain invisible to them all, and she could safely listen and watch.

"Derryth," said Cull, from outside the door of the tent. "Come. It is time."

Though he stood on the other side of the tent wall, he may as well have been just beside her. She reacted to his voice, and his presence, that strongly. She closed her eyes, and for a moment stood very still, gathering her courage—and hardening her heart. She would not allow him to weaken her. Taking deep breaths. She reached for her cloak, which she pulled over her shoulders and with its hood, she covered her head.

When she emerged, Cull did not look at her. He only touched her arm near her elbow, and led her away. Effric watched in silence where he stood beside the destrier, brushing the animal's gleaming coat.

They walked in silence toward the edge of the camp, garnering the attention of all they passed. With each step, Derryth felt the tension in her rise. Inwardly, she exhorted herself to be brave. Perhaps there would be no more opportunities like this to observe Buchan, the Kincaid's greatest enemy, firsthand. She must seize the opportunity and glean what she could.

Cull moved tall and masterful beside her, the ruler of his domain. Despite his silent scowl and his disregard for her, being with him made her feel safe. No voice called out a vulgar compliment now. Nay, each man held silent, stood rigid in a display of respect, and bowed his head as they passed.

Passing into a small copse of trees, they arrived at a black-and-gold-striped tent, at least three times larger than Cull's quarters. Laughter—male and female— emitted from within, which gave Derryth some relief, because if ladies were present then at least some degree of manners would be upheld. There was also the music of a lute. Warriors guarded the tent, and when they grew nearer, one stepped forward and drew back a panel of embroidered velvet so they could pass through.

Derryth lifted her chin, squared her shoulders, and preceded Cull inside.

Chapter 9

Derryth braced herself as some ten or twelve faces turned toward them, Buchan, Robert, and Duncan among them. All richly dressed, and all, she realized, men of importance.

She also knew instantly that she had misunderstood what sort of ladies would be present.

They were beautiful, every one—their eyes, lips, and cheeks painted and wearing rich layers of shining silks, velvet, and brocade. They sat among the men, smiling broadly, their gazes bright and sharp. More than one bejeweled hand was pressed against a male thigh, more than one arm draped seductively across muscular shoulders. No doubt there was not a single wife among them. Several cast obvious glares of suspicion on her.

"Cull," Buchan called out.

"And his prize," added Duncan, his gaze striking

dark and hot on her, above the gleaming head of a dark-haired woman who perched on the bench beside him. "Very different from what I expected, I must say. Tell us, *Nameless*, what is your woman's name."

Beneath her cloak, Derryth bristled at the words. *His* woman. She most certainly was not that.

"Derryth," Cull replied in a low, even voice. "Her name is Derryth."

She felt as if all eyes pinpointed on her then, dissecting her face, her hair, and her clothes.

"Derryth! What a pretty name!" exclaimed one of the women, a striking red-haired beauty who leapt up. She extended her arms in enthusiastic greeting, and rushed near, her forward movement clouding the air with the scent of flowers and spice.

"Come and sit," she said extravagantly. To Derryth, she said, "I am Sorcha! Buchan's favorite, at least for the moment." Everyone laughed, including Buchan, whose dark gaze moved from his lover to Derryth.

Taking friendly hold of both of their arms, Sorcha led them inward. "Come and sit. Servant, take Derryth's cloak, and see that their goblets are filled with wine."

A glance at Cull's face showed him to be at ease with these people.

He guided her into a seat at the long wooden table—actual chairs rather than benches, which seemed very impractical for an army camp—before taking the one beside her.

The next hour was a blur of wine and music. Coarse jests, and vulgar stories. For the first time in her life she felt dull and out of place in the midst of a celebration, whereas Cull, dignified and quietly spoken, seemed to easily belong, though she took some satisfaction that none of the offensive words came from his lips, nor did he laugh at the filthier jests.

Still, she felt alone and self-conscious. Though Cull sat beside her, tall and long-limbed, he did not speak to her, nor even glance her way. Sorcha, during this time, moved from one seat to another, talking to everyone, and ultimately returned to a seat beside Cull, to whom she spoke in a stream of flirtations, her hand often resting on his arm, which threw Derryth's emotions into disarray. More than one couple drifted away, to kiss and grapple and laugh in the corners, their hands moving over each other's bodies in ways that made Derryth's cheeks burn.

However, it was Buchan, always, who remained the center of attention, as if everyone found his sly words and easy boasts the most charming and pleasing words they'd ever heard. She did not, and kept her face averted so that he would not see the gleam of hatred that most certainly resided in her eyes. She would not be dazzled by his wealth and importance. She would not forget that he was a murderer, whether by deed or intent.

On the other side of Cull, Sorcha yawned and stretched like a cat, then leaned forward to turn her green gaze upon her.

"You're so pretty, Derryth, and I am so *bored.*" She smiled brightly. "Would you like to try on one of my gowns? I would love to see you in something besides that sackcloth you are wearing. Really, Sir Cull, can you provide no better for her than that?"

Cull's gaze met Sorcha's, his manner distant, and

after moment, he replied, "Nay, Sorcha. I cannot, for she is not mine for which to provide."

"Derryth. Truly?" She leaned forward, smiling, and again clasped his muscular arm. "I thought you were his prize! But no? I beg you, tell me all. Sir Cull remains such a mystery to all of us women, I would have you spill every one of his secrets."

Cull narrowed his gaze upon Sorcha, but she only smiled effusively between the two of them.

"I don't think Derryth knows how to speak," said another of the ladies, her voice laced with unkindness.

It was enough to inspire her voice. With a hard look at the woman, Derryth replied, "Alas, there are no secrets to spill, as I likely know less about him than any of you."

"Sir Cull, tell me that isn't true." Sorcha's hand spread tight and claiming on Cull's thigh. Derryth's temper flared, seeing the familiarity, which he allowed.

It occurred to her that Sorcha was interested in Cull. That she *wanted* him. Or that they had previously been lovers. Her mind filled with images of the two of them, in a naked embrace, twisted in linens and furs. Her spirit grew dark at the thought. He could have been intimate with any of the wicked women in this room— or perhaps even all of them at once!

But what did it matter to her? She did not care for him. She did not want him for herself.

Duncan leaned forward from where he sat, his eyes glazed with drunkenness. "Are you saying Cull hasn't claimed his prize?"

Everyone laughed, as Derryth's cheeks filled with heat.

"No truly, I want to know," he persisted cruelly. "Has Cull the Nameless, claimed Derryth, his prize? See how lovely she is? Is it not somehow against nature that they should share his quarters, but no lovemaking has occurred?" The dark-haired girl beside him glared at Derryth.

Derryth wanted to rise up and run from the tent. She wanted to flee.

Buchan watched silently, his eyes dark and piercing on her, from where he sat.

"Leave her alone, Duncan," Cull warned, his expression gone utterly cold.

Duncan laughed, and looked at the faces around them, before scowling at Cull. "You do not give me orders." His lip curled. "I don't even know why you are here. You are not even one of us, not really."

"Aye, Duncan. He *is* one of us, and he told you to leave her alone," said Robert in a firm voice, surprising her with his intervention.

Sorcha cried out, "All of you men are behaving like unchivalrous beasts, and making Derryth uncomfortable. You're going to ruin dinner before it is even served. There is also to be a special announcement, I am told by my own very knowledgeable Buchanbird." She winked at Buchan, to which he eased back in his chair, smiling indulgently in return. "A reason for celebration. Come now, Derryth. I've a blue gown that matches your eyes. I cannot have you wear garments so unworthy of the occasion, not when you are my guest of honor."

Derryth could not tell if Sorcha was truly being friendly or making fun of her. She only knew that the woman was close to Buchan, and therefore she did not trust her. She could not trust anyone in this room.

Not even Cull.

Duncan still stared at her from across the table, his eyes gleaming. "Dearest Derryth, I did not mean to make you feel unwelcome. Indeed, I only wished you to know that if *he* does not wish to be your master, that I am happy to take his place."

Her master. As if she was a servant, to be submissive—and claimed. Her hands curled into fists, and she buried her angry retort.

"You go too far," said Cull, leveling a look upon Buchan's son that made the smile fade from Duncan's lips, replaced by a glare of outright hatred.

"Aye, Cull, and I will take it further—" he snapped.

"Stop it, the both of you," Robert warned, leaning forward, his expression fierce and concerned. "Must the two of you always provoke each other?"

Buchan chuckled, from where he sat.

Sorcha stood, and placed a hand on Derryth's shoulder. "Come, my new dearest friend. Let us leave these men to their boorish bickering."

Though Cull had all but ordered her to remain by his side, she wanted nothing more than to escape her present company. Eagerly, she stood and allowed Sorcha to hook her arm into her elbow, as if they were indeed friends.

"This way," said Sorcha grandly.

Another woman stood as if to join them. "I'd like to come as well."

"Unfortunately, you are not invited," Sorcha sniffed, and in a rustle of silk, led Derryth away.

They passed through another curtain, into a small chamber littered with cushions and chairs, before going to another where a large bed was visible in the light of a wide bowl-shaped brazier. Wind pushed against the sides of the tent, and the walls moved.

"Stand there," said Sorcha, pointing to a circular carpet. Going to a trunk, she searched for a moment before returning with a garment of gleaming silk, the color of a male peacock's feathers. She lay the garment over the back of a chair.

Glancing into Derryth's eyes, she smiled and helped her remove her kirtle, and her *léine*, so that Derryth stood only in her undertunic, hose, and shoes.

"Oh, just look at you. They are perfect." Before Derryth could react, Sorcha ran her hands over the linen, cupping Derryth's breasts and squeezing them. "I'm so envious I could cry."

Startled, Derryth stepped away with a gasp, and blocking any further touch with her arms. "Please don't touch me like that."

Sorcha looked at her, as if momentarily confused.

"Oh, forgive me." She bit her lip, and clasped her hands into tight fists, looking truly mortified. "Sometimes I forget myself, and the wanton I have become. I promise, I will remember myself from this moment on."

True to her word, without any further trespass of her hands, she laced Derryth into a fitted scarlet *léine*, and atop that, the blue kirtle, before standing back and walking in a slow circle around her. "I knew the gown would suit you. Now sit. I can see you have done everything possible to hide your hair."

She gently pushed Derryth down into a chair, and Derryth wondered what would happen if she simply jumped up and ran away. Aye, she loved pretty clothes, and hair and woman talk, but she felt very strange with Sorcha, almost as if she was allowing herself to be seduced in some way, into the sort of life Sorcha lived.

It made her want to return to Cull immediately, and beg for him to take her away from this place.

"So . . . tell me the *truth* about Sir Cull. Though you both tried very hard to deny it . . . I can see there is something between the two of you." She tilted her head. "A delicious tension, which only comes when two people are lovers."

Derryth's chest tightened. *Lovers*. No, they were certainly not that. There had only been the kiss.

Sorcha leaned close, so close that Derryth could see the golden flakes dusted across her nose and her cheeks, and whispered conspiratorially.

"Is he good in bed?" She smiled giddily. "Does he make love for hours on end? I have heard told that he can make a woman scream in pleasure, but I do not know if it is the truth or if those women merely tell lies to make others, like me, jealous."

Some part of her felt relief at hearing Sorcha's words. At least she knew she and Cull had not been intimate, which was what she'd feared when they were at the table. And yet imagining Cull giving pleasure to any other woman made hear heart grow cold. She did not want to talk about him anymore.

"I know nothing of that," Derryth answered stiffly, averting her gaze. "He is nothing to me, nor I to him."

"You're such a sweet child. You lie! I know you do!"

The woman loosened the braids at Derryth's nape, setting her tresses free to fall down her back, while the rest remained in place. "Such a beautiful color. Rather like angel's wings, I would think, while mine is the color of sin."

Spinning away, she returned with a small metal basket.

In the following moments, Derryth submitted to having her eyes lined with kohl, and her lips stained, but when Sorcha sought to dab more color on her cheeks Derryth shook her head. "No more."

The smile faded from Sorcha's lips, and Derryth sensed the sudden downturn of her mood. Suddenly, the woman knelt beside her, and looked up into her face.

"Though he is called Cull the Nameless, Buchan often calls him Cull the Incorruptible. Is that true? If he has not claimed you, one might surmise that perhaps he prefers men—"

Derryth shook her head, and moved to stand. "I would like to leave now."

But Sorcha held her in place, both hands gripping her arm. "Or is he the *finest kind of man*? One with honor, who does not abuse the heart or body of a woman."

Derryth stilled.

"Friend, listen to me." Sorcha took Derryth's hands in both of hers and squeezed them tight. "Be careful here, with these men, and even the women. If allowed to do so, they will smother your soul, as they have done mine, and you will find yourself dressed in the richest garments and wearing jewels bestowed from their favor, but there will come a time when you are left alone with your finery and cast off by all who once celebrated you, and you will want nothing but to die."

Sorcha's green eyes now glittered with tears. Her face, without its smile, seemed transformed, and sad. She was young, Derryth realized. No older than herself.

Sorcha continued. "If there is any chance to take a man like that for your own, to claim his heart, and win his protection, then you must do so. Do not let him go." She stood and turned from Derryth, as if gathering her emotions. "But come, we must return to the others. We have already been gone too long."

They left the chamber, Derryth eager to return to Cull's side, only to be confronted with a shocking sight, illuminated by the light of a lantern. Duncan, sat on a padded bench, his booted legs spread wide as he clenched he head of the dark-haired woman who knelt on the carpet before him.

"Ahh!" he groaned, staring downward, as her head raised and lowered at the juncture of his thighs.

For a moment Derryth was confused about what she was seeing, but then she saw his trousers unlaced, and realized Duncan's sex was in the woman's mouth. A wicked smile turned the corners of his lips.

Looking up, his gaze met Derryth's, dark and unblinking, and his smile broadened.

"Yes," he urged. "Just like that. Don't stop."

"Mmmmm!" the woman moaned in response, and her head bobbed faster.

"Duncan!" Sorcha exclaimed, laughing, having resumed her guise. Claiming Derryth's wrist, she dragged her past, muttering, "Men! They can never get enough of *that*."

Flames burned Derryth's cheeks. She hurried past, trying to block out Duncan's moans of pleasure.

The moment they passed through the curtain, Derryth felt Cull's eyes fix immediately on her, as if he had been watching for her return.

To her surprise, he stood. The room fell silent.

Sorcha led her to him. "Just look what I found hiding under that ugly garment. Isn't she a jewel? She is my gift to you."

"She was just as lovely before," said Buchan, his eyes narrowing on her with sudden interest. "Cull . . . where did you say you found her?"

Sorcha, smiling, attempted to pass Derryth's hand to Cull, but Derryth refused, not wanting to be anyone's "prize" or "gift" to be treasured one moment, and when she lost her shine, to be thrown away.

She seized her hand away, and moved past him to sit on the bench in the same place as before, wishing more than ever that she had never stumbled into the path of Cull the Nameless, and those with whom he kept company.

Cull did not answer the Wolf's question, pretending not to have heard.

He did not want to share one detail about Derryth. As the night had gone on, he had only wanted to protect her from these hard-eyed, sometimes vicious people whom he'd spent his life observing, and learning to understand.

He had already intended that they would leave upon

Derryth's return. He could barely suffer the present company when he imagined them through her eyes.

Something had upset her. He saw it in her averted gaze, her flushed cheeks and blanched skin. Had Sorcha said something? Or Duncan, who some time ago had, along with his companion, disappeared?

Aye, she looked beautiful in Sorcha's rich garments—a bright-eyed queen in blue—but the stricken look on her face demanded some sort of intervention from him.

He turned to Buchan. "Thank you for your hospitality, but the day will begin in just a few short hours and as you know, the camp will be moving toward Inverhaven. I'm sorry to leave so early, but—"

Buchan stood and rested a hand on his shoulder. His dark brows gathered.

"Nay, you cannot leave. Not yet. I forbid it." He grinned, showing his teeth. "Not until I have shared my announcement. Sorcha, the food."

Cull forced his expression to remain unaffected, though inside he cursed at having been so flatly denied. He wanted to get Derryth away from here.

Sorcha crossed the tent, her red hair shimmering in the lamplight, and within moments, Buchan's servants arrived, bearing fragrant, steaming trenchers.

Buchan rose again from his chair. "Everyone sit. Servants, refill their cups. I have something important to say." His eyes narrowed, and he searched the room. "*Where* is Duncan?"

"Here," replied a voice.

Duncan appeared, pushing through the curtain, followed by his female companion, both of them flushed and laughing. The woman's hair was loose and wild at her shoulders, where before, it had been carefully styled. The color that stained her lips also stained Duncan's cheek and neck, leaving no doubt as to what had occupied them.

But Cull did not miss how Duncan's eyes went straight to Derryth, darkly taunting—nor the way her cheeks further emptied of color.

He returned to her side, and sat, gently touching her back—regretting when she flinched. Leaning close, he murmured in her ear. "What has happened to distress you?"

Derryth looked up at him, her blue eyes flashing . . . and *pleading*. He saw that Sorcha watched them from across the table, and smiled as if pleased.

Derryth did not reply before Buchan's voice commanded his attention away.

"Sir Cull the Nameless."

"Aye, lord," he replied. He stood, wondering why his name had been spoken so loudly, and with such intent.

Buchan's eyes regarded him warmly.

"I have been accused by some of showing you too much favor. You are young, that much is true, and I have always taken interest in your progress." He tilted his head. "But you've *earned* your glories. Without a doubt you have *proven* your worth not just to me, but to whatever Stewart sits on the throne of Scotland. Know this bestowal of honors . . . this sworn promise, comes not just from me, but directly from the king."

Cull's heartbeat quickened. Bestowal of honors? Sworn promise? To what did he refer?

Chapter 10

Cull bowed his head in acknowledgment. "I am grateful for whatever regard the king may have for me, as well as you, my lord. I always have been."

The room held silent, all watching and waiting.

"Good," said Buchan, his smile widening. "Because it has been decided that you will command all forces in this endeavor, from this moment on. Your company of men, and the two others which have joined yours here today, combined."

The warriors at the table, who were noblemen of the King's Guards and the commanders of those three companies, raised their goblets to Cull.

"Well deserved!"

"Lead us to victory."

Cull had no chance to thank Buchan or even to speak because Duncan let out a bitter bark of a laugh, and addressed his father. "Unbelievable."

The room fell silent.

Duncan pressed his hands against the table and stood, glowering. "It is I who specifically requested command."

Buchan's eyes flashed, but he replied evenly. "You will have your chance to lead, Duncan, when the time is right." He paused, taking up his goblet—which he lifted high. "But the siege of Inverhaven, and the reward for taking the castle there, will go to Cull."

Cull could only stand, and watch, stunned by what unfolded. He had not expected this at all, but took boundless pride at the announcement.

Everyone stood, raising their goblets as well—except for Derryth, who stood stone-faced and with her hands at her sides, until Sorcha moved to stand beside her, and pressed the cup into her hand.

"Reward?" Duncan spat. "What reward?"

But it was to Cull whom Buchan spoke. "Take the castle, Sir Cull the Nameless, and the castle is *yours*—along with the lands, and a title . . . a name to be determined then, by the king and Parliament."

Warmth spread through his shoulders, and his scalp. He had not expected this at all. Buchan's words promised everything he'd ever wanted. Land, and even a castle, which he could fill with sons and daughters. But most important, a name to give them.

"You can't be serious," Duncan muttered, in clear disagreement.

"Congratulations," said Robert, standing and coming near to grip his hand.

But strangely . . . his smile did not reach his eyes, something that Cull felt could not go unmentioned.

"You don't agree that I should lead?" he said quietly, so that only Robert would hear.

Robert gripped his hand and pulled him close, speaking into his ear. "There is no one more deserving than you. I am troubled by other thoughts, which have naught to do with you."

Robert squeezed his hand hard, and moved on. Cull made his way through the wall of well-wishers who encircled him, back to Buchan.

He blinked, his heart still beating with excitement. "Thank you, my lord, for this opportunity. I won't disappoint you."

"I know you won't," Buchan replied, staring into his eyes. "You've Ainsley to thank for this as well. She's very persuasive you know, and sang your praises repeatedly to the king."

Ainsley . . . Buchan's dark-haired, dark-eyed daughter and Robert and Duncan's youngest sister, of whom he had barely thought about since departing on this campaign. Indeed, he could hardly call to mind the image of her face, because . . .

From the first moment outside the bath house, there had been only Derryth.

Aye, he was bewitched by the little Highlander. But what good could come of that? He returned to his seat, and her side, where she sat silent and alone, while everyone else laughed and talked around her.

"Derryth—" he said.

Her gaze fixed on him sharply. "I wish to leave," she whispered, her lips turned into a frown. "You may return if you wish and stay as long as you like. Just please take me away from here."

Inwardly, he flinched. He needed no more proof that he should set aside his fascination with her, before it developed one degree more. They were from two different worlds, and she judged him for his. Moments before, he'd actually felt *pride* that she had been present to hear of the honors that were given to him, and even more that she, such a beauty, sat beside him for all to see.

But she had refused to lift her goblet. She did not congratulate him as the others had, or even attempt a smile. Despite the hardness of his warrior's heart and years of shielding himself from weaker emotions, he had desired her approval. But now anger sparked inside his chest, that she somehow expected him to be ashamed for his place at this table, where other men would sacrifice anything to be.

He was *not* ashamed. He was proud of all he had achieved and the opportunity he had been given, and he would not allow her to lessen his feeling of accomplishment.

He turned in his seat, closing the distance between them, ensuring their privacy with the wall of his body.

"Just a while longer."

"Then I will see myself back to your tent." She moved as if to stand.

He snared her wrist. "No."

Her head snapped toward him. "Let me go."

"Can you not glare at me as if I am some devil?"

"You *are* a devil," she whispered. "Just as much as he."

"He" being Buchan. He knew she despised the earl, for his impositions upon the clans, and aye, truth be told, even he had flinched at times, hearing of the Wolf of Badenoch's cruelties. But his mood went black, hearing the condemnation on her lips. He was a warrior . . . a King's Guard and a knight, not a diplomat. It was a life he valued and took great pride in, considering from whence he had come.

"I wilnae apologize for who I am, Derryth," he said, his anger rising.

Her gaze flashed into his. "I want no apology, or anything else from you."

And yet in the same moment he saw heartbreak in her eyes that she desperately tried to hide. Tears welling against her lashes . . . the result of pain inflicted by him.

All anger fled him, replaced by self-loathing. She was no warrior, adept at wearing false faces as necessary to advance and survive.

"Cull, is something amiss?" said Buchan's voice from behind, sounding amused.

He turned in his seat to find a silent room, with everyone watching. Despite his determination to remain dispassionate, blood rose into his cheeks. Damn, but he'd let her get deep under his skin, here, where it was most dangerous to show it—both for her and himself.

"Nay, sir." He stood. "But I am fatigued from this long day, and doing my best to convince my companion to leave."

"Clearly she does not want to spend the night with you," Duncan muttered.

"Shut up, Duncan," Robert muttered.

Cull's chest warmed with satisfaction when Derryth willingly took the hand he offered. A moment later, after saying a round of good-byes, he led her toward the door.

In the blink of an eye, Sorcha was there. "I have so enjoyed meeting you, Derryth. I do hope we will see each other again soon."

"Thank you, Sorcha," Derryth answered, before looking down at the kirtle she wore. "Your dress. I will return it."

"Keep it," the woman replied. "As my gift. The color looks better on you than me, as I knew it would. I will send a servant in the morning with your other garments."

Buchan moved toward him then. "A moment alone, Cull, before you go."

Cull allowed himself to be drawn aside, and after a sideways glance toward Derryth, turned his attention fully to the earl.

Buchan grasped his arm, and spoke in a quiet tone. "I will not go with you to Inverhaven tomorrow, but rather will withdraw to Lord Nester's castle at Carven." Lord Nester being a longtime ally of the earl. "As you know 'tis but a day's ride from here, so please, send couriers and keep me informed as to how the siege unfolds, and your estimation on when we can expect a surrender or . . . battle—at which time I will come."

The words surprised Cull. "I had thought you would be coming with us?"

Buchan nodded. "Unfortunately, there are . . . other matters that require my attention." His eyes darkened.

"Cull, tell no one of this, but I have received word that my father is ill and not expected to survive. There is no time to go to him. I simply await word."

Cull's heartbeat stalled, hearing this. The king, on his deathbed. "My prayers are with you and your brothers, sir."

And yet he knew this was no mere matter of grief.

The earl murmured gravely. "I must make plans to protect my interests in the time of . . . uncertainty that will most *certainly* follow."

Cull realized that he too must prepare himself.

Buchan's father, Robert II, had not ruled for years as he suffered from a frailer constitution of mind and physicality. Instead the country had been largely governed by his two eldest sons along with Parliament, but had never been without infighting, betrayals, and intrigue. Even the three Stewart brothers were rarely of one mind, at times turning against one another to further their own ambitions. It was only with care that Cull had managed to keep the respect of all three men.

"What do you expect will occur?" Cull inquired carefully.

Buchan exhaled, as if already weary of the future to come. "I do not doubt that Carrick will be named king, despite his physical ailments. He is eldest after all, and birth order has its rewards in our imperfect society." The earl let out a low growl of annoyance. Cull knew the Wolf had always considered himself a greater man than either of his brothers, and competed fiercely against them to prove himself. Without a doubt, he would continue to do so, even now, as gray threaded their hair.

Cull remained silent. He would not speak against one Stewart or the other. Despite his connection to Buchan, he considered them all very much one and the same.

Buchan crossed his arms over his chest. "No doubt Fife will continue on as he has since Carrick's accident, as Guardian of the Realm. Where will I, the third and youngest brother, fit into this new order? Only time will tell." He grinned, but without warmth.

As for himself? Cull could only follow the path he'd followed for so long. He forever owed a debt to Buchan, but as a King's Guard, he would serve the *King* of Scotland, and do so honorably. He would not stray from that path. In that way, he hoped he would somehow carve out a place for himself—a place that he could for the rest of his life call home, and a sanctuary away from this life. That dream was within his grasp. He had only to fulfill his sworn duty to achieve it.

"Then one final matter," said Cull.

"Aye, commander." Buchan rested a hand on Cull's shoulder. "Whatever you need."

"Have you the official edict issued by the king and Parliament against the Laird Kincaid? I should like to have possession of it when I meet with him to demand the surrender of Inverhaven."

"Of course." Buchan nodded. "'Tis at Carven awaiting me, with the rest of my important documents. I'm a fool not to have brought it with me. It's just with this news of my father, my thoughts have been a bit . . . disarrayed."

"Understandably, my lord."

"I shall have it couriered to you straightaway."

"Thank you, Earl. Then good-bye, until we are victorious."

He turned back to Derryth—

Only to find Duncan standing very close to her . . . his hand spread on her lower back as he bent to speak intimately into her ear.

Jealousy flared up inside Cull, so suddenly the intensity of it stole his breath.

But he saw then that their closeness was not mutually desired. Derryth grimaced and leaned away, clearly seeking to escape. However, Duncan gripped her arm, his eyes dark and his teeth clenched behind a predatory smile.

Cull's vision went black.

"*Duncan*," he barked. His voice silenced the room.

Duncan's head snapped up, and their gazes locked. Tension reverberated between them.

"Come here, Derryth," Cull said evenly.

A sly smile spread across Duncan's lips.

"Go, peasant," he said, releasing Derryth, and backing away. "Your master summons you."

Derryth turned. Color stained her cheeks, and she did not meet Cull's gaze as she hurriedly joined him.

"Duncan." Buchan scowled, rebuking his son.

But Duncan was already gone, disappearing into the deeper shadows of the tent.

Side by side, Cull passed with Derryth into the night, he draping her cloak over her shoulders, but she stepped away, putting several paces between them as she fastened the garment at her throat.

"What did he say to you?" he demanded in a low voice.

"Why does it matter?" she answered tightly, crossing her arms over her chest as she walked.

She looked so small, fragile and alone. And was she *not* alone? He had done little to protect her inside, and though he could not think of what he should have done differently, he could not help but feel regret.

A strong gust of wind moved through the trees, sending her hair sweeping back, to gleam in the night. She caught it, and with a quick turn of her wrist, twisted it upon her shoulder, and pulled her hood up to cover her head. A moment later, the sky sprinkled them with drops of rain. She walked faster, through the trees. With long strides, he easily kept up, his blood warming just from being alone with her again.

"It *does* matter what he said to you," he said.

"Because you and he hate each other?"

Hate Duncan? He hadn't until he'd seen him touching Derryth like that, but perhaps now, at last, it was true.

"Nay, Derryth, because whatever he said offended you, and I would not have you offended. Tell me what he said."

Had Duncan made her some sordid offer? Had he declared some intention to seduce her? Duncan would do that. No doubt he would. Seduce Derryth, just to provoke him. And then when she was used up . . . destroyed, he would cast her off.

"Aye, his words *did* offend me," she answered softly, staring ahead. "But do you know what offends me more?"

"What?" He caught her by the shoulders, and gently pressed her against a tree, in an instant craving the intimacy they'd shared just hours before. Wanting to kiss her again. Was that all it took? A moment alone with her, for him to be drawn back in?

In the shadow of her cowl, her eyes widened, and he thought he saw the gleam of tears.

Damn him to hell. She was afraid and he was aroused. What sort of beast did that make him?

"It doesn't matter." She moved as if to push past him but he held her still, by her arms. Tension rose between them, something he found almost painful, and yet infinitely sweet. He was not accustomed to being so caught up in someone else. Never before had he *ached* to touch a woman. Why her? The feeling both unsettled and intrigued him.

"Tell me," he repeated. "What offends you more than Duncan?"

Him. She would say that he did. He needed to hear it. Then, he could break free. Then, he could forget her.

Rain fell in earnest now, pattering increasingly hard, all around.

Her eyes widened. "That you are one of them, and I wish you weren't—" she choked, and a tear fell over her cheek. "Because you are so much finer than that. Finer than any one of them."

Him . . . *fine*? Her words struck through his heart. How could she say something like that about him, a former slave? A warrior with no true possessions but his horse, armor, weapons, and pride.

"But I'm not," he said, his voice gone hollow.

If only she knew from whence he had come. From nowhere. From darkness. From the pit of a slaver's ship.

"Aye, but you *are*," she said. "You pay an old man wages, when he is far too old to work. Because he has nowhere else to go, and because you are kind. You allowed me to see my kinsmen, calming my fears and theirs. Because your heart is good and honorable. I know there is more within you. So much more, because I can *see* that man when I look in your eyes."

Her praises ignored the violence of his past and the blood he had spilled. They had nothing to do with his ability to hold a sword, or clear a field of the enemy. They were words he had never in his life realized he wanted to hear.

Until now.

She pushed past him, into the rain, but lunging, he caught her and brought her into his arms, against his chest. "You're crying for me?"

He still couldn't believe. Still didn't understand.

"Aye, Cull, I cry for you," she exclaimed hoarsely. "And everyone else who will be hurt by you after tomorrow."

With a sudden wrenching of her shoulders, she broke free from him then, and ran again into the rain, away from him, away from the camp. Away from Buchan's tent.

He followed at a distance, striding over the uneven earth, and found her stopped at the edge of a clearing, her arms at her sides, drenched. She turned to him, her eyes wide, her expression stricken.

"I don't know where to go," she said.

Something powerful rose up inside him then, a warmth that defied the chill of the rain on his skin. A soul-deep need he had never felt for any other living thing. How could she have done this to him, in the mere passing of a day? When for so long he had existed and fought and survived, needing no one. Trusting no one.

He strode toward her, rain striking the planes of his cheeks, and soaking through his garments. She made a sound when he touched her arms . . . a low sob. He lifted her up into his arms, just as he had, one day before, like a child. But it was no child who looked up at him in the night, her face pale, her eyes wide and encircled with dark lashes. Derryth was a woman, and he kissed her like one then, tasting rain and passion on her lips. He knew bliss when her hands came up to frame his face.

"Oh, Cull," she whispered.

His every muscle contracted tight, and he was consumed by an urgency that set his heart beating faster. He carried her through the quiet camp, through a torrent of rain that would make the next day a misery for his army and the move they would make, but that did not concern him now. Most men had crowded into their tents. He'd given orders because they were so near the location of their intended attack, that there would be no large fires, no music. No shouting or laughter, which could draw attention.

Effric did not greet them, and no doubt slept in the shelter of his covered wagon. For that, Cull was grateful, for he did not want the old man to see the look of blatant desire on his face, plain evidence of his need for the woman in his arms.

Inside, it was warm and dry, and for the first time he did not give a damn that his boots muddied his carpet. He set Derryth on her feet beside the brazier, inside its circle of warmth. Water dripped from the hem of her cloak and from his face. He did not hesitate. Standing so near that their garments touched, he reached over her shoulders for the fastening of her sodden cloak, removing it and discarding it to the chair.

"Cull . . ." she said.

"Yes," he murmured in her ear.

She breathed heavily as with impatient hands he divested her of the sinful blue gown that hung damp and heavy as it slid from her arms, and with a silken hiss, fell to the floor, leaving her standing in a deep red undertunic.

She stood silent, still taking deep breaths, still turned from him, and he sensed she did not know what to do. That despite their attraction . . . the powerful connection they shared, he was still her captor, an enemy of Highlanders, and therefore an enemy to her. All that was true, and perhaps made the moment feel all the more forbidden. He could not recall ever having wanted a woman so badly. Need tightened his groin, and his sex lengthened against his thigh. But he knew his desire went deeper than lust, and he wanted to claim her heart just as equally as he wanted her body. He knew if he was to have her, that he must take extra care.

Slowly . . . he touched her hair, which was damp from the sodden hood he'd just removed from it. The silken, white-gold tresses that had fascinated him from the first moment. Gathering the softly curling mass in his hands, he bared the nape of her neck—God, her *beautiful* neck—and bent to press an open-mouthed kiss there, tasting her with his tongue.

"Cull . . . please." She shivered and sighed, emitting an uneven, broken breath.

He kissed her neck once more before releasing her hair to cascade again down her back. Grasping her slender shoulders, he rubbed her there with the flats of his palms, before enveloping her in his arms, and gathering her tight against his chest.

"Don't be afraid," he murmured against her temple.

Wind and rain lashed the tent, as there, in the light of the brazier, he held her for a long moment, simply standing, his heart beating heavily in his chest, before turning her in his arms.

"Put your arms around me, Derryth," he said quietly.

She did so, and her hands flattened against his back. He touched her cheek, cupped her chin, tilting her face upward so that her eyes looked into his. She trembled . . . and closed her eyes, but did not pull away.

Bending, he kissed her. Gently . . . his lips grazing hers, teasing himself with their unbelievable softness. She moaned, leaning against him. That was all it took for his wall of restraint to come crashing down. Desire surged through him, strong and wild, and he tilted his head, losing himself in her.

Open mouthed and commanding, he seduced her with his lips . . . tasting her . . . delving deeper with each thrust of his tongue, until she responded with equal fervor, her hands grasping at his arms . . . and sliding up around his neck. Aye, he knew how to kiss a woman, how to make her crave more, but he was no less intoxicated by Derryth.

"You feel so good in my arms . . ." he murmured, his mouth never leaving hers. "You're so lovely."

Without thought, he lifted her, and carried her to his bed, and lay her on the furs. Quickly, he divested himself of his boots . . . his wet jerkin and the tunic beneath, before returning to her arms. The night was so dark, and the shadows so deep, there was only their mouths joining, and their hands touching. His hands moved over her waist, sweeping up over her ribs—at last—to her breasts, which he cupped and caressed through the linen that covered her. She was so slight, he was startled by their fullness. She arched, and gave a soft cry. He pulled at her *léine* where it gathered at her hips, pulling the linen higher.

Chapter 11

"Wait . . ." she cried.

Her body suddenly rigid, she caught his wrist, even as the rapid breaths that emitted from her parted lips told him she was still as aroused as he.

His need for her was so powerful, and the instinct that they should be together so true, it took all his strength to pull himself back from the edge—but draw back he did.

"Derryth, I want you," he murmured, the weight of his body on his hip, as he sprawled half atop her. "But I would never force you. Will you share my bed? Will you share my night?"

More words gathered on his lips. Promises to protect her. Sworn vows to never let her go. Oaths his heart demanded of him, and yet—

He dared not make.

"Cull—"

"Answer me," he replied, lowering his head to kiss her, but she turned her face away. Instead he lowered soft kisses along her collarbone, and then her neck . . . until her lips found his again. The passion between them rose up hotter than before. His tongue delved deep into her mouth, and she buried her hands in his hair.

Only for her to break away again, gasping . . . half crawling away.

"What do you expect me to say?" she said, agonized.

Aye, he was in agony too, his sex hard and aching for satisfaction.

"You don't have to say anything, Derryth," he replied, exhaling through his teeth. "Just don't say no."

Derryth stared at him, wanting him . . . her heart near breaking. But losing herself to this passion would be a betrayal to all she loved. No matter how strongly their souls connected. No matter how honorable a man he might be.

"No," she whispered, hating the word, even as she spoke it, for Cull was everything she wanted in a man. And yet she could not have him.

"I . . . understand," he said, his eyes black in the night. He eased away from her, and rolled onto his back to stare straight above, his arms extended over his head.

How magnificent he looked, lying beside her. His muscles delineated by the firelight. His face stark with passion. He still breathed hard, but swallowed, as if he sought to assert control over himself.

"I'm sorry," she whispered, her heart clenching. Wanting him still.

"You mustn't be," he murmured, his voice deep. "It is I who lost control."

She closed her eyes. *She wanted more than anything to lose control.*

He was silent for a long time. At last, his shoulders eased and he breathed out through his nose. "Tell me . . . is there someone who waits for you, at the end of this journey?" he asked. "Are you married . . . or betrothed?"

"No," she answered, with a shake of her head. "There is no one."

Perhaps she should have lied, and told him there was. But she did not want to lie to him anymore than she already had.

He nodded slowly, a half-grin turning his lips. "Well, good. There is that." He turned his head to peer at her. "But you are innocent?" He spoke the words softly. "A virgin?"

"Aye, Cull," she whispered, heat rising into her cheeks. "I am that."

He looked away then, his arms behind his head, to again stare at the ceiling above. "Then you are right to have stopped this. I am not the man you should give your innocence to. A woman's innocence is something worth protecting, and I will protect you, even from myself."

Her gaze swept over his muscled shoulders. The long, rigid line of his torso. If he only knew how much she wanted to make love to him.

"I think it is best that you go to sleep," he said.

"Aye," she whispered, her heart heavy with regret. "Good night."

Shivering from the cold of the night air, she moved to leave his bed for her pallet.

He rolled toward her, and caught her wrist. "I meant here with me."

Again, his eyes stared into hers, renewing the connection between them, just as certainly as any kiss. He released her. He drew back the furs, and slipped his legs beneath but continued holding them up in invitation to her.

"We have already passed one night together, side by side," he said. "What is one more?"

Without hesitation, she joined him, and sighed with conflicted contentment when he pulled her close . . . and bent his head to kiss her again, softly . . . sweetly, his tongue tracing her lips and teeth, as his fingertips caressed her jaw, urging her mouth wider as the kiss grew deeper and more urgent.

He growled low, in his throat, and ended the kiss . . . but he did not release her.

"Close your eyes, and go to sleep."

Derryth savored the sound of his voice, and the vibration of his chest beneath her hand as he spoke. Though she wanted more of his kisses, she understood why he'd stopped.

Held in his arms, his hard body pressed against hers, she rested her cheek against his shoulder. Though she closed her eyes, she prayed the night would never end.

Cull awakened to darkness, and the sound of men's muffled voices, quietly speaking nearby. Feet trodding

heavily through mud. They were the sounds of the encampment awakening. Despite the thoughts that had
troubled him deep into the night, it was the first night
he could remember that his sleep had gone uninter-
rupted by dreams of smothering darkness. Of fear. Of
a dank, stinking ship.

It was no small thing. Indeed, nothing short of a
miracle, and he could not help but believe it had something to do with the woman sleeping in his arms.

She did not snore now. Nay, he had learned from
two nights passed in a shared bed that she only did that
in the moments after drifting off to sleep. Since she
still slept, he could examine her face unobserved, without her seeing his fascination with her. He memorized
everything . . . her long lashes . . . her small nose, and
her lips, pink and swollen from his kisses the night before. And ears, so perfectly shaped.

Unable to resist, he placed a single kiss there, just
behind the lobe, thinking that after he would slip from
the bed.

But she stirred against him, her bare legs align-
ing against his . . . her bottom nestling warm and soft
against his groin. Her innocent movement was all it
took—

He closed his eyes, and clenched his teeth, as his
cock stiffened deliciously against her. When he opened
his eyes again, she was looking up at him through
sleep-hazed eyes.

"'Tis morning," he muttered gruffly. "I must go."

"Not yet," she whispered, rolling onto her back to
look up at him.

With sleep still clouding his brain, and darkness all

around, it was all the encouragement he needed. He rolled onto his back, dragging her atop him. Framing her face, spearing his fingers into her hair, he pulled her down for a kiss, one that became instantly hungry and ruled by passion, his tongue thrusting inside, to be met by hers.

Atop him, her body melded to his, her breasts brushing heavily against his chest, her nipples hard and apparent. Her thighs parted and she settled naturally . . . perfectly against him. God, she was soft, and lush. A fantasy in the shadows. Only the trousers he still wore protected her from his arousal.

Her arms came round his shoulders. His hands slipped underneath her *léine*, to her bare bottom. He kissed her mouth as he squeezed her there, savoring the smooth, warm skin, against his palms. He inhaled her breath, and moved . . . lifting his hips beneath her, pressing his sex against the luxurious, soft heat of her body. She moaned. The sound was enough to shatter him inside, and take him to the edge of something dangerous.

He let out a groan of agony, into her mouth. Not daring to tempt himself a moment more, he turned, rolling her onto her back. She peered up at him, her breasts rising and falling with her deep breaths, looking as unfinished and tortured as he did.

"I cannot stay with you here in this bed a moment more." He pressed one more kiss to her mouth, before slipping out of the bed. "Not without being inside you."

The brazier glowed warmly, which mean Effric had entered as they slept. In the dim light, his swollen arousal was more than apparent against the garment that constrained it. She pushed up from the bed, and stared at him there, her cheeks deeply flushed.

"I am sorry," she said earnestly.

"Don't be."

"But I *am*. I did not intend to . . . *inflame* you, or myself . . ."

"I know you did not," he replied, looking over his shoulder, his eyes burning on her. He could not help but smile at her innocent words. "It just something that happens very easily between you and me, that I should have known better than to have allowed. But damn Derryth, you tempt me."

"You tempt me too," she said softly.

He pulled a tunic over his head and shoulders. "It is a wonderful thing to experience with another person. A rare thing, if you must know. And 'tis nothing to be ashamed of, as long as it stops there, before something else happens that we can't take back."

She sighed miserably, and burrowed into the pillows, which pleased him, because he was miserable too. Aye, he had enjoyed awakening in such a way. He'd enjoyed it immensely. But he wanted more, and he couldn't have it. He'd meant it when he said he'd protect her from himself. One day, she'd find a man she loved, and he cared for her enough to make sure she arrived at that day without regrets.

"Go back to sleep."

But Derryth did not go back to bed. Instead, she arose and helped him dress . . . lifting his hauberk onto his shoulders and kneeling to bind his boots. But strangely, as the moments passed, he sensed a darkness falling over her, and a paleness to her skin. Her hands shook as she helped him fastened his sword.

"What is wrong?" he asked, his hand encircling her wrist.

She peered up at him in silence. Tears gathered against her lashes.

"Derryth?" He frowned.

She pulled away, turning from him.

"'Tis not an easy thing," she said, her voice thick with emotion. "Thinking of you going off to fight. To possibly be killed."

His chest clenched. Just like last night, her words struck him deep. No doubt there were many who would grieve his loss if he fell in battle—but because he was a valuable fighter for powerful men, and would be difficult to replace among the leadership of the king's warriors. But no woman had ever cried out of fear he might come to harm.

Lust was a much easier emotion to manage. He did not want to care. Too bad he already did.

"It is all I know," he said. "It is the life I prefer." He smiled rakishly. "And if you didn't already realize, I'm very good at what I do, so do not fear for me."

She threw a glare at him, as if his attempt at humor offended her. "But I do fear for you."

"Because you are a good person," he said, moving to stand behind her. "With a good heart."

Pulling her near, and turning her toward him, he bent . . . kissing her eyes . . . her lashes . . . her soft, parted lips. Thinking to banish her tears. Her emotion unnerved him. What could he do to reassure her?

Nothing. His loyalty was sworn to the king—and to his own ambitions. Though she had made no demands, he could make no such vows to her. Certainly, he had made that clear.

He kissed her once more, hard on the mouth, and backed away feeling shaken.

"I have already tarried too long, and must go," he said, pulling away, hardening his heart . . . and speaking to her much as he had before. Brusquely, as he turned to take up his leather gloves. "Today you will ride in the wagon with Effric. I'm afraid it won't be comfortable, but you will stay dry and warm."

"One step closer to Inverhaven," she said pensively.

Aye, he thought as he left her without looking back, a shadow darkening his heart. And one step closer to their good-bye.

When Cull left the tent, Derryth shed more tears, but quickly recovered her determination. She had kissed Cull, yes, but neither of them had made any promises to each other, and for that she was thankful. She had not asked to be put in this terrible situation, where she must make terrible choices, but she would do whatever she must to protect those whom she loved—

And she did not love Cull.

Though her conscience lingered over that silent declaration, she refused to ponder why. When Effric came for her an hour later, Derryth was ready. Ready to move on to the next stage of . . . whatever was to come.

"Put on your cloak, lass," the old man instructed. "Where is yer trunk? Give it to me. It is time for ye to go to the wagon."

From there, wrapped in her cloak, and furs, she watched as he instructed a group of soldiers in packing Cull's belongings and tent onto another wagon. She could not help but feel as though the memory of their time together was being dismantled as well. *No*, she did regret having passed the night in Cull's arms. But she knew she must not repeat the same intimacy with him again, at the risk of her heart.

One day soon, he would know she was a Kincaid. There was no way to avoid that inevitability. The deeper she allowed her feelings to grow for him, the more the pain of that moment would hurt. But Cull would respect her decision, once he knew. She *knew* that he would. Somehow that made her secrets all the more painful to bear.

Before long, the wagon lurched to a start, with Effric urging the animals on. Derryth looked back at the line of men and wagons and the rutted, muddied earth they left behind. In the distance, she saw a smaller traveling caravan—Buchan's, departing in the opposite direction. Eventually, she turned around to look with dread toward Inverhaven.

Hours passed. The travel was excruciatingly slow, giving her plenty of time to replay the most meaningful moments of the night before in her head. She felt certain she would live the rest of her life regretting that she and Cull had not met each other under different circumstances . . . in another life.

But they had met in this life, and there was no way to avoid what would come. With each moment that passed taking them closer to Kincaid lands, her agitation and fears grew. More than once she caught sight of Cull, though he never rode close. He remained always at a distance, and flanked by men. She also spied Deargh and the other Kincaid men working as a team to drag a great sled stacked with wood.

Then suddenly, Cull was there, riding alongside the wagon, ordering Effric to halt. When the wheels rolled to a stop, he guided his animal to the back where she sat.

"Ride with me?" he said, though his expression revealed nothing of his intentions.

Despite all of her morning resolutions to hold herself distant from him, she stood, and climbed onto the back of his horse and held tight as together they rode away from the rest of the army, skimming around the bottoms of several hillocks, before coming to a stop beside a narrow river, amidst a cluster of trees. It was a beautiful place. A place she had never visited before.

He swung his leg over and dismounted first. Reaching up, he helped her down, and in the process, held her close, lowering her against him, her softness against his muscled brawn. Instantly, a fire lit inside her, a passion for him so strong, she feared it might never be extinguished—not by time, or distance . . . or death.

Before her feet even touched the ground, his mouth was on hers, demanding and hot, leaving her dizzied and equally wanting. With the hard trunk of a tree at her back, he tilted his face, kissing her again, before his lips left a scalding trail down her cheek and her neck.

He stopped, holding her tight against him, breathing deeply near her ear.

"I am in command of an army," he growled. "And yet for the last hour, all I've thought of is you."

His words filled her with guilty pleasure. She loved hearing that he had been thinking of her, just as she'd been thinking of him, but their whole reason for being here, in this beautiful place together, was *wrong*.

He kissed her mouth once more before backing away, unsmiling, his eyes descending the length of her body, bold and admiring. There was an air of tension about him that made the air feel charged.

"But I did not bring you here to ravish you," he said. "I have food."

She let out a small sigh of relief, for if he had intended to ravish her, she did not know if she had the willpower to stop him. Turning back to his destrier, he removed a rolled blanket and a small leather pack. "We can't stay for long."

He spread the blanket, and together they sat very close together—he with his long booted legs crossed before them, and she with her legs curled beneath her gathered skirts—sharing bread, cheese, and wine. Though he did not touch her, his eyes continually fell on her lips . . . and her breasts, and she perceived in him the same longing she felt. Heat warmed her cheeks, and a feeling of agitation rose within her, shortening her breaths. She remembered his lips on her skin. The way his strong body felt against hers. She barely tasted the wine, for the unspoken desire between them.

But then he glanced at her with a certain darkness in his eyes, and pressed his lips together, as if there was something he felt reluctant to say.

"What is it?" she asked.

He held silent for a long moment before speaking. "I . . . wanted to apologize to you for this morning. For being cold to you before I left my quarters. You . . . expressed your fears for me, and I can only confess that I did not know what to do or say." His jaw drew tight, as if the mere speaking of the words made him uncomfortable. "I am . . . not accustomed to someone caring for me in that way."

She inhaled, breathing past the sudden pain in her heart. "I do care. And I wish, more than anything, that you were not here on Buchan's behalf."

"Because you are a Highlander, and that puts me on the wrong side. The side of the enemy, in your eyes. An unforgiveable side."

She nodded. "Buchan is—"

"I know what he is, Derryth," he replied solemnly, looking away, over the surface of the water. With his hands, he snagged a few sprigs of grass, and tugged them from the ground. "But . . . I owe him my life, and for that reason, I am here."

"Your life?"

"I am . . . Cull the Nameless." He looked at her directly, and she saw blackness in his eyes. "Orphan. Slave."

"Slave," she repeated, her breath stalling in her throat. "Do you mean . . . he paid your man-rent?" She did not understand. She imagined him to simply be a hired soldier, obligated to take up arms on Buchan's behalf whenever called upon.

"Nay, Derryth," he replied, his voice gone flat. "Nothing so civilized as that. He found me among the Moors and Slavs on a Venetian slaver's ship, anchored off the coast, and he purchased me. And he set me free."

"A slaver's ship? H-How did you come to be there?"

"I . . . don't know. I have no memory of anything before that. I do not even know my true name—if I ever had one."

Derryth's heart shattered, hearing the words. She could only imagine Cull as a small boy, on that horrible ship. Alone and afraid. Receiving lashes and who knew what other punishments instead of warm hugs and kisses from someone who loved him.

She stared at him in stunned silence, emotion weighing her chest, and tears rising in her eyes.

"The scars on your back—" she choked out.

"Are from when I was a boy," he supplied. "I was . . . twelve or thirteen when he found me. He asked if I would like to fight for Scotland. After that, he took me to a castle near Holyrood, where I trained with a weapons master for years with other boys, before being summoned to Edinburgh."

"And now he uses you to carry out attacks on his enemies," she said.

"No, Derryth." A quiet laugh broke from his lips. "For a time, I served the king's household, at Scone or Edinburgh, or wherever he traveled, but mostly I have spent my years on the border with England, skirmishing . . . negotiating . . . warring, there. I have escorted emissaries to London to discuss treaties, and other matters. I've seen Buchan only rarely, although I know he has watched my progress from afar. It is by my own efforts alone, I became a King's Guard, and a knight. Buchan has never asked me for anything."

She whispered, "Until now."

Chapter 12

"Until now," he repeated.

Derryth did not speak. She did not know what to say. She could summon no argument to disarm him. No reason to dissuade.

Cull's eyes burned with intensity. "Not only that, but he has given me a chance to rise above a past that would otherwise still chain me. A chance to have property, and a castle of my own. But more important, a name to give daughters and sons." He paused. "It is all I have ever wanted. It is all I've ever striven for. I will not allow the chance to slip away."

Something else occurred to her then. "Like other men of such position, you will marry a noblewoman, to strengthen your position."

"That is . . . the expectation," he replied softly.

"Why have you told me all of this?" she asked, forcing a brave smile, though tears stung her eyes. "You could have just gone on as before, until you let me go."

"I wanted you to know why."

"Why you can't choose me," she said, her heart breaking, just a bit, because of the finality of it all.

He dipped his chin. "Perhaps one day you'll forgive me for what I'm going to do there, in Inverhaven, but I know you won't be able to forget." He touched her hand, where it rested on the blanket. "I just wanted you to know it's all right for us to be on opposite sides. That you can hate my actions, and I don't blame you."

He did not know how opposite their sides were. Not yet. But he would soon. She did feel greater peace now, knowing he would understand when the time came. That there would be no accusations of betrayal or duplicity.

She nodded, blinking away tears. "We don't have to hate each other."

She felt such sadness. As if they were saying good-bye. Desperately, her gaze swept over his lips . . . the line of jaw . . . to his throat below, memorizing his every feature.

"I could never hate you," he said, leaning closer, his blue eyes spearing her through with such intensity, she shivered. "And soon . . . I've no choice but to let you go."

One last kiss.

Her pulse rising in her ears, she moved toward him, her hands touching his chest.

His mouth crushed down on hers, with a passion that stunned her. Feeling helpless against his desire and her own, she clutched at him, kissing him back. His mouth slanted on hers, tasting of wine, and his hands came to her shoulders. Derryth was so centered on him, on *remembering* every detail of these moments that might be their last, she did not protest when he lay her back onto the blanket. His eyes glazed with passion, he lay beside her and deftly unfastened her cloak. She stared up through the tree limbs, her hands in his flaxen hair as his mouth moved to her neck . . . and his hands to the lacings of her kirtle, the front of which he parted.

"Again," he murmured. "One kiss, and I am lost."

She gasped, as his fingers pulled down the neck of her *léine*, exposing both of her breasts to chilly air, and the wet heat of his mouth, as he cupped and stroked them both, one and then the other, licking her nipples to rigid points. Her misery at losing him only intensified her emotions and the sensations she felt. When his hand moved lower, finding its way under her kirtle, to stroke between her legs, she could only arch her back in pleasure, and moan. She was innocent of such things, but she did not want him to stop.

"Cull," she whispered, her hands grabbing fistfuls of the blanket as her passion pitched higher.

"I love the way you say my name."

He stroked again . . . and again . . . coaxing her toward the edge of some mysterious paradise. She shifted against the blanket, miserable and delirious all at once.

The things he did to her body made her bold. "And I love the way you're touching me."

Looking down into her face, Cull's eyes darkened

as his cheeks flushed. "I am selfish, for wanting to see you like this." He peered down at her, his gaze hot and wanting. One finger found its way deeper, to slide against her slickness. "It is how I will remember you always. Beautiful, and wanting me."

Again, his head bent to her breasts. At last, when she felt as if she might scream from need, he eased his fingers inside her and continued the rhythm.

"*Cull.*"

Light flashed behind her eyes, and the earth beneath her quaked, sending pleasure rippling through her limbs. His mouth closed on hers, urgent and sweet, and pushing her kirtle down, he gathered her into his arms and held her tight against his chest.

"Oh, Derryth," he breathed into her hair. "I should not have . . . but with you, I lose all control."

But he had not lost all control. If he had, he would have made love to her, and she would forever belong to him. She clung to him, knowing this was good-bye. Moments later, he pulled her up to standing. Together, in silence, they returned her garments to order. Cull kissed her one last time, long and passionately.

Within moments, they rode back in the direction from whence they'd come and soon rejoined the lumbering caravan. He drew the destrier alongside Effric's wagon. The old man's lips formed what could only be described as a disapproving line, as he slowed the animals and allowed her to climb back inside. Only when Effric's face was turned, did Cull throw her an intimate look that made her heart clench before riding away.

Hours passed, and they continued on until at last, the army stopped. As twilight gathered, she perched in the wagon, shivering, staring at Cull's tent, once again pitched upon the earth. She had spent the hours in the wagon thinking of Cull. Of everything he had told her. Of the way she felt for him. She'd unsuccessfully tried to work out some resolution, where every trouble in their world would turn out right.

Suddenly a figure passed close by. One she almost didn't recognize. It was Nathan, carrying an armful of firewood. His face was gaunt, and his skin and clothing filthy. Glancing around, he furtively made his way closer to her.

"Nathan, are you well?" she whispered, her gaze scanning all around, fearful that someone would see them together talking. "Is everyone well?"

"Aye, all are safe and unharmed, and at last we are allowed to move freely as long as we work and feign loyalty to our commander, Duncan Stewart." He all but spat the name. His gaze moved over her face and her garments, almost as if taking note that she had received far better treatment than the rest of them, and for that she could not help but feel a strike of shame. "Deargh has told me to tell you to be ready tomorrow night."

Furtively, he passed a small bundle over to her, which with a glance, she found to be a soldier's tunic and a snood.

"Ready?" Her pulse skipped at the import of his words.

If Deargh sent word to be prepared, then a firm plan had been made. For whatever reason the decision had been made not to simply wait until they were freed by Cull.

They would escape—and she would never see Cull

again. Her emotions were torn between joy at the idea of seeing her sister—and perhaps even her bairn, but sadness that everything she'd known with Cull would come to an end.

Nathan murmured, "Someone will come for you and we will all flee the camp together, and make our way into the castle."

Without another word he was gone, hoisting the bundle of wood onto his shoulders. Left alone, she let out an anxious sigh.

Two soldiers emerged from Cull's quarters, followed by Effric, who lurched toward the wagon, wincing in pain.

"Effric," she said, concerned for him after such a long day's journey. She climbed down, unable to simply watch, as the old man had commanded her to do. "Tell me what I can carry or do. You *must* rest."

"Aye, lass. I will now that all is in place for Sir Cull, and for you." He gestured that she should accompany him. "Come with me now, and I'll see you inside, then I'll make me own bed 'ere."

Inside, all was just as it had been before. Cull's armor. The chairs. The bed. She took one blanket from the bed. The one Cull granted her the first day, and turned to Effric.

"Where is the pallet?" she asked. "In the wagon still? Stay here, and I will go get it."

"I did not believe it was needed," he said quietly, averting his gaze.

Her heart clenched in her chest.

"Well it is," she cried, tears stinging her eyes because she knew tonight must be different.

She could not sleep in his bed again. She could not allow him to touch her the way he had that afternoon. She could not allow herself to get any closer to Cull . . . and then leave him on the morrow. She turned from Effric, her cheeks on fire, her composure gone, and a moment later he returned with the pallet.

"I am sorry to have spoken to you so sharply," she said, regret weighting her shoulders.

"Sharply!" he chuckled. "It is clear you have not spent much time in an army camp."

"That much is true," she replied, taking comfort in his humor. "And though I think you are dear, I hope to be gone from this one soon."

"I hope that for you as well, lass," he replied earnestly before leaving her.

Hours passed. She lay on her pallet but could not sleep, restless, her ears listening for Cull's approach, at times her fears nearly spiraling out of control. What would the coming days bring? Death. Destruction. For those she loved—or for him?

But there were the normal sounds of the camp, which she knew would continue all night. Never the solid, confident cadence of his boots on the earth. No doubt he was occupied with making plans for his attack on Inverhaven. Perhaps he slept elsewhere or, like her, not at all.

Then suddenly he was there, pushing through the flap, a tall, broad-shouldered shadow in the night.

A wave of emotion rose up in her so strong that she pushed up to sitting on the pallet. Her heart pounded, tangled up with a need to hear his voice . . .

He froze, seeing her, then continued inward, his

face averted . . . as if displeased . . . angry even, at finding her on the pallet.

There was nothing she could do about that. She lay down again, pulling the blanket high beneath her chin.

Turning away from her, he undressed quickly in the shadows, his scarred back painted by the light, the terrible, tragic proof of his unfortunate childhood that only made her ache for him more. She closed her eyes, wanting so badly to go to him, and to feel the comforting strength of his arms around her.

In his *braies*, he turned and, without word, climbed into his bed, turning to face away from her, his shoulders a mountain ridge beneath the dark furs.

She closed her eyes, and willed herself to sleep. She burrowed into the pallet, seeking to create warmth. Her breathing slowed . . .

His voice jarred her awake from the darkness.

"I cannot possibly sleep with your teeth chattering like that," he said from the bed, the words sharp-edged with annoyance.

"I did not realize my teeth were chattering," she replied, stung by his tone. "I will try to stop."

She rolled to her other side, and clenched her eyes shut. Just as she dozed off, she heard his sharp voice again.

"That abominable sound. You are doing it again. Get in the bed where it is warm," he ordered.

"No," she replied. "I will not."

"Well I cannot sleep with you chattering away like that," he growled. "It is important that I sleep."

"Then sleep. But I can't sleep with you."

"I won't touch you, Derryth," he bit out. "Never again, if that is what you wish."

She sat up, and looked through the darkness at him.

"It *is* what I wish," she replied, remaining in place. "Don't you understand, Cull? Why I can't be near you? What happened this afternoon . . . it can't happen again. I already feel too much."

He let out a low breath, but still, he did not turn toward her. "I understand. But I don't have to like it."

"I don't like it either," she said. "But it is the way it must be. Can you not just give me one of the furs?"

"It wasn't a request, Derryth. Get in the bed, or I'll put you there myself."

She knew he would follow through with his threat. She heard the promise in his voice. She could not allow him to touch her, even in anger. If laying rigid and miserable at the edge of his bed would keep that from happening, then she would do it.

She stood, still holding the blanket, and moved toward the bed, her chest tight with emotion.

She wrapped the blanket around her, as if it would provide some barrier of protection against his closeness, and crawled in beside him, taking care that they did not touch.

For an eternity, she lay rigid and unmoving, until she was certain he slept. Only then did she allow the tension to leave her limbs. The tightness of her throat and her chest, suddenly released to a rush of tears over a feeling of loss so deep she could no longer keep it hidden inside.

If only she could keep them all safe. Those she

loved inside the castle . . . and Cull. If only she could sway his loyalty from Buchan to the Kincaids.

It was a fantasy that would never come true. And yet still she ached for his arms around her. The comfort of his chest against her back. His warmth. His kiss.

Suddenly, his hands were there, rolling her onto her back. Cull's face peered down into hers, stricken.

"Don't cry," he said gruffly.

His warmth radiated through her blanket. His fingertips grazed the outline of her face. His nostrils flared, and his gaze darkened.

"Derryth . . ."

She knew he intended to kiss her.

She shoved at his hands, and pushed away, springing from the bed. Gasping for breath, she retreated into the darkest shadows.

"I cannot stay here with you," she cried, blinking through tears that fell more earnestly now.

He arose as well, throwing back the blankets and rising tall and imposing to stare at her from across the bed.

"Do you think I do not feel too? That I do not have a heart?" he said. "Do you think it will be easy for me to say good-bye?"

She covered her face with her hands, unable to look at him for the longing that nearly overwhelmed her. "Please Cull, just let me go. Let me go now. Anywhere. Back to my kinsmen. Anywhere that is not near you."

"No," he said, with a finality that startled her.

Her hands dropped away.

"No, not now . . . or no, not ever?" she asked, something akin to fear rising up inside her.

"I don't know," he said, his face inscrutable in the night.

"What do you mean you don't know?" she demanded hoarsely. "You must let me go. You promised you would. . . . Cull? What is it that you intend to do?"

He did not answer. With shoulders hunched and angry, he strode toward his garments and yanked them on, along with his boots. With a final, dark glare at her, he stormed from the tent.

She thought of the time they'd spent together that afternoon. How perfect those moments had been, and she'd remember them always. But the words had been said. She had no place in his world, and he, no place in hers. She had guarded her heart as best she could, and now he had to let her go.

Watching him go, she saw two guards posted nearby, standing with spears.

At just that moment, a great clamor of men's voices filled the air. Alone, she did not know what to feel. Fear, or anticipation?

A chill went through her, because intuitively, she knew something important had happened. Something had changed.

Chapter 13

At the center of camp, Cull pushed through the wall of men, some of whom held torches. He fixed his eyes on the sword embedded in the ground there, with colorful streamers tied to the hilt, flying in the wind.

"It's from the Kincaids," shouted one of the Highlander mercenaries. "They know we are here."

Robert joined him, his eyes fixed on the weapon. "The Kincaids are old Norse stock. Like their Viking ancestors they've thrown a sword into the midst of the enemy before battle, as a challenge. As a promise of their bravery and skill." He spoke in a tone of obvious admiration.

"Whose side are you on?" said Cull, with a glare.

Robert chuckled. "Yours, Cull. But you must agree with me. They know how to send a message."

"Then let us send one as well." Cull turned to his

commanders. "There is no reason to wait. Let us advance now on the castle, and say a hearty good morning to these Kincaids. Let our army be the first thing they see when the sun rises."

Their shouts and cheers filled the air.

They moved quickly, and in less than two hours, his army was in place, just outside the range of Kincaid archers. The catapults groaned and creaked, pushed to the forward edge of the line, where they would await his order. Teams of men carried wood for the barricades and fortified walls, and on his orders set about to building those structures immediately.

Just before dawn, Cull walked the entire line, from beginning to end, inspecting and encouraging the men, and making changes where he saw them needed. When he arrived at the company commanded by Duncan, he paused, seeing Deargh and his kinsmen intermingling with the other warriors, and bearing weapons.

"What is this?" he demanded of the nearest captain. "I did not approve that these men would receive weapons and fight. They were only to build the barricades. My orders were clear."

He had all but decided to give them their freedom today. To let them take Derryth, and go, as he knew he must.

"We need more men on the line," came a voice behind him that he recognized as Duncan's. Cull turned and watched him approach. "And these men are willing. I take full responsibility for them."

Cull did not reply. Instead, he strode toward Deargh, whose gaze darkened as he grew nearer.

"You," he said. "Come here."

Deargh complied and waited in silence, with his tattooed head bent, for Cull to speak.

"Am I truly to believe that you are my ally now? Because I don't."

Derryth was a Highlander through and through, and abhorred the idea of the Crown's interference here. Was he to believe Deargh and his kinsmen did not believe the same?

Deargh answered, "We do not need to be allies in order to fight side by side. We only have to prefer fighting over farming." He shrugged. "The Kincaids are not MacClellan allies."

"Neither are they your enemies."

"That is true." He nodded, and spoke in a quieter tone. "But Duncan Stewart there has offered to pay us generous daily wages t' shore up his part of the line. So we'll stay until we feel like moving on, if that's all right with ye." His eyes gleamed. "Perhaps we'll go in the night, before anyone can complain of paying generous wages to Highlanders who have no intention of staying for the fight."

Cull's eyes narrowed on the man, but he understood. The Highlanders needed the money, and if Duncan was foolish enough to pay them, so be it. It meant one more night with Derryth . . . perhaps two, spent in utter misery, for he must not allow himself to touch her again for both their sakes. But curse him to hell, he would seize upon any chance to keep her with him, if only to delay their inevitable good-bye.

"Send word to me when you intend to go," he muttered. "Derryth will be ready to travel with you when you do."

* * *

Derryth would never forget the moment Effric's wagon crested the hill and started its downward descent toward Inverhaven.

They'd traveled behind the army, and so she had seen the famed Castle in the Clouds, a place she so deeply loved, surrounded by the ugly, dark line of Cull's combined force, with catapults in place. The sight struck fear, and deep sadness, into her heart and made her more determined to make her way inside so she could be with those she loved, no matter what the consequences. How could she have believed, for even one moment, that her loyalty might be swayed?

Just as before, Cull's quarters were constructed, his every belonging put in place. Everything was the same. And yet everything was different.

Once night fell, Derryth lay on the pallet, a blanket covering the garments she wore—those given to her two days before by Nathan. She waited. Though she urged herself to be calm, fear all but consumed her blood.

Would Nathan come, or had the plan changed? She only knew she had to be ready.

Cull had not returned to his quarters once since the army had advanced on Inverhaven. Now that they were here, outside the walls of the castle he intended to take, he would be consumed with planning the attack and setting all of the pieces and parts of his army into place. It saddened her to think she might never see him again without a high stone wall between them. But neither could she bear the thought of seeing him now.

Hours passed, and her eyes grew weary. For a while, she dozed.

Suddenly, Nathan was there, just inside the door.

"Derryth," he called softly, into the darkness.

She started up, standing, sleep instantly gone from her mind.

"Yes. I am here!"

"Come now. Hurry."

She hurried to the door of the tent, her heart pounding with fear.

"Your hair," he hissed. "Cover it."

She had forgotten, and quickly pulled the snood up.

He grasped her hand, and after a moment's glance outside, dragged her behind him, so fast and so headlong into the shadows, it took a moment to orient herself. There was no moon, and the night was black and concealing.

Unlike the earlier encampments, all the soldiers were crowded along the forward line, stationed or sleeping behind walls that had been built from the transported timber. It allowed them a clear path, down the stony incline, toward the castle. When they reached the bottom of the hillside, he knelt and pulled her down beside him, behind a small rise of earth.

"Why are there no soldiers here?" she asked, looking around.

"They cannot be everywhere," he replied in a hiss. "They are spaced far apart, with only sentries in between, and I know their movements."

"But where are the others?" she said.

"Crossing now as well," he answered. "You just can't see them for the night. Come on now . . . *run*."

He yanked her forward, and her feet struck the ground, doing her best to keep pace with him.

She could not think of Cull. *Oh, but she did.*

The wind stung her eyes, which she blamed for her tears. To think that she might never see his face again. Feel his touch. His kiss. Their last words to each other had been spoken in anger.

She thought of Elspeth, and the bairn, that might even now be swaddled in his mother's arms, awaiting his aunt's first kiss.

"Hurry," Nathan ordered, running, shouting over his shoulder. "You must keep up."

She flew through the darkness behind him, as fast as her legs would carry her.

High above, a sudden flare of light appeared, illuminating them. Derryth stopped, paralyzed by fear.

A burning arrow soared over them, revealing their position on the field—and a moment later, struck earth, blazing brightly as they raced past.

Another arrow *hummed* past her, and another, *thudding* into the earth, these without flames. These, most certainly intended to kill them. Were they Kincaid arrows? Or had they come from the camp? Would she die on this field, trapped between two worlds?

But darkness again surrounded them . . . and the arrows stopped falling.

There came the thunder of a horse's hooves from behind them. A sound that struck her heart through with terror. They were only halfway across the field. How would they ever outrun a rider?

Was it Cull?

"Faster!" Nathan bellowed, for certainly he heard the sound too.

The horse drew closer, as if its rider could see in the dark and knew exactly where they were. She looked over her shoulder, just as another flaming arrow lit the sky.

A massive black steed emerged from the curtain of night, racing up behind them, stones flying out from its hooves. To the side of its flying mane, Cull's face appeared—a mask of fury as he positioned himself in the saddle to reach down for her. She cried out in fear that she would be trampled instead.

An arrow *whizzed* above her head.

Thwick.

The sound of a hard strike.

Cull pitched backward, out of his saddle—

Thud.—to land on the ground.

Derryth stopped, shock rippling through her limbs. She took several steps away from the castle, toward Cull.

He lay on his back, motionless, only the soles of his boots at the ends of long sprawled legs visible to her.

Dead?

"Cull!" she screamed, her heart exploding in her chest.

He could not be dead. Just thinking it made her feel dead inside.

"Derryth, come," Nathan ordered, his voice urgent.

All she could think was that she had to find out if he was alive. She had to go to him. He was there because of her. He'd come after her.

Someone seized her arm and pulled. Nathan. She wrenched free, and stumbled away.

"Go on with the others! Go on without me," she sobbed.

Racing toward Cull, she saw his leg come up, bending at the knee, and he wrenched himself up into a sitting position. She threw herself down beside him, and in the darkness touched his chest . . . his shoulder, and there felt the wetness of blood, along with the hard stalk of an arrow.

"No," she gasped.

If he died she would not be able to bear it.

"Damn you, Derryth," Cull cursed, in a guttural tone. Even in the dark, his eyes shone bright and furious. She knew relief then, that he was alive, but still fear that he would fade away before her very eyes.

Suddenly a wall of warriors appeared, raising their shields. A King's Guard bellowed orders. Burly armed men lifted Cull and dragged him away. The heels of his boots dragged heavily across the earth. Clutching at his arm, she followed, flinching . . . *gasping* as arrows struck the shields. A dark shadow streaked past— his war destrier, returning to camp.

By the time they reached the edge of the field, he'd shrugged off the help of his men and was walking, his hand clenching her forearm, pulling her along behind him. With his other hand, he wrenched the arrow out of his shoulder.

Robert stood there, among the warriors, looking between them in dismay.

Only then did she realize Nathan had been captured

as well. He stood, his arms held by two men, his tunic torn and his chin bloodied.

"Where are his kinsmen?" Cull growled.

A scowling King's Guard answered. "Still on the line, Sir Cull. None are missing, save this one."

Derryth looked at Nathan, who stared at her with a sort of hatred. She did not blame him! But . . . he had told her they were all escaping together. Had he lied to her, or had there been some sort of misunderstanding? It did not matter. She was to blame for his capture, and any apology now would be meaningless. Not that she even had the chance to speak one.

"Secure them all," Cull growled. "But keep *him* separate from the others. I will deal with him later."

Deargh and the others! What would happen to them because of her attempt to leave?

"Nay, Cull," said Duncan, appearing with a personal guard of his own men. "Let me deal with that unpleasantness. I owe that much to you. It was I who trusted these men, that one included. And my men who allowed these two to pass through the line. I'm sure you have your own punishment planned for the girl."

He smiled at Derryth a long moment, before turning. He gestured to one of his men, who came forward, and bound Nathan's wrists before leading him away.

Cull still did not look at her, but led her up the hillside, his hand tightly gripping her wrist. Men lined the way, watching as they passed. Cull said nothing, only proceeded toward his quarters, his hand a vise on her arm, his face a snarl. Effric watched, looking mournful as they passed him, going directly into Cull's tent.

Cull all but hurled her inside. She whirled round, waiting for him to storm forth and confront her . . . but he did not. Tears blurred her eyes, as she waited for the accusations of betrayal that did not come. There was only silence, as with a growl he sank into the chair beside the brazier, his face a frozen, blank mask.

She blinked away her tears. "If you're not going to kill me, then . . . then let me tend to your wound."

He did not answer. He only stared at her in the darkness.

She had never closed a wound before, but she couldn't just let him bleed, untended. It was her fault he'd been wounded.

With trembling hands, she opened her trunk, where she'd packed away Effric's sewing basket, and returned to his side with a needle and thread. Still, he did not move or speak. The tension radiating from him sent a shiver through her. But she would not hide in the shadows from Cull. She would not be a coward, when there had been so much between them before.

She exhaled, staring at his shoulder, where blood stained the leather. She would have to remove his garments to sew the wound. She set the needle on the table, and nervously set about unfastening his hauberk.

Without warning, he seized both her arms, and pulled her toward him.

She gasped. Despite the wound, he was still terrifyingly strong. He held her half suspended above his lap.

"You and the others," he growled. "You're Kincaids. Not MacClellans."

"Aye," she answered, free of the lie at last, but in

the next moment she feared her honesty put more than herself in danger.

She breathed heavily, not knowing what the next moment would bring.

He pulled her closer still, unbalancing her so that she sprawled across his legs, her hands flattened against his chest. He stared into her eyes, the lines of his face drawn and stark.

"I'll release them," he uttered in a low, thick voice.

She stilled, staring into his eyes. Had he truly spoken the words she thought she'd heard?

"What?" she said, her voice soft with surprise. With hope.

"I'll let them go, but you . . . Derryth . . ."

She did not move, waiting for the words. That he hated her. That he would keep her as his prisoner. That he would punish her, for all the rest.

"Choose me." He clenched his teeth, and repeated. *"Choose me."*

His voice . . . his words . . . filled her ears, along with an understanding of what they meant. Warmth flooded through her, out from her heart.

He did not say please, or tell her that he loved her or that he would make everything right between their two opposing worlds. But the words were a plea all the same, one from a man with so much to lose.

"I choose you," he rasped, as if the words came straight from his soul.

She did not waver. There was no decision to make. Her heart insisted there be no other reply.

"I choose you too," she said, trembling at the import of what they'd both just said.

Though he held her arms still, she brought her hands to either side of his face, and with a quiet sob, kissed his warm, firm mouth. His hard-boned cheeks. His jaw, rough with stubble. The lids and lashes that lowered to cover his beautiful, pale eyes. A harsh breath broke from his lips, drawing one from her own. Their mouths met again, in a kiss that was both hungry and achingly sweet.

Aye, everything in the world outside the tent was wrong. But between them, this was right. She did not know how their conflict would be resolved tomorrow, but it didn't matter in this moment. All that mattered was being with him.

The night shifted around her as he stood, lifting her against him, gathering her fiercely in his arms, kissing her until she was light-headed. Three steps, and he lowered her onto his bed, his intentions more than clear.

"Your wound—" she murmured.

"Can wait," he uttered, his eyes glittering in the night, fixed on her.

The intensity in his manner took her breath away, and gave increased life to the sensations rushing through her own body. In mere moments, she and Cull would make love. Just knowing that sent a surge of heat into her breasts, and between her legs. Her nipples, where they grazed against the rough wool of the snood, became achingly aroused and sensitive.

Stepping back, his hands went to the fastenings of his hauberk, which, with a grunt of pain, he impatiently removed, before his tunic, which he lifted over his head, revealing the muscular expanse of his chest and shoulders, and the dark stain of the wound there.

Derryth did not lay there, simply watching. The danger of loving him hung heavy in her mind, and the knowledge that tomorrow would most certainly tear them apart. This might be their only night together, and she was impatient to spend every moment of it with him. She pulled off the snood, and standing, her breasts bared to his hungry gaze, pried off her shoes. Watching her, he gave a sudden, needful grunt, which made her feel shy and unprepared. But still, she pushed the woolen trousers from her hips—

Only for his hands to join hers. He hooked his thumbs into the waist, grazing . . . teasing her bare skin, and with a push, dropped them to the floor— where a moment later they were joined by his. He stood naked in front her, his manhood so large and erect and beautiful that she could only stare.

"Derryth . . . ?" he asked.

"*Yes*." She moved into his arms.

Chapter 14

Derryth knew only joy as he swept her up, his mouth hungrily claiming hers. Holding her under the shoulders . . . he lifted her body higher . . . *harder* against his, tilting her back, devouring her breasts, sending her body into a delirium of pleasure, before lowering her to the bed. There he joined her, his body stretched long and lean atop her, on the furs.

"I can't touch you enough," he murmured roughly. "Taste you enough."

Again, he smothered her with kisses . . . her lips, her body . . . *everywhere* . . . trailing lower, across her torso and stomach, to dip between her thighs, where he kissed her intimately, and tasted her with his tongue, until she writhed, her hands in his hair, gasping out his name.

She felt the same wild need to know every part of him, and when he returned into her arms, kissing her, with the taste of her passion on his lips, she did not deny herself. Her hands explored his chest, and his torso, his smooth skin and the muscles that flexed when he moved against her. How magnificent he was! And yet her curiosity led elsewhere, and she boldly touched that part of him that pressed so hard and urgently against her.

"*Ah* . . . your hands on me . . . they feel so good," he murmured, his lips and breath on her ear. "Like this."

His hand encircled hers, showing her what to do, how to stroke him and bring him pleasure, proven by the sharp gasps that came from his throat. It seemed only right and perfect when his sex was suddenly there, between her legs, prodding . . . *thrusting* into the damp, aching part of her that so desperately wanted him inside.

"Your body . . . god, you're so sweet," he murmured, gripping her thighs, spreading her, and thrusting harder. "I can't hold back . . . *ah* . . . but I don't want to hurt you."

"Don't stop," she whispered, feeling no regrets, no shame—only the desire to join with him, and become his woman. "I want this hurt. I want you."

His invasion stung . . . *hurt*, but she took pleasure as each inch of him drove deeper, sweetly stretching her, tearing her. She cried out in torment as at last, he filled her completely—

"It is done, Derryth," he murmured, his cheeks ruddy with passion. "You're mine."

She stared up at him, dazed, still fevered. Aye, she was changed forever now—and she would remember the sight of him like this always . . . his shoulders taut and bunched in the firelight, one darkened by the arrow's wound. His torso, tight and rippled beneath her hands. His muscular hips and long, powerful legs sprawled between hers.

Her warrior. Her love.

"You're mine," she murmured, arching beneath him, wanting to find pleasure in the pain.

"Aye. Only yours." His mouth lowered onto hers, teasing her with kisses, soothing her . . . seducing her with the rhythm and pleasure of his lips and his tongue, so that she almost forgot the pain and pressure his sex rendered inside her.

"Let me show you how good we can be," he murmured against her lips.

Vaguely, she realized his hips moved also, in time with his kisses, stroking his sex inside her. With each foray of his body inside her, he coaxed her desire to life.

She wrapped her arms around him, wanting to be closer to him, feeling the need to move too, to claim *him* as well. Soon . . . everything changed. There was no more pain, only the smooth glide of pleasure, the rhythmic creaking of his bed, and their undulating bodies touching everywhere. His every kiss . . . his every *thrust* took her higher, made her hungrier, made her need more, even as his blood stained her skin.

"Oh, Cull," she murmured feverishly.

Would she ever feel *more* than this?

"Yes." His hips moved faster, and at the urging of his hands at her hips, she did the same. "Oh, god, Derryth. Now. *Yes*. Like that."

She felt it. The same wild urgency. The same rising wave of pleasure. But where would it take her?

The next thrust of his sex inside her answered that question—sending her spiraling high, soaring into a place she'd never known. Her body and her soul shattered into brilliance, and a love for Cull so intense she thought she might die from it. . . .

Her womb clenched again and again around Cull's throbbing staff as he seized her tight, groaning her name into her hair, arriving at the same paradise. She clung to his shoulders, her legs twined tightly with his, and gasped, her eyes wide, into the night, knowing only joy that he filled her womb with his seed.

Afterward . . . they lay in each other's arms, warm and still breathing hard. It was then that the magnitude of what had just occurred truly struck Derryth, straight through the heart.

Cull lay, staring into darkness, still trying to calm the beat of his heart and his racing mind, when he realized Derryth was crying.

He half turned on the bed to peer down at her, his heart tight in his chest. "I should have waited. You weren't ready. I hurt you and—damn, I bled on you like a savage." Seizing a corner of linen, he gently removed the stain from her shoulder and breast as best he could, which only made him feel like more of a savage. "Curse me to hell for being so—"

"No," she interrupted, holding him tighter and pressing her face to his neck. His vision blurred with the pleasure of her embrace, her voice in his ears. "That isn't it."

"Then what?"

She sat up, eyes glistening, her tousled hair falling over her pale shoulders, to frame her pink-tipped breasts. One look at her like that was all it took for his body to come alive again. But he forced himself to be still. To listen. She looked at him so earnestly. He wanted to hear what she had to say.

Tenderly, she touched his face. "I didn't know it would be like that. That it would mean so much." She exhaled softly, her eyes filling again. "At least to me. You're a man, a handsome and desirable man. I know you've been with other women—"

"Hush." He touched his fingertips to her lips, his throat closing. Not wanting any other person between them. No part of his past in their present. "Everything is different with you."

He whispered the words, feeling vulnerable just speaking them. Perhaps . . . perhaps he should guard himself as he always had . . . but somehow, he knew he could not. He could only speak the truth to Derryth. His armor had been pierced, and she would forevermore be his weakness.

"I feel the same." She nodded, and squeezed him tight, her scent—now something he craved—filling his nostrils. "But it makes me so afraid."

Her voice broke.

"Come here," he murmured, pulling her tight against him, and touching his hand to her hair. With his thumb, he wiped the tears from her cheeks.

He wanted to protect her from harm and heartbreak. But how would he protect her—and still be true to himself, and all he had striven for? The answers did not present themselves, but he would not regret claiming her for himself.

"I can't lose you," she whispered. "But Cull, neither will I turn against them."

He flinched inwardly, hearing the words . . . but they came as no surprise. Her heart was loyal, and she loved fiercely. It was just one thing that made her Derryth, and one thing that made him want to be loved by her.

Indeed, he could not muster one bit of anger toward her for hiding the truth of her Kincaid relation from him. But she belonged to him now, and she might very well be carrying his child when this night was over, a possibility that sparked a flame, deep inside his chest. Did he not now owe it to her to do everything in his power to protect not only her and himself . . . but her loved ones as well? And yet he must do that while satisfying his duty to the Crown.

"Don't worry about that now," he said. "Trust me. Give me time to think."

Already, his heart weighed heavy with the prospect of morning, but when Derryth suddenly left the bed, his attention shifted instantly to follow her.

He stared at her naked bottom and legs as she disappeared into the shadows on the far side of the tent. The *slosh* of water sounded, and he knew she was washing. Reappearing just as gloriously naked as before, she cast him a shy smile and returned to the chair. There she lit a small lantern, bathing her hair and her naked skin in golden light. Desire hardened his cock, causing it to jerk against his thigh, as his gaze moved over her round breasts, and her pink nipples. Her rib cage . . . her waist . . . and the shadowy space between her thighs. But he had just taken her innocence. She would not be ready for his passion again just yet. Perhaps not again that night.

"Come here," she said softly. "Let me stitch your wound."

He arose from the bed, and after also taking a moment to wash, he lowered himself into the chair. Her gaze swept over his nakedness, and rested briefly on his aroused member. Color rose into her cheeks, making her even more beautiful.

"I've never closed a wound before," she said, lifting the threaded needle, and looking slightly nervous— but also mischievous. She bit her lower lip.

"As long as you're naked," he replied wickedly. "I doubt I'll feel a thing."

He meant it. This close to her, all he could think of was sex. Already, desire enflamed his blood and his hands ached to touch her.

She bent over him, and as she did, her breasts swayed, full and tempting, just beside his face. In a flash, his hands were on her waist, and his mouth latched onto a tight pink nipple.

"Stop!" She wiggled against him, laughing, pulling away—but only an inch. "I almost stabbed you in the eye with the needle. You must be still."

He loved the sound of her laugh, and this new familiarity between them. It felt so easy and right.

"I *will* be still." He pulled her near again, kissing her . . . smiling, gently dragging her astraddle his hips. "But I think you'd have a much better vantage *here*, to do your work."

"You are wicked," she exclaimed, her eyes alight.

"Mmmmhmmm." He chuckled, pressing a kiss to her collarbone. "But am I not right?"

"Cull, what is that, underneath your arm?" She bent to examine his torso. His mood dipped.

"'Tis nothing—"

"Another wound?"

"No."

"A bruise, then?"

"'Tis the slaver's mark," he replied, too sharply. But she looked into his eyes, and he gentled. "Forget it please. I would remove it if I could."

"Of course," she said softly. "I'm sorry. I did not know."

"There is nothing for you to feel sorry about." His hands squeezed her buttocks, and his sex grazed against hers.

She sighed blissfully, and kissed his temple . . . his cheek.

"You are making this difficult," she said in a quavering voice.

"I'm making this better," he growled, playful again.

"This must be done." She pointed the needle at him. "Don't move again, until I am finished."

Though his cock was hot and hard, and torturously near her sex, he did as she ordered, and did not move, or even flinch as she stitched his skin. Such pain was minor compared to that which he'd survived in the past, and easy to ignore, especially when he could occupy himself looking at her face, and her body.

"There," she said, as she tied off the knot, and cut the thread. "I think I did very well."

A downward glance toward his shoulder showed an even row of neat stitches.

"No kittens?" he said, chuckling, pretending to be disappointed.

But he did not wait for an answer. He pulled her against his chest, delighting in the crush of her firm breasts and the tight peaks of her nipples against his skin. His mouth closed on hers.

"No kittens," she breathed, laughing . . . blindly setting aside the needle on the table, meeting his tongue with her own.

Their laughter faded as they grappled, touching each other, each kiss more passionate than the last. Their hips moved, mutually rubbing . . . teasing, until his growing need made him selfish.

His hand twisted in her hair, and tilting her head back, he peered down into her eyes.

"I want to be inside you again," he said, breathing hard . . . his body aching so fiercely. "But I don't want to hurt you."

"I want you too," she panted, her hand sliding down over his stomach, to curl around his aroused length. "Now, Cull, please."

His cheeks filled with heat.

"Then take me," he replied, kissing her, eyes open to hers.

Exhaling unevenly against his lips, she shifted against him, rising onto her knees. Still holding him . . . guiding him, she carefully eased her body down on his. A groan broke from his lips as her narrow, wet heat ensheathed him.

Releasing him, she gripped his shoulders, and let out a sound he knew to be half-pleasure, half-pain.

He cursed himself for wanting too much, too soon. She wasn't ready, having just made love for the first time. But he couldn't back away. He couldn't stop. Not now.

"Don't move," he murmured—commanding himself to do the same. At least as far as his lower half was concerned.

She complied, swaying, watching him through half-lidded eyes as he bent, dipping his head to capture her nipple between his lips and his tongue. She gasped, arching. His cock responded with a hard jolt, and his vision blurred.

He smiled, gasping. "I said . . . don't move."

She stilled again. "But you torture me."

"And myself, but 'tis for the best. You'll see." His hands worshiped her . . . measuring her waist, sliding over her delicate rib cage and upward, to cup and caress her breasts, which he slowly . . . languidly kissed, licked, and sucked.

Her head fell back, and she rocked her hips hard against him, clenching her thighs, agitated.

"Please, Cull," she pled. "I want to move. I need to."

She already did so . . . testing his resolve, pressing her womanhood against him.

"Aye, love," he replied, watching her, transfixed by her passion—her desire for him. "Go on, then. Take your pleasure from me. But go easy . . . go slow."

Tentatively at first, she eased along his length, before repeating the same sweet movement again. Before long she found a rhythm . . . she found what felt right, nearly shattering him with each slick stroke. Gripping her hips, he felt her arousal as her body tightened around his cock. She moaned intensely, rocking back, so that her breasts thrust toward him and her silken hair teased his thighs.

In that moment, he half lost his mind. His vision blurred, and his bollocks seized tight. His cock surged in size as he emitted an anguished groan.

"Cull, now . . . I need . . ." she said desperately, sounding tortured. "I need—"

Nor could he wait a moment longer. Bracing on one palm, he lifted his hips to meet her, driving deeper—

They came simultaneously, his body jerking with sudden release, exploding inside her. She gasped, her arms and legs tightening around him, her womb seizing him as their mouths joined, and their bodies embraced. Again, he arrived at a place of pure bliss, tangled with the soul-deep strike of understanding that he must protect her, and their future together, at all costs. With his life, if need be. He had never felt for another person in such a way. In a world where he'd seen life end quickly, a fearsome burden weighed his heart, just as strong as his satiation.

As their passion eased, he held her for a long time, her body against his, her head on his shoulder, kissing her cheeks and her eyes and stroking her hair. How amazing that such sensual passion could in moments transform to tenderness.

As each moment passed, the darkness crept in around them. Trepidation over what would come.

Lifting her, he carried her to the bed, where he

dressed her in one of his tunics. Laying down beside her, he pulled the furs over them both. She pressed against him, quiet . . . pensive. He knew from the tension in her body that she was afraid.

"You must trust me," he said again into the darkness. He held her until at last she slept.

The next morning, before dawn, Derryth glanced up from where she knelt, fastening his boots to find his jaw tight and his pale blue eyes staring hard, over the top of her head, at nothing. After making love to her once more, just before dawn, he had fallen quiet, and had remained deeply in thought since. And yet he'd been so gentle with her, his touch lingering on her hand. Her hair.

While she still wore his tunic, he was dressed in the garb of a commander, and moments away from leaving her. Her pulse increased, and fear tightened her heart, at the thought of being separated from him. She did not want to be left alone.

"What will you do?" she asked.

Chapter 15

"I don't know," he answered quietly. "Not yet."

She nodded. "Buchan wrongly conspired against the father of the present Kincaid. I was not there. I cannot say what happened, but he was responsible for the deaths of the laird, his lady, and many others. What he did here, those years ago, was no honorable intervention on behalf of the Crown, but a crime."

He nodded once—a sharp downward movement of his chin.

"All believed the Kincaid sons to be dead, but the eldest, Niall, survived that night and returned to reclaim his birthright. Another son, Faelan, is alive as well. Whatever the Wolf has done to gain the support of Edinburgh in this, was done to finish them. Perhaps to conceal his crime."

Cull exhaled. "I believe you, but . . . give me time

to think," he replied. "To ask questions. To come to my own understanding."

She nodded, accepting his answer for now. She would not make demands on him. He had already promised her so much. Other matters weighed heavily on her mind, which only she herself could resolve. There was one more secret she held from him . . . that she was not just a Kincaid, but sister to the Laird Kincaid's wife. Not only that, but daughter to Inverhaven's prior laird—a man who had once conspired with Buchan to destroy the Kincaids.

And she would reveal that truth to him. There would be no more secrets between them, only complete trust.

But she must talk to Deargh first, who, along with the others, Cull had promised to release. Somehow she had to explain to Niall's second-in-command why she was choosing to stay here, with Cull. That while her loyalties remained just as strong with her family, Cull also had her heart.

She would send the old warrior with that message to Niall and Elspeth, and pray that instead of inspiring disbelief and anger, that they would find some solace in knowing she was doing everything in her power to ensure this conflict came to a peaceful end.

If that was not possible, she must convince Cull, if not to join the Kincaids, then to relinquish his position as commander. For if he raised one hand in violence against the Kincaids, she would be left with no choice but to leave him forever. That possibility caused her the deepest pain, but after passing the night with Cull, she took comfort in knowing he would understand.

"I must go," he said from behind her, his hand touching her waist.

Her entire body swayed toward him, drawn to his warmth, to his strength.

He turned her, holding her close, his manner different from the night before. Gone was the playful, sensual lover, replaced by a solemn and quiet man. Tension emanated from him, revealed in the hard line of his jaw. No passion burned in his eyes for her, only thought.

"I will be here," she answered. "I only ask that before you release Deargh and the others, that I be allowed to speak to him."

He nodded. "Of course."

He bent, pressing his forehead to hers, touching her cheek with his gloved hand. He closed his eyes, pressed his mouth to hers, and exhaled against her lips. "Trust me, Derryth. It is all I ask."

She nodded, and watched him step back, so tall and magnificent in his quilted leather jerkin, his sword affixed at his hips, that he took her breath away. He was hers, and she was his. No matter what occurred from this moment on . . . their night of love would bind them together always. Even if they were forced apart.

"I'll return before noonday, to see that you're all right."

She nodded, smiling.

Only a short time later, Derryth had just dressed when a voice summoned her to the door.

"Lady."

Two warriors stood just outside the door, their gazes averted, and their manner respectful. Effric was nowhere to be seen. No doubt he was still at the wash-house with the linens he'd gathered just a short time before, his manner quiet and kind, as always, though she felt certain he knew what had taken place between her and Cull the night before.

The older of the two warriors spoke. "Our commander has sent us to bring you to him."

"Your commander?" she inquired, unwilling to trust anyone but Cull completely.

"Aye . . . Sir Cull, the Nameless," he answered.

Her suspicions eased.

"A moment to get my cloak," she replied, backing away.

No doubt Cull summoned her to talk to Deargh. Nervousness twisted her stomach, and she prayed she would find the right words to say. When she had donned her cloak, and covered her hair with its hood, she rejoined the men and followed them.

The morning camp thrived with activity, and one warrior led the way while the other followed behind. She passed men shodding horses and others sharpening sword, spear, and knife blades that she hoped they would never find cause to use. Her glance lifted, resting on the castle that protected the people she loved, and who loved and cared for her. How would Cull resolve this impossible quandary, while also remaining true to himself and his own ambitions? Ambitions she respected and admired, for of all men, did he not deserve a name? Her mind strove for the answers, but none became clear.

Moments later her warrior escort slowed, drawing to the side . . . and she saw it was not Cull who awaited her, but Duncan, dressed in a leather jerkin, trousers and boots, so much like Cull, but lacking in every way. Fear weakened her legs as she eyed him with suspicion.

"You summoned me?" she asked, her voice tight with tension. "For what reason?"

"Aye," he grinned wolfishly.

"Why?" Beneath her cloak, she trembled with revulsion, remembering the last words he'd spoken to her in Buchan's tent. That he'd imagined it was her kneeling between his legs, doing those things to him with her mouth. "And why the lie?"

He meandered closer, his boots crunching over the earth, and it took all her courage not to flinch away.

"My apologies for the false pretense," he said, standing far too close, in an intimate manner that made her skin crawl. "But I knew you wouldn't come if you knew it was me."

"You are right. I would not have come. What do you want?" she demanded, shifting . . . turning to face him, because she did not like that he stood behind her.

"What's wrong? Don't you trust me?" he murmured darkly. "That's good, because you shouldn't."

Her pulse tripped anxiously through her veins. She knew nothing about the camp, having remained inside Cull's tent since they'd arrived. But she feared she'd unknowingly been led deep inside Duncan's territory, where Cull would have no idea she'd been taken. If she turned and ran, Duncan and his men would easily capture her if they wished.

Duncan's eyes swept from her lips, downward over her breasts, and hips. "I thought certainly you would want to say good-bye to Nathan before the poor man is executed."

"Executed!" she exclaimed in horror.

He nodded, resting his hand on the hilt of his sword. "He did, after all, come to this sad and far-too-early end trying to save you."

Two men dragged Nathan forward, then, sending him sprawling into the dirt, his hands bound behind his back.

"You can't execute him." She glared at Duncan. "Sir Cull promised to release him along with the others."

"Did he? Why would he be so gracious, I wonder, as to promise something like that?" He chuckled, low in his throat. "I can only imagine that your negotiating skills must be very good." His brows gathered suggestively. "Very good indeed."

She ignored him, focusing her attention on the man who knelt behind him.

"Nathan!" Derryth stepped toward the young man, but Duncan seized her back. Nathan glared up at her, before shifting his gaze to Duncan.

"Give me another chance!" Nathan shouted, his eyes flashing.

"Another chance?" Derryth murmured, her mind grasping for explanation. The words implied there had been a first. "Nathan, what do you mean?"

Duncan growled into her ear. "I would . . . suggest that you and I enter into . . . *negotiations*, but I fear no good would come from it. I am already resolved. Poor Nathan was given one task. You see, Nathan understands who is truly in charge of this camp, and for that reason he sought me out, confessing that you were all

Kincaids, and in doing so betraying his kinsmen in an effort to ingratiate himself to me." He shrugged. "At first I sent him away, thinking him useless. What good are traitors, but for information—and he had already spilled his secrets. But then I realized I could make use of him from the inside of that castle there behind you. As a spy. And that I wanted him to take you with him."

"Why?"

"Don't you see?" He drew back, his eyebrows going up as if she missed the obvious. "Cull has taken something important from me." His lips transformed into a snarl. "Inverhaven should have been mine. But for some reason my father gave this opportunity to him." He stared at the ground for a moment. "I wanted to take something that meant as much to him. And we all know he wasn't exactly punishing you inside that tent last night for your attempted escape. Oh, don't play the virgin and try to deny it. Half the camp heard the sounds of your pleasure."

It wasn't true. She knew it. But he leered at her, and heat scalded her cheeks. How she hated him.

He gestured to Nathan. "But back to the matter before us." He took a few steps, pacing, before turning back to her. "Nathan failed. I can't let your lover know that he and I conspired, and no doubt Nathan would talk. Even if he did not talk to Cull, he would talk to someone, so I've no choice really. Death must be his consequence."

He intended to kill Nathan to silence him. And what of her? She knew the answer, and it weighted her heart like a stone. Now that he'd spoken those words to her, he wouldn't let her go.

As if to prove that, his hand suddenly caught her by the arm.

"Let me go," she insisted, trying to pull free.

But he only held her tighter. "Don't look at me with such fear. It's not as if I intend to kill *you*. What kind of a beast do you think I am?" His gaze grew solemn, and with his other hand, he touched her cheek. "But it is me whom you must please from this moment on."

His words and manner chilled her to the soul.

"You're a horrible man. Just like your father." Derryth broke free of Duncan's hold, and moved quickly to put as much space between them as possible, but his warriors, their expressions hard and cold, their hands on their weapons, herded her back. She was trapped. His prisoner. Helpless—and completely separated from Cull, her protector.

Duncan strode toward her, his eyes narrowing. "What do you know of my father?"

She stiffened. "Just stories I have heard."

"I see. Well . . . what can I say? I do take after him." Abruptly, he turned on his heel toward Nathan.

"I'm sorry, dear boy," Duncan said, his face a mask of feigned sympathy. "Stewarts aren't known for giving second chances. So let this thing be done."

Duncan crossed his arms over his chest, and stepped back, nodding to one of his warriors, who pulled his sword free of its sheath.

"No!" Derryth screamed, horrified. Would she be forced to stand here and watch as the young warrior was executed?

The executioner moved nearer.

"But I've something to tell you," Nathan shouted,

his eyes wild, his shoulders and legs straining toward the man who held his life in his hands. "Something you'll want to know."

Suddenly she knew what he would say.

"Nathan, no," she pled.

Though in truth, she knew he had no choice, if he wanted to live.

The young man glared at her. "She is not just a Kincaid clanswoman," he spat. "Her sister is the Lady Kincaid."

Everything went silent and still. The blood drained from Derryth's face. Now this enemy knew her secret. And Duncan was not only her enemy, but Cull's. He would no doubt use it against them both. Her stomach clenched. How she wished she'd told Cull the truth, but now it was too late.

Slowly . . . Duncan pivoted on the heel of his boot, his burning gaze falling on her.

"Well then." Pressing the palms of his hands together, he lifted his fingertips toward his chin and peered at her as if he had never seen her before. "To think, I just thought you a pretty peasant." A grin spread across his lips, one that bared his teeth. "You are far more valuable than that."

Midmorning, Cull strode toward his quarters. Despite the weight on his shoulders, the thoughts crowding his mind, he was eager to see Derryth, and lose himself in her again, at least for a while.

He had made some decisions. Some difficult ones, but ones with which he was at peace—as much peace as he could hope for, given the circumstances.

As he had this morning, he would continue to lead these men, and build the fortifications and entrenchments that would be required for the coming siege. When the preparations were done, he would send word to the castle to meet with the Laird Kincaid, and do his best to negotiate some settlement, some manner of peace between the Highlander and Buchan.

In this moment, he could not imagine what solution might satisfy both sides, but he would press through the coming days, and allow the answer to arise. However, if no resolution could be found, he would relinquish control here to whomever Buchan chose. And then . . .

His mind presented no further answers. And perhaps, yes, it was best he not consider that far ahead. He only knew he would do as his heart and his honor commanded, and marry Derryth, and spend the rest of his life protecting her from hurt and harm, whatever that meant, because she . . .

She was the greatest prize.

But truth be told, the warrior in him prayed that somehow, he could win this battle, for himself and her, and surrender nothing of his ambitions. That he could one day have a name, and lands, and Derryth too. Damn, more than anything, he wanted it all.

But right now, he wanted Derryth, in his arms. In his bed. Aye, he would make love to her all night long, because she, more than his ambitions, gave him strength.

He pushed through the door of the tent—

Effric stood there, his shoulders bent. The old man

turned to him, his face pale in the circle of his dark snood, and his eyes wide.

"She is gone," he uttered, his arms going out.

Cull looked at Effric, the words echoing in his ears. "What do you mean she is gone?"

His gaze swept about his quarters. Not finding her there, his heart turned to cinders. The world dropped from beneath his feet.

"I mean that she is gone." The man's eyes widened. "The girl is not in your tent."

His heart thundered with fear. She'd been taken, and at this moment, might be suffering harm.

Curse him, he'd left her alone, unguarded, without specific instructions to Effric not to leave her side. Someone among the camp had seen her attempt to escape with Nathan the night before as an unforgivable offense, and sought to punish her.

His blood crashed through his veins, the sound filling his ears. He had to find her. He turned toward the door—

But Duncan was there, ducking to enter.

"The girl is gone as well?" A dark scowl etched his face. "What a damned coincidence. I was just coming to tell you that our prisoner has escaped."

Cull felt the first crack of ice in his veins.

"*Which* prisoner?" he demanded.

"Nathan?" Duncan waved a hand. "Aye, I do believe that was the churl's name. The same one who was with her last night. Though I caged him myself last night, this evening when I went to issue his punishment for attempting that run to the castle last night, he was gone."

Cull felt as if he'd just taken a battering ram to his gut.

"When . . ." he said, barely able to speak.

"It had to have been before dawn," Duncan replied. "Else someone would have seen them."

Before dawn . . . just moments after he'd asked her to place her trust in him. Was Nathan lurking just outside, waiting for her, even then?

"Where would they have gone?" said Effric. "Should we send riders out to track them?"

"No need, old man," said Duncan with a shake of his head. "I can all but guarantee you they have made fools out of us, and fled to the castle after all."

Cull turned, his chest hollow, and stared at the inside of his tent with different eyes. Open eyes. There was no sign of a struggle. No tipped chair. No overturned goblet or spilled ale. The signs were clear. She had gone willingly with whomever had come for her.

Last night, had she sacrificed herself to appease him? Only to gain his trust so that she could escape again? He closed his eyes, remembering her face as he'd made love to her . . . the way she'd touched him. Kissed him. The words they'd spoken.

No. He couldn't believe that.

But she was gone just the same. He could only surmise that in the light of day, her loyalty to her clan and kin was stronger than what she felt for him. That when he'd asked her to trust him to find some resolution . . . she hadn't.

So she'd left him. She had made her choice, and in doing so, had left him free to do the same. And without her . . . what other choice did he have than to return to being the warrior he'd been before?

"What do you intend to do about her?" said Effric, pressing close.

"Nothing," he growled, feeling numb . . . humiliated by his feelings for her . . . and increasingly angry. "She is gone. If that is what she wants, then I don't want her back."

Without her, he could only go on as before. Once, they had told each other that it was all right to be on opposite sides, and indeed it was. But she no longer had his loyalty. He would not sacrifice himself—or his ambitions—for one who would abandon him without so much as a good-bye.

He turned to leave his tent then—only to find Duncan still standing there.

"I'm truly sorry, Sir Cull," he said gravely. "I know you had come to care for the girl."

He did not reply. Stone faced, he strode past him, into the clouded light of day. There, he immersed himself into the construction of the perfect siege camp. He barked out orders to his men, and toiled beside them, sweating . . . heaving timber and stripping down to pound posts deep into the ground. That night, beside a blazing fire, he ate among them, and listened to their songs and stories. Shunning the shelter of his quarters— and the bed he'd shared with Derryth last night, and the nights before—he stared through the darkness toward the castle, wondering if she peered out from inside.

*   *   *

Derryth shivered, and inched as close to the fire as she dared, having no blanket or fur to cover her. Only the garments and cloak she wore.

Tears slipped from her eyes, as she thought of Cull. What must he think, having found her gone? Was he afraid for her? Did he realize she'd been taken against her will? Or worse . . . did he think she'd escaped with Nathan again?

Nathan, who lay on the opposite side of the fire, turned away from her, just as silent and hateful as he had been every moment since their failed escape. His betrayal may have gained him his life, and for that she forgave him. But she could not forgive him for having aligned himself with Duncan before that. In doing so, he had been disloyal to not only herself, but Deargh, and Fiona, and the entire Kincaid clan. Even so, where had his duplicity gotten him? He was a prisoner, just like her. Still, she would not trust him again.

At Duncan's orders, four stone-faced warriors had taken them away while darkness still shadowed the camp, though he himself had not accompanied them, to her relief. That was her *only* relief, for she did not know what he intended, only that he would use her in some way against the Kincaids, and no doubt against Cull.

They had traveled for hours, riding southwest and away from Inverhaven, moving quickly, and stopping only to rest the animals, until night fell and they made their camp. One of the men caught several small hares, which they roasted on a makeshift spit, and split one between her and Nathan. Now, as she pretended to sleep, they sat all around her, silent and vigil, giving her no opportunity for escape. Even when she'd demanded privacy under the pretense of relieving herself, two had stood just a stone's throw away, behind the trees, stepping into her path when she darted in the opposite direction. But they'd been careful not to harm her, touching her only when necessary, and she feared that meant she was being saved for something else.

She closed her eyes, and willed herself to sleep—warming herself with the hope that soon Cull would come for her.

Chapter 16

The next morning, his skull splitting from the endless cups of wine he had drunk the night before with Robert and Duncan, Cull dispatched a missive to the castle, inviting the Laird Kincaid to discuss terms for his surrender. Within an hour, the reply came that the laird would meet him at the gates. Only then did he return to his empty tent, a place that no longer held solace for him, only privacy, which he desired in that moment as he prepared himself to meet with the man he intended to defeat.

And kill? He had no lust for blood or destroying families, only for winning. He considered some of his greatest triumphs to be conflicts he had won without bloodshed. If he could in some way allow the laird and his family to live, and go elsewhere, he would do so. Then, as promised, he would claim Inverhaven as his prize.

As for Derryth . . . what of her? Who was she to the Clan Kincaid? Did she live inside the castle, or in the village? Was she a servant to the laird's family? A seamstress perhaps, to the Lady Kincaid? Or a friend? He realized he did not know her at all. There'd been no time.

Despite the anger he'd felt the night before, he did not hate her. Could never hate her. But neither would he attempt to claim her for himself, if their paths crossed again. For one night, he had been a weaker man because of her, and he would never allow himself to be that weak again. Briefly he had considered going to see Deargh, to question him about what he knew beforehand of Nathan and Derryth's plan, but in the end, he merely gave orders to his captain that the older man and the others, including Fiona, should remain in the camp as prisoners, without the freedom to move about or take up weapons.

He washed and dressed, and avoided looking at the bed . . . and the chair . . . and at Derryth's wooden trunk, which remained neatly packed in the corner, having been left behind, no doubt too cumbersome to carry as she'd made her way through the darkness away from him.

Alone, he donned his armor . . . all but his helmet, and outside his tent, he climbed atop his horse. Effric handed him the reins. His men gathered round, shouting out encouragements to him, and insults against their enemy, a roar that grew so loud that no doubt those on the ramparts could hear. Perhaps even those inside the castle.

At the base of the hillside, Duncan and Robert, on

horseback, fell in behind him, along with a company of twelve warriors, all chosen by him. The camp was left in the command of his fellow King's Guards.

They left the shelter of the barricades and crossed the field, and in the distance, observed a wide and rushing river. They wended their way through rows of abandoned cottages and hovels, which he had ordered to be left intact, for no doubt most of the same villagers who now cowered inside the walls, fearing his attack, would return to their homes after he had won. He had seen it time and time again through his years as a warrior for powerful men. The lure of home and hearth had a way of blurring the lines of loyalty, and though there might be hard feelings and mutterings against him for years after, most would decide to stay.

As Kincaid warriors watched from the ramparts above, silent and solemn, they made their ascent up a wide road.

"The castle 'tis beautiful, is it not?" said Robert quietly.

"Indeed," replied Duncan in response. "'Twould be quite a prize for any man."

Cull did not miss how Duncan avoided speaking his name, as the future lord, but he cared little what Duncan thought now. Large and sprawling, with towers that most certainly on some days touched the clouds, the fortress was also strangely familiar, as if it had always been there in the back of his mind, and in his dreams. Perhaps that meant Inverhaven was truly his destiny, and that he should feel no regrets for making it his.

Arriving at the entrance, they all stopped their

horses, except for him, who rode to their forefront. In that manner, they waited as the heavy wooden gates groaned, swinging open.

A man stood there at the center—tall, and dark haired, wearing no armor, but only a tunic and plaid. He stood as proud as a king, and stared directly into Cull's eyes. He knew, without introduction, that this was Niall Braewick, the Laird Kincaid.

Behind him, several stone throws away, stood a beautiful, raven-haired woman who was very pregnant, whom he could only assume to be the Lady Kincaid. To her side, and a few steps back, glowered a striking pale-haired warrior, and a lovely redheaded woman, who if his information was correct, would be Faelan Braewick and his wife, the Laird and Lady Alwyn of Burnbryde Castle, who had no doubt arrived with countless Alwyn warriors to assist in the defense of Inverhaven, just before his army had arrived.

Beyond them, the bailey was filled with hundreds of warriors and villagers, including children, all looking at him in surly silence. He searched every face in the crowd, as well as he could from that distance, but did not see Derryth. It did not mean she was not there, watching him, hating him, at this very moment.

"You must be Sir Cull," said the Kincaid, his gaze piercing him through.

"I am," Cull replied. "I have come to offer terms."

"What terms?" the laird demanded darkly.

Cull shifted in his saddle. "Surrender the castle and your lands and you will be allowed to live."

"Whose terms are those?" the laird replied, sounding tired and unsurprised. "I don't think I have to ask, with Robert and Duncan Stewart sitting there behind you. Tell me, where is Buchan?" He stepped forward, his eyes gleaming with challenge. "Where is the Wolf?"

Though he'd intentionally not asked the details of the conflict between Buchan and the Kincaid, it was clear there was hatred between them.

Cull answered evenly. "The terms are issued by the king and Parliament."

The Kincaid laughed, the deep sound bearing an edge of sarcasm, as if he doubted Cull's words. "Well then . . . before I respond to your very generous offer, I would see the formal charges against me, issued by said king and Parliament, signed, and given his seal, so that I may know the reasons why I'm being commanded to forfeit my castle and my lands."

'Twas a reasonable request, and strangely, one rarely made by those facing attack.

Cull tilted his head in assent. "I shall have possession of the orders shortly, and will present them when they arrive. Until then, consider your castle under siege."

The laird's eyes went flat. "I think we've already assumed that."

With a jerk of his chin, the gates moved again, slamming closed.

Cull stared at the closed gate, his mind churning.

"Delightful people," said Duncan, sarcastically. "I don't know why Father so despises them."

To Robert, Duncan said, "Did you see Magnus—"

Magnus. The name was unfamiliar.

"You mean Faelan, as he is now known," his brother replied.

"He was standing off to the side."

"I always liked him," said Robert.

"I did not," Duncan growled. "He was such an arrogant bastard."

"But he isn't a bastard," Robert argued. "Don't you remember?"

"I meant the words as a general insult."

The words meant nothing to Cull. Always before, he'd preferred not to know the stories of the men he would meet on the field of battle. The more faceless and heartless they remained, the better for his conscience. But something about the story of the Braewick brothers, Niall and Faelan, intrigued him. He wanted to know more. He would have the story from Robert in private, without Duncan to interfere and taint the truth.

Cull turned his mount, and rode in the direction from whence they had come, the others following him.

Duncan still spoke behind him. "Faelan left his own castle and lands, to come to his brother's aid. Would you do that for me?"

"No," said Robert plainly.

"Nor I for you," said Duncan.

"I did not see your faithless lover, Cull," Duncan teased. "She must be in one of those fine towers, hiding from you. Hopefully not with that strapping young warrior who saved her."

Cull ignored the taunt, though he wished more than anything to reply with his fist. As much as he liked to believe he'd hardened himself against Derryth, his feelings were raw where she was concerned. Aye, she had made the decision to return to her people, but he did not have to like it. And though he'd confess the truth only to himself, he'd wanted nothing more than to have glimpsed her face.

Riding in silence for the remainder of the way, they returned to camp and an hour later held council in his tent.

"Father would want us to attack," said Robert, holding a cup of ale, and staring into the brazier.

Cull replied, "I am a knight of Scotland, and by my honor, I will follow the accepted rules of battle. I will present the laird with the orders he has requested to see, which by the laws of the land, he is owed. Your father promised to send them. Why have they not yet arrived?"

Robert shrugged. "Perhaps Father is distracted. Perhaps the king is dead, and word has simply not yet arrived here."

"Well we can't wait forever. The men want to fight, and soon will grow bored." Duncan stood and turned to him. "Give me leave, Sir Cull, to take a small company of men to go and retrieve the orders." He shrugged. "Likely I will meet the courier along the way. It isn't as if anything is going to happen *here* for a long while. Either way, it is not so far to Carven. If all goes well, I will return within a sennight, the orders in hand."

"Yes, go," said Cull.

Any excuse to send Duncan away had its attractions.

Duncan stood immediately. "Then I will go, and return as soon as possible. In the meantime, my company will continue on under my captains—under your direction of course."

After he was gone, Robert sat with Cull in silence for a long while.

He leaned forward, suddenly, his eyes, darkly intense. "Commander, I ask with all respect that you do not inform my brother, nor my father, of the request that I will now make . . ."

Cull scrutinized Robert's face. "What is it?"

But Robert's face gave nothing away. "I would beg your leave as well. Not to depart camp, but to dispatch a letter, written by myself."

"What sort of letter?"

Robert peered down into the goblet he held. "I feel . . . overwhelmingly compelled to send a trusted rider straightaway to Edinburgh, where Parliament last met, to request the original orders for this action there, at their source."

Original orders. Why would Robert feel the need to circumvent his father, and request such a thing?

Cull tensed, his scalp drawing tight. "You do not believe the orders were issued? Or that those we receive will be false?"

"I don't know . . . not yet," Robert replied, leaning back, his expression suddenly hard. "But I feel that for whatever reason, my father intentionally delays, and there is no guarantee Duncan will return with them. I . . . understand and respect your need to proceed in this mission with honor, and wish to do the same, as much as that is possible in battle. In war. Obtaining orders that we know to be true and correct will allow us both to do so, with a clear conscience."

Cull could not help but suspect there was something

else, buried within Robert's words. A warning that even here, between just the two of them, he dared not speak.

Would Buchan have truly dispatched him, with an entire army, to these Highlands, to fulfill a personal quest for revenge? Without the approval of the king or Parliament? Being that Buchan was no longer Justiciar of the North, he no longer commanded such authority. 'Twould be an egregious transgression, not just against the king and Parliament, but against Cull himself. One that despite the debt he owed to Buchan, he could never forgive.

He recalled the faces of the Kincaids, who had looked out at him from the gates, those of the Braewick men, and their wives, and their people. Long ago, he'd learned to block out the emotions . . . the empathy and care. But he could only admire the Kincaids, and wish duty had not brought him to this place. Even his desire to claim Inverhaven faded, which astounded him, because for a brief moment in time, it was all he desired. It was then he heard a voice inside his head that was not his own, compelling him to press further, to know more. It was Derryth's. His chest tightened, and his skin warmed, and in that moment he ached for her so deeply. Was she a part of him now, even if he did not wish it?

After glancing away, he again held Robert's gaze. "What grievance does your father have against the Braewick men? Don't tell me it's better not to ask. I must understand the truth of what's going on here."

Robert nodded, his face grim in the firelight. "You

deserve to know. You must understand that much of this I myself have heard secondhand, as my father all but refuses to speak of the true details of the matter."

"Go on."

"At one time, before Robert was king, and David still ruled the land, my father and the Laird Kincaid were allies of a sort, brought together by their disagreements over David's policies, and his plundering of Scotland's coffers."

"Allies you say."

"Aye. The Laird Kincaid was a powerful man here, in the north. Many smaller vassal clans swore their allegiance to him. But the night he died, two of those clans turned on him. The details have always been . . . muddy. Shrouded in secrecy. No one speaks of what happened that night, almost as if there is shame involved."

"The Kincaid was killed," said Cull.

Robert nodded. "Some allege betrayed and murdered . . . along with his lady wife, their three young sons, and many Kincaid men and villagers."

"His three sons, you say." Cull leaned forward, for if he had seen two of the sons that day, the words made little sense.

"Aye, and there is the source of today's conflict. You see, some two years ago, a man claiming to be Niall Braewick—the eldest of the sons who had long since been declared dead—*murdered* along with their father—appeared. He seized control of the castle at Inverhaven, which had been granted by the Crown to a Lord MacClaren, a suspected conspirator in his father's and mother's deaths. Indeed, he married the MacClaren's eldest daughter. But many, including my father, allege he is an imposter."

"And that therefore, we find ourselves here in a dispute over land." Cull nodded slowly. "There was another Braewick there today—"

"Faelan, who lived for years believing he was the bastard of another conspirator, the Lord Alwyn . . . defeated last just year at the hands of the Kincaids, in their quest for vengeance."

"Another imposter, I suppose."

Robert nodded. "So some claim."

"What do you believe?"

Robert remained silent.

"Robert," Cull demanded forcefully. "*What do you believe?*"

"I believe they are Kincaids," he blurted out, standing, to pace beyond the brazier. Turning back to Cull, he said, "I believe their claim is true and honorable."

Cull also stood. "And you believe that those years ago, your father was somehow involved in murdering theirs."

Robert clasped his eyes shut, and clenched his jaw. "I don't know. Truly, I don't but—"

His words stalled.

"But what?" Cull demanded, his muscles tense, for perhaps he did not want to hear what Robert would say.

"An old warrior told me once, when I was trying very hard to understand the earl's motivations against this northern clan, that my father once admired the Lady Kincaid, when she was young." His voice softened. "Before she married the laird."

No. He did not want to hear this.

"Your father has admired many women," Cull replied, tamping down the anger that grew in his chest.

"But loved only one, it seems," Robert concluded quietly. "The same man also told me when he traveled through the Highlands years later, and allied himself with the Kincaid, that he loved her still, and endeavored to have her for himself . . . and that she did not feel the same."

A whole clan destroyed . . . for the love of a woman? *That* was what had brought him here, to the gates of Inverhaven, with an army and catapults? *That* was what had driven him and Derryth apart?

His hands curled into fists, and he seethed. "You are saying that your father plotted against the Kincaid, because the Kincaid's wife rejected his advances, and that because of that they were all murdered? Including *children*?"

Just speaking the words chilled him to his soul.

"I did not say that," Robert bit out, glancing toward the door of the tent.

"But you *believe* it," Cull alleged. He closed his eyes, disgust rolling through him, like plague. Damn, what crime did he find himself complicit in?

In the shadows, Robert's countenance appeared to pale. "I only know that some say that there were not only MacClaren and Alwyn warriors present there that night. That there was a third conspirator, never identified, who provided many well-trained warriors." He sighed, aggrieved. "And that since hearing the words, my soul has never rested easy since."

For a long time, silence held the room.

"Write your letter," Cull said at last.

* * *

The sound of a rider's approach awakened Derryth. Her eyes flew open, and she lurched up, to stare across the top of the fire, to where Nathan lay curled on his side sleeping, and beyond the men who stood watch over them, diligent, their stances alert and their hands resting on the hilts of their swords. 'Twas early morning. Just before dawn. Darkness concealed the identity of the traveler, and weariness dulled her mind, but hope rose up inside her with each thud of the horses' hooves.

Cull, her heart sang. He came for her.

And yet when the rider arrived, the eyes staring down at her did not belong to Cull, but to Duncan. Disappointment speared through her, sharp and grievous. The dark seemed darker then, and the cold all that much colder. The distance between the camp and Inverhaven, herself and Cull, far too vast. She gathered her cloak around her, and stared into the fire, though its warmth did nothing to remedy the chill in her bones. Moments later, she heard the sound of him dismounting, and his boots crunching across the earth toward her. She closed her eyes, and braced herself for his unwanted presence.

"Wake that churl," he ordered, with a jerk of his chin toward Nathan. "Take him away so that I may speak privately to the lady."

One of the warriors kicked Nathan, and as he roused, they dragged him away.

With Nathan gone, Duncan stepped closer, his intimidating presence towering above her. Firelight revealed his lips drawn into a teasing smile.

"Good morning, love," he said.

Her blood curdled at the offending words. She offered no greeting in reply—only a warding glare. And yet she stood rigid, her feet fixed in place, undeniably curious about what he would say to her. If he would share some news of Cull or the Kincaids. But could she trust anything he told her? She knew she could not.

"I saw you there," he murmured, glancing to the place where she'd first stood after wakening. "Filled with such *hope* until you saw it was me."

She looked away, into the darkness, so he would not see the true depth of pain he inflicted upon her with the truth of those words. Just days ago, she had never felt so alone as in Cull's quarters, separated from her kinsmen. How strange that now she hoped with such a wild and desperate fervor, to be returned to him. To face the future and any conflicts or consequences with him. Here, she felt lost and entirely out of sorts.

But he moved nearer. "But he won't be coming for you. All it took were a few words from me, and he believed."

"He believed what?" she demanded, as a gust of wind swept her hair across her lips.

He shrugged, his manner easy, though his eyes gleamed hard and cold. "That you attempted again to escape with Nathan, and this time the two of you succeeded. He believes you're inside that castle back there."

Derryth's spirit plummeted. No doubt his words were true. Cull had no idea she was here, being held as Duncan's prisoner, and that she had been forced to leave him against her will. Instead, he believed she'd willingly escaped . . . run from him . . . after they'd sworn their hearts to each other. Weak kneed with despair, she sank down beside the fire, perching on a log.

No. *No.*

She must be stronger than this.

She inhaled deeply, drawing on Cull's strength and her own, and pushed the misery away. Things were different now. She had to believe that despite Duncan's lies and interference, Cull knew in his heart and soul that her words and her actions had been true. That she would never betray him. That they would find each other again, and never be torn apart.

But the question remained. Why had Duncan brought her here?

"Why have you done this?" she whispered harshly, making no effort to conceal the hatred in her eyes. "What do you intend?"

He crouched beside her, so close she felt his warmth.

"I don't really have to tell you anything, do I? But I will." He gestured between the two of them, his tone intimate. "Because you and I are going to be partners from this moment on."

"Partners," she repeated the unpalatable word, her voice devoid of inflection. "In what way?"

"In that you will do as I say," he said almost amiably—but the curl of his lip grew cruel. "Today. Tomorrow. Always. And if you do, I will allow him to live. Defy me, and . . . I make no promises."

Her heartbeat increased. Was he threateneing Cull's life? Despite his having abducted her from the camp, his threat shocked her still. She had known the two men did not like each other, and that Duncan seemed to perceive some sort of competition between them, but now the true depth of his hate for Cull had been made clear.

Derryth's blood went cold. Duncan was just as wicked as his father.

"What is it that you want?"

"I want Inverhaven," he replied, peering at her down his prominent nose. "I always have. Properly governed, those lands would be a bastion of northern power. And they will be mine, once I convince my father that Cull is not deserving. I also intend to marry you."

Marry her? She peered at him in stunned silence as the words thundered inside her ears. She could not marry him. Her mind rejected the very idea. There was only Cull. Her heart would accept no one else.

When he grazed her cheek with his knuckle, she flinched.

"What's wrong?" he chided. "Do you find my touch so distasteful? Or are you troubled that Cull never offered to marry you? Of course he did not. He thought you were just a baseborn peasant, worthy only of being his mistress." Duncan chuckled. "All this time . . . he had no idea of the jewel he held in his hands. The key to the northern realm."

Derryth's breath hitched in her throat. She closed her eyes, feeling cold and numb, wanting nothing more than to cover her hands with her ears. To block out the words. But why, when she already knew what he would say?

Duncan leaned closer, and purposefully closed his hand atop hers where it rested on her leg. "You are the daughter of the man who by right and royal edict should never have been ousted from those lands. Your sister foolishly chose to marry that imposter. What a grave mistake on her part. Once the castle and lands are taken, a marriage to you will only strengthen my claim."

He looked out over the landscape, which the dim, creeping light of dawn had just begun to reveal.

"It is my sons . . . *our* sons, who will rule the north."

Chapter 17

Cull spent the next sennight waiting. His days, he immersed himself into leading his men and tirelessly maintaining the siege. Each night he spent in restless misery, thinking of Derryth inside the castle. When at last a courier arrived, riding from the south, and presented Robert with a sealed missive, the two of them withdrew to the privacy of Cull's quarters. Watching Robert's face as he silently read, he understood what the written words would say before they were spoken. Still, he read each word, until fury blackened his gaze and he could read no more.

"Damn your father," Cull cursed, his fist clenched atop the table where he'd crashed it down on the crumpled missive.

"Aye," replied Robert tersely, already pacing the room. "While he'd convinced a good number of Parliament to support him in his attack against the Kincaids, there was greater dissent against any action. No orders were issued. This attack against Inverhaven is being undertaken without proper consent." He covered his mouth with his hand for a moment, before dropping it away. "He lied to you. He lied to us all."

Cull stared into the shadows. It took everything within him to contain his rage. The man who had once saved his life . . . who had given him a future, had manipulated what Cull had considered an almost sacred bond between them, and used him like a pawn.

"It is not the first time he has lied to me," said Robert, his voice edged with bitterness. "Even so, time and time again, I played the dutiful son, and carried out his orders, seeking to gain his approval—and his trust. Toward what end? Even knowing him so well . . . his history of aggression toward those who displease him, and duplicity to have his way . . . Cull, this time he has gone too far."

Cull hissed, and paced the floor, his quarters suddenly feeling too small and confining. "He has compromised my honor as a warrior, and as a King's Guard." He fixed his gaze on the other man. "Not only *my* honor, Robert, but yours and even Duncan's—and that of all our men."

Robert stared back at him, his features drawn in anguish.

What outcome had Buchan thought to achieve, in the end? The deaths of his enemies, before any intervention could come from outside? That he would seize these lands, and defend his claim to them later? One thing he knew for certain, Buchan had no right by the laws of Scotland to promise the lands to him as any sort of prize. That the earl had dangled such a false reward in front of him, to gain his cooperation, only infuriated him more. Certainly Buchan, knowing Cull's past, also knew his heart's desire. To have a name. To possess lands, and a family. That Buchan had used Cull's deepest, most private yearnings against him, to draw him into this wicked plot, was the greatest of unforgiveable betrayals.

And though Buchan's deception had brought Derryth into his life . . . it was also because of him that he'd lost her forever.

Or . . . had he?

Everything was changed now. He could not give his loyalty to a man who clearly stood for everything he despised. With his mind now freed to rebel against the man who had betrayed his trust and his soul, his heart returned instantly to her.

"What do you intend to do?" Robert asked pensively, watching him.

He would end this thing with Buchan. As far as he was concerned, his debt was paid. He was done. No matter what kindness was done to him those years ago, he could not carry out Buchan's personal campaign of hate and vengeance.

"I must go to Carven," said Cull. "I will relinquish my command of this siege. If he proceeds, he must do so without me."

Only then could he return to her.

"This green color is very pretty on you," said Ainsley, with a smile. "I'm so glad we chose it. Duncan will be so pleased."

The dark-haired, sharp-eyed young woman held up one of Derryth's new kirtles, sewn by Mairead's personal tailor—Mairead, being Buchan's wife. Not his church-wed wife, who was named Euphemia and from whom he was estranged, but his Gaelic handfasted wife, who was mother to seven of his children, including Duncan and Robert. Ainsley had explained all of this soon after Derryth had come to Carven Castle, where they were all guests of Lord Nester, Buchan's trusted ally.

Derryth had learned many things from Ainsley, as most of their conversations were one-sided, and the young woman loved to talk. Although everyone repeatedly called Derryth a guest, she was a prisoner—held here against her will—and no pretty garments or gracious words would change that. But her first night, locked alone in her windowless tower room, she'd decided that though she could not bring herself to smile and laugh, as if she was in any way happy here, she would play the quiet and docile girl in order to learn all she could about her enemies. Some detail . . . some passing comment might later be useful. For that reason she passed each day silent and sullen, watchful and listening.

In this manner she learned that Mairead was *not* Ainsley's mother, but Buchan *was* her father. Other than that, the details of her birth were not exactly explained and Derryth did not pry. She only knew that Ainsley moved about the castle at ease, and seemed to get along well with Mairead.

They were not in her room at present, but in Ainsley's, preparing for the evening meal. Derryth had napped for hours at midday, burdened by a soul-deep weariness that she hadn't been able to shake since arriving. Even now she could feel the pull of sleep behind her eyes. She could only assume her psyche sought to escape the strain of being at Carven by seeking to hide away in dreams.

But she would be expected belowstairs. A deft-handed maid had styled Derryth's hair. She wore a new scarlet kirtle, which might as well have been sack-cloth for all she cared, because the garment had been paid for by Buchan.

Buchan . . . who remained very much a mystery to her, passed in and out of her days, speaking little. Glowering much. He kept mostly to his chamber, accepting and sending missives, which, according to a passing comment by Mairead to Lady Nester, kept him informed of the king's health and the ever-changing alliances being formed between his two older brothers with the nobles and powerful men of the country—something he seemed fixated upon, and yet at the same time seemed to shun by hiding away here at Carven, his days and nights filled with rest and entertainment.

Dreading the evening before her, when she would be returned to Duncan's company, Derryth glanced out the open window again, searching the deepening night for something . . . *someone* she feared would never come.

"I cannot wait to have you as a sister," Ainsley exclaimed, allowing the maid to fasten a bracelet at her wrist. "I will help you with your wedding to Duncan, and when the time comes, you can help me with mine."

A wedding to Duncan that had not yet been agreed

to by Buchan, something she knew from the terse conversations between the two men each night.

"Marriage can be such a magnificent thing," declared the young woman. "When two people are in love."

Ainsley hadn't always been so friendly. She'd circled Derryth warily for days. Likewise, Derryth had done very little to encourage a friendship between them. She could only believe Ainsley wanted someone her own age to talk to. This afternoon, it was as if a font had sprung open. Since then, Ainsley had been a nonstop stream of chatter.

"Have you a betrothed then?" asked Derryth, if only to fill the silence.

"Not yet . . . but soon," the girl replied slyly . . . *giddily*, her cheeks flushing scarlet. "The man I love is not a nobleman, and has no land or titles, but he is a well-respected King's Guard. Soon, his circumstances will change, and then he will approach father to ask for me."

Derryth tensed, for the description of Ainsley's suitor seemed too familiar.

Ainsley stood, and peered at herself in a small looking glass that hung on the wall. Apparently liking what she saw, she smiled, and stroked the gleaming length of her hair. "I cannot wait. I love him desperately, you see. And I know he loves me too."

Anxiety twisted Derryth's stomach. She could hold silent, and ask no questions. But no . . . if it was Cull, she wanted to know. He had spoken vaguely of marrying into the nobility. Was it Ainsley's hand that had been his intent?

"What is his name?" Derryth asked, suddenly finding it difficult to breath.

But just then, Mairead appeared on Ainsley's threshold, dark haired and severe. "Come Ainsley and . . . you . . . Derryth . . . it is time to go belowstairs."

Ainsley swept close, taking hold of Derryth's arm.

"Later," she whispered. "I can't speak of him in front of her. She doesn't approve of him for me."

Neither did Derryth.

They joined Mairead in the corridor, where the older woman cast a sharp gaze upon Derryth, her hair and her new garments. "Better. At least you are presentable now."

Derryth's cheeks burned. When she'd arrived at Carven, she'd been filthy from three days of travel, her garments muddied and torn, and had been made to feel like a savage being accepted into civilization ever since. But she would not be provoked into speaking, or challenging Buchan's other wife. Instinct told her she was just as dangerous as he.

Tension settled in her neck and shoulders, with each step they descended, for each night in the great hall meant torment for her.

Belowstairs, they entered the shadowy great room, lit by wall sconces and candles. From what she had gathered, the lord of Carven Castle had hosted Buchan and Mairead here for nigh on a sennight, as they awaited word of the king's health, which from the last missive arriving from Ayrshire, had neither declined nor improved.

Suddenly Duncan was there, his hand at her back, possessive and claiming.

She had learned not to flinch so obviously at his touch. Though there had never been an easy moment between them, and he had made clear to all his intention to marry her, he had never attempted to force himself on her in any way, not even for a kiss. She had, however, caught him more than once staring at her with blatant interest, and remained wary of the moment his tactics would change.

"Come," he murmured near her ear. "Tonight you will not hide away among the women, as you have on previous nights, but sit where you belong, between my father and me. I insist."

At last, Carven rose up before them like a dark raven perched on the earth. It was hours after nightfall when they arrived in the courtyard, but Cull had refused to stop for the night, choosing to press on, for the sooner he was finished here, the sooner he could return to Inverhaven to issue final orders to his men to withdraw from Buchan's folly, and to find Derryth.

Would she go with him, if he asked her? Despite her loyalty to her clan, he thought she would if the conflict between them was removed. Though now, with his world upended, he had difficulty imagining what a future between them would be.

But a life without Derryth seemed just as unimaginable. Each time he thought of seeing her again, his pulse quickened, and he felt half sick at the idea of her being in danger. Did that not mean something? Hell, he had not slept a sound night since she'd gone, for he lay awake, tormented by the fantasy of her, intermingled with the dark memories of his past. He was ready to sleep again, but he would only sleep with her returned to his side.

Moments later, after passing through numerous guards who instantly recognized them, and allowed them to pass, Cull and Robert strode through the castle doors, where music and voices and sounds of the evening meal underway emanated out from a great hall. A servant rushed forward, offering to take their cloaks, but both brushed the man's efforts away.

Cull kept away from the open doors, uninterested in the revelry or entertainments. Already tension pulled at his shoulders, and his mind burst with the words he would say.

To Robert, he said, "I have no wish to sit with him at a table and pretend that we are in good stead."

Robert responded with a curt nod, and eyes that burned as angrily as his own. "I'll let him know we must speak to him alone, and that we have no wish to wait until tomorrow."

Striding away, he disappeared inside—

Only to return moments later, his jaw clenched. He avoided meeting Cull's gaze, and issued a vile curse.

"What is it?" said Cull, knowing Robert had seen something.

Something inside the room behind him. His torso tensed, and his arms tightened. He moved forward, but Robert's shoulder met his, halting him in his tracks. His hands grasped his arm.

"Don't go in there," Robert growled between clenched teeth. "Not yet."

Cull froze. "Why."

"*She's there.*"

Who was there? What woman would provoke such a response in Robert, and a warning to keep him away? His mind hurtled out only one reply.

"*Derryth*," he murmured.

His soul thundered. Was it true?

Here? Not at Inverhaven? *How?*

He moved toward the door.

"Robert?" called a woman's voice—one he vaguely recognized. "Is that you? Oh, come back!"

But it was Cull who entered to search for one face among the shadows.

Duncan's hand closed over hers. Derryth tore it away. They had long since finished eating, and now sat on benches near the fire, intermingled with Buchan and Mairead, Lord and Lady Nester, and others. Everyone laughed and talked all around them, unaware or unconcerned about her growing distress.

Duncan leaned close to growl into her ear, "What will it take for you to warm to me? Have I not played the part of the gentle suitor? Have I not shown you that I am capable of patience?"

Derryth bristled at the intimate tone of his voice. His attentions . . . his expectations closed around her, smothering and offensive. Even the lingering smell of roasted meat became too much, threatening to turn her stomach. She had thought she could play the submissive captive, but she'd been wrong. She could not abide his touch, or his words.

"You are no suitor of mine," she blurted. "I am a prisoner here. I am being held against my will. Your father seeks to destroy my clan, as do you, and I will never forgive that."

"Oh come now," he chided, his gaze brightening with anger. "You wouldn't be the first captive bride to fall in love with her husband."

What he proposed was impossible. She was in love with Cull, her heart filled to overflowing, and there was not one smidgeon of room for any other man. That would never change. She could not even force herself to pretend.

"I will never love you." She turned her face, looking away, toward the doors, wanting to escape, but knowing she would never make it past the guards.

Suddenly, Cull was there—his pale hair gleaming in the light of a wall sconce—tall and arresting, dressed in dark oiled leather, scowling into the shadows—

"*Cull.*" Ainsley stepped into his path, her dark hair shining down her back, and in the next moment—threw herself into Cull's arms.

Derryth also moved to stand from her seat, her emotions tangled, fear and love—

And pride, for was not Cull the most magnificent thing?

Only for Duncan to ensnare her by the arm, and force her back down.

"Do not make that mistake again," he growled near her ear, any vestige of his former gentleness gone. "You will remain beside me. Your *eyes* will remain on me. Do you understand? Remember what I said?"

That he would kill Cull, if she showed any preference for him.

She didn't believe it. Cull would slay Duncan in an instant, if provoked or given no other choice. She did not doubt his fighting prowess. But she must consider their surroundings. Buchan was here, and Lord Nester, each of them boasting scores of men, who would act on their orders.

"Aye," she hissed, furious at being controlled in such a way when she wanted nothing more than to rush to Cull's side.

"I meant it," Duncan gritted.

She waited for Cull to approach, her heart beating wildly. She heard the even fall of his footsteps on the stones . . . saw his boots, but that was all, because fearing for him . . . wanting to keep him safe, she kept her face averted. And yet. Seeing the hem of Ainsley's kirtle appear so close beside him . . .

Her gaze darted up.

Cull stared at her where she sat beside Duncan—his gaze cold and flat and dangerous. Ainsley clung to his side, smiling and vibrant.

Duncan's hand squeezed her wrist, and she reminded herself once more that they were surrounded by men with swords who would intervene within seconds—on Duncan's behalf—if any conflict arose. She quickly diverted her gaze away, never having felt such frustration.

"Sir Cull, where are your manners?" said Buchan, his voice low and questioning. "And your greetings.

Say hello to Mairead, and to our hosts here at Carven."

"Greetings, Mairead," Cull all but growled. "Greetings all." He added pointedly, "Duncan. *Derryth*."

"Truly, Cull, why so serious?" Ainsley questioned, offering up a nervous laugh.

"It's because I took his favorite captive." Duncan replied bluntly, and Derryth clenched her eyes shut. "I'm sorry you are angry, Cull. But once I learned she was the Lady Kincaid's sister . . . daughter to the deceased Laird MacClaren—"

He paused dramatically, allowing his breath to ease out of his throat.

In the silence that followed, Derryth felt as if her heart were being ripped out.

"Oh . . . Cull," Duncan said softly. Cruelly. "You did not know? Well . . . now that you know the truth, certainly you must understand why I had to get her out of that camp. So filthy and dangerous, with men everywhere. And keeping her within sight of the very place where her clan will be destroyed?" He sighed, as if aggrieved on her behalf. "Even you must concede she deserves better consideration than that."

Duncan's hand closed on hers. She opened her eyes and stared at the offending sight.

"And to my amazement and I'm sure to hers, as we traveled here, we discovered fond feelings for each other."

Derryth's head dipped at that, feeling too heavy to hold high another moment more.

"Duncan," said Buchan in a warning tone.

"As far as the Mistress MacClaren is concerned,

your duty is done," he said to Cull. "I am her protector now."

Buchan spoke then, sharply. "*I* am her protector, Duncan. Mairead and I. Until I decide differently, which I have not." He paused. "Robert, take Cull there, to the table. I know you must both be hungry and travel-worn."

"I would ask instead to speak to you, my lord," Cull said darkly. "Alone."

"Tomorrow," Buchan replied brusquely. "There will be time then. Tonight, rest. Perhaps tomorrow, you will be more yourself. Nester's servant over there—the very tall man, do you see him?—he will see that you are given a chamber in which to rest."

Lord Nester stood then. "For Sir Cull the Nameless, we can do far better than that. What an honor it is to welcome you into our home, Sir Cull."

Derryth snuck another glance, to find Cull looking at Lord Nester, and Ainsley smiling radiantly beside him.

Cull replied quietly. "Thank you for your hospitality."

"It is not given freely," replied Lord Nester, laughing.

"My lord?" Cull inquired.

"I insist that while you are here, you instruct my men in their morning weapons practice. It is rare they have the opportunity to observe a renowned warrior such as you."

"Good god," muttered Duncan beside her, derisively.

"Of course he will," said Buchan magnanimously.

"We can all watch!" cried Lady Nester, clasping her hands together. "We can make a sort of tournament of it. If Sir Cull agrees."

"Aye, my lady," Cull replied politely—but without true enthusiasm. "As you wish." He redirected his gaze toward Buchan. "As long as it does not delay my appointment with you, my lord."

"'Twill not," Buchan replied testily, his eyebrows raised. "Now go, and eat. Drink wine. Flirt with my daughter. Stop glowering at everyone."

Laughing, Ainsley led Cull away.

Duncan called for more wine and filled Derryth's cup, but she did not drink for fear the rich liquid would cause her to reveal her emotions, for all to see. Several of Buchan's men joined them, and told stories, the details of which she did not hear . . . for as every moment passed, her attention remained focused elsewhere.

Though she did not dare look at Cull, she felt his presence, just as surely as she felt the heat from the fire. She listened, craving the sound of his voice, and heard him offering courteous, but short, replies to Ainsley's endless questions and attempts to draw him into conversation. Aye, he was angry to have discovered her here, and most certainly to learn she was a MacClaren. But she could not help but wonder if there had been a romance between him and Ainsley, as Ainsley had inferred. It was apparent that Ainsley had expectations.

Suddenly, Cull was gone, and Ainsley with him. Misery weighted Derryth so heavily she found it difficult to breath. Even if he was angry with her, he'd been here, in her sight. After these endless days apart, she hated being separated from him. She needed to talk to him. To tell him everything that had occurred, so there would be no misunderstandings between them.

So as not to raise suspicion, she waited a long while before at last speaking to Duncan, who had long ago fallen brooding and silent. "I am tired. Please, I would like to retire."

"You look pale," Duncan said, sounding more accusatory than concerned. "Are you feeling unwell?"

"Only fatigued, as I rose very early this morning," she replied, though she *had* felt sickly earlier that morning. Unsteady and dizzy. But how else was she supposed to feel when awakening to this place and these people? Or perhaps it was that she'd eaten very little these past few days. She'd had no appetite.

"I will walk you," he said, standing.

As he had each night—for she went nowhere unescorted. With his hand at her back, they paused so that she could bid good night to Buchan and Mairead, and Lord Nester and his family. He then guided her toward the tower stairs. She feared being alone with him there, in that shadowy place. Now that Cull had returned, she did not know what to expect.

When they had gone two steps up, Robert suddenly appeared behind them. "Duncan."

He did not meet Derryth's gaze, but spoke only to his older brother.

"I need to speak to you."

"In a moment, when I return," Duncan replied, urging Derryth up another step.

But his brother persisted. "It's important—a matter having to do with your men who remain at the camp." Robert caught the attention of a finely garbed old woman, wearing an old-fashioned kirtle and jeweled girdle, who approached, walking very slowly. Derryth knew her to be the Dowager Lady Nester.

Robert bent his head, and raised his voice. "Lady Nester, would you mind seeing Mistress MacClaren to her room?" Turning to Duncan and Derryth, he whispered, "Remember, she is not very good of hearing, so if you wish to have a conversation, you must speak loudly—but don't shout, because she thinks that is rude."

Duncan glanced at Derryth. "And even if you are thirty winters old, like me, she'll pinch you for it, and it hurts."

If he wasn't Duncan, she might find his humor amusing.

"Very well," muttered the lady, exerting some effort to place her foot on the first step, and glancing toward Derryth. "I'm going that way myself."

"Then I suppose this is good night," said Duncan in a disappointed tone.

Lifting Lady Nester's hand, Robert pressed a kiss to her knuckles, before pressing her hand into Derryth's. But as she already knew, the lady was not a friendly or affectionate sort. She dropped Derryth's hand, and ascended the next step.

With an air of reluctance, Duncan removed his hand from Derryth's back, and with a lingering glance that made her uncomfortable, he turned away.

Derryth let out a shaky sigh of relief, watching him

and Robert stride toward the doors that lead into the bailey.

As always, four guards stood watch there, protecting the entrance, in addition to many more she knew to stand vigil outside. It was something she did always . . . assess opportunities for escape, but there had been none at Carven. The Wolf kept himself too thickly guarded, and where she was concerned, there was always someone watching.

Not that she wanted to leave now that Cull had arrived. Even heartsick over him, and fearing he hated her, she had no wish to flee if there was a chance of seeing him again. Her blood ran warm, just knowing he walked the same floors. And yet with each step up the stairs, she felt more removed from him than ever. Forgotten, even. As she followed the dowager slowly, up each step, tears blurred her eyes, but it was all right because the stairs were dark, and only sparsely lit with small lanterns. At last, they arrived at the first landing, and turned, pacing through a space of inky shadows before reaching the next rise of steps.

"Watch your step," the old woman warned sharply, moving upward into the dim light. "And do stop *rushing* me."

Suddenly, powerful arms pulled Derryth into the blackness.

A hand firmly covered her mouth, capturing her gasp.

Chapter 18

Derryth did not need to see the face of the man who held her. His body and his scent were as familiar as her own.

Only the way he continued to hold her so tightly could not, under any circumstance, be called an embrace. Though his hand lowered slowly from her mouth, he continued to impose his power on her, clenching her helpless against him so tightly she could barely breathe. She was his prisoner, and utterly under his control.

"Cull," she whispered, trying to pry his hands from her.

But then he turned her again—quickly . . . pressing her back *hard* against the stone wall.

She gasped, her hands coming up against his chest. Head lowered, he pressed his forehead to hers, his every muscle drawn tight against her, his manner terrifyingly intense.

His eyes stared into hers, agleam in the dark.

"If you did not understand what I meant when I said that I *chose you*, and when I asked you to *trust me*"—he whispered harshly, the words spilling from his lips—"then let me be clear."

"I *did* trust you," she whispered back, frantic—and terrified that someone would discover them together. That suddenly Duncan would appear on the stairs, and kill Cull, and she would never leave the shadows again.

"I meant that I loved you." He held her tighter. His nose touched hers.

"Oh, Cull."

"*I love you, Derryth*. God help me, I do."

She seized handfuls of his tunic in her fists, filled with a wild craving for the power and muscles she felt beneath.

"I love you too." Her eyes filled with tears.

"Then why—"

"I was going to tell you who I was, that I was a Mac-Claren, but please understand and forgive me, I wanted to tell Deargh first—that I was going to stay with you, so he could tell my sister, and explain."

He responded with a nod . . . exhaling. The tension in his muscles eased.

But there was still so much she needed him to know. "And then soldiers came, and I thought you'd sent them to bring me to you, but it was him—"

The words spilled from her mouth in a feverish whisper.

"It doesn't matter now." His lips pressed against her temple, and his arms came around her in a fiercely tender embrace. She stilled, overcome by his comfort, his touch, inhaling his scent . . . but she had not said all she needed to say.

"Cull, I—" she murmured.

"Shhh." His hand came up gently beneath her chin, to trace the lines of her jaw with his fingertips, and his mouth closed on hers—the kiss saying more than any words. Derryth's spirit, which had been so low for days now, soared as she held his body, so strong and beloved, tight against hers.

She stiffened, hearing something on the stairs. He'd heard it too. She shifted . . . sheltering her with his body.

"Where are y' girl?" called the dowager, from just out of sight.

It was enough to fill her with terror again. Perhaps it was only the dowager, but next, it would be someone else who would tear her and Cull apart forever.

"You must go," she whispered. "Duncan said he will kill you if he finds me talking to you—or even looking at you."

"He said he will *what*?" Cull growled beneath his breath, his eyes flashing in the dark.

She pushed out of his arms. "Don't trust him. Don't trust any of them."

Breaking free of the shadows, she rushed toward the stairs, praying the shadows concealed the feverish flush on her cheeks.

"I'm so sorry," she called out. "My slipper fell off my foot, and I fell behind looking for it in the dark."

"What did you say?" the woman said grumpily, squinting at her, before giving an impatient wave of her hands and turning away.

Derryth followed, but looked over her shoulder once more. Cull still stood there, a shadow in the night.

"What were we thinking when we chose that color for you?" Ainsley said as she and Derryth passed through the garden the next morning. "Here in the light, that shade of green turns your skin the most unpleasant cast."

It had gone on all day. The sharper, sideways glares. The slights about her appearance and manners. Those few bitter words spoken between Cull and Duncan in Carven's great hall the night before had been enough to make Ainsley realize that Cull had feelings for Derryth, and it was enough to make her Ainsley's enemy.

And yet the words did not wound. Cull loved her. He had come to her, and their feelings for each other were just as strong as before. She carried that knowledge like a talisman. She wore it like a shield.

The night before, her hours alone had been spent restless, and wanting him with her. She had so many questions. Why had he come here? Certainly not to find her. He'd believed her to have escaped to Inverhaven. Why had he seemed so . . . intense toward Buchan the night before, as if displeased with the earl? Angry, even? Was he still loyal to the Wolf, or had something occurred to change that?

As the night had gone on, there had also been fear. Fear for Cull. Fear for herself. Fear for her loved ones, still under siege at Inverhaven. By the time morning had come, she'd nearly been ill from it and had barely been able to swallow a bite of her breakfast. She felt so tired from lack of sleep, and would have remained in her room if not for the hope of seeing Cull again. Of speaking to him.

Perhaps lack of sustenance and rest made her sharp now, for she could not help but reply curtly to Ainsley. "I would be more than happy to return the kirtle to the tailor, and go back to wearing the garments I came here in. Would you like me to take it off now?"

Ainsley paused in her step, and sidled closer. "I can't imagine why my brother would want to marry a backward little Highlander like you. No castle or lands seems worth that trouble."

With a toss of her head, Ainsley moved more quickly, walking ahead to join Mairead and Lady Nester, leaving her behind.

Derryth almost smiled. Alone, at last. It was just the sort of opportunity she'd have waited for to attempt an escape, but now that Cull was at Carven, she must find some way to speak to him again. Was it possible that they could escape together?

And suddenly, Cull was there, passing through the trees, garbed in a fitted leather jerkin, his long, lean legs encased in dark trousers and high boots. He gripped his sword in one hand, mid sheath. Her excitement at seeing him grew as he moved very close beside her, so close their garments touched.

"Good morning, Derryth," he murmured sensually.

She exhaled, startled and thrilled by the clandestine moment. But then his hand found her waist. He pulled her close and bent, kissing her hard and long on the mouth. Possessing her. Branding her as his own.

Then he was gone, and she left standing in place, breathless and flustered, her heart pounding over the forbidden kiss, watching him go, so tall and so commanding, without even a pause in his booted steps.

Fear quickly took pleasure's place. What if someone had seen?

"Didn't you hear what I told you last night?" she hissed after him.

"Aye, lass, I did," he replied over his shoulder, almost nonchalantly. "*Let him try.*"

Only then did she see Robert, emerging from the trees to walk beside Cull. He chuckled low in his throat. "You daring bastard."

Clearly, he'd seen Cull kiss her, and yet he did not challenge Cull for what he'd done. With a start, she remembered the night before. Robert's sudden appearance at the bottom of the stairs, drawing Duncan away. Were the two men friends then . . . allies, even? Was it possible that Robert could be trusted?

She arrived at the practice field. Shunning the company of the women, she was more than pleased to stand by herself. It appeared that Lord Nester's men had already gathered, and waited for Cull to arrive. Lord Nester and Buchan stood at a distance, arms crossed, watching. Duncan as well, though he wore a sword. With narrowed eyes, he watched his rival take the field, with Robert at his side.

"Wait!" called Lady Nester. "Champions! Do not begin without receiving your favors!"

Ainsley untied a blue ribbon from her wrist. "Did you not bring a ribbon?" she said to Derryth. "Forgive me. I forgot to tell you."

It did not trouble Derryth in the least not to be included, but Lady Nester, who had always been pleasant to her, moved nearer, several ribbons streaming from her hands. "I have several. Here, one for you, Derryth, to bestow upon your chosen champion." Her eyes twinkled, as she pressed a scarlet streamer into her hands. "Although we all know who that is!"

She meant Duncan, of course, for everyone in this household persisted in the myth of their romance, rather than acknowledging that Derryth had been brought here, and remained, against her will.

Lady Nester distributed several more ribbons to several other ladies before turning again to the field. "Men. Come, and accept the colors of your fair ladies!"

For a moment she felt dizzy . . . unsteady. She ought to have eaten this morning. A piece of bread, at least.

But then Derryth's eyes met Cull's, and she became strong again. She watched . . . heart beating as he strode directly toward her.

I choose you.

Aye, she had chosen Cull too, and if he was brave enough to stand against Duncan, then she was too. Though she glimpsed Ainsley's forward movement beside her, she strode forward as well. To the sounds of surprised gasps, she met him halfway. There, they stopped and stared into each other's eyes, and she did not care who saw. Aye, she was frightened, but she'd never felt more alive.

She tied the ribbon just below his shoulder, around the flexed muscle of his arm.

"Thank you, fair lady," said Cull, his voice husky with humor.

"Win the day," she breathed.

"I intend to," he murmured. "And the lady as well."

He backed away, his eyes fixed on hers. She returned to the periphery of the field, where she avoided the gaping stares of the women who waited there. Ignoring them, she turned back to watch.

Cull drew his sword, and handed the empty sheath to Lord Nester's grandson who'd approached him, appearing intent on acting as his squire. The boy drew back to stand beside Derryth, his eyes trained on Cull, his eyes alight with admiration.

After that, Cull did not hesitate. He lifted his sword.

The air sounded with the clash of metal. He moved with lightning quickness, meeting the first challenger with easy confidence, and encouragements, though eventually the man fell away—red faced and yielding victory. Nearby, Robert performed much the same exercises with a line of challengers.

Duncan remained in place, his features carved into stone. Of course he was furious that she'd tied the ribbon on Cull's arm. No doubt he already plotted some punishment against them both. But she was tired of being afraid, and she would not beg his forgiveness for what she had done.

Lord Nester strode forward, gesturing toward Cull. "There, men, do you see? The way he lunged forward and swung his sword, as one movement, without hesitation? Continue to watch this man. There is a reason his name is spoken with such reverence among the fighting men of Scotland."

"And among the ladies as well!" called Lady Nester.

Laughter filled the air. Cull himself appeared not to have heard the compliments. He smiled easily, speaking to Robert and several other men, one of whom bent over his sword, as if to examine its craftsmanship.

At last, Lord Nester moved into their midst, hands raised. "Enough. The contest is done. I think 'tis clear who must be declared champion."

"Unless Duncan wishes to offer challenge," said Buchan abruptly, moving forward. He looked between Cull and his son, who remained fixed in place.

Silence fell over the gathered party, along with an almost palpable tension. It was as if Buchan sought to provoke his son against Cull, and perhaps vice versa. Derryth suddenly felt very warm . . . and cold at the same time. Aye, she was agitated by the scene unfolding before her, but why did she feel so strange? The dizziness returned, teasing along the edges of her vision. Was it only that she had not eaten? Or could it be that she was ill?

Or . . .

Her breath caught in her throat.

She had missed her monthly courses. With everything else happening, she hadn't realized.

Duncan lifted his chin. "Of course Sir Cull is an *impressive* warrior. Who would dispute that?" He spoke the words with a distinct edge of sarcasm. "It is all he knows. He is nothing more than a savage dog, trained to fight for his master. For that reason I decline."

"For what reason?" Robert demanded.

"Because he's a damned *slave*," Duncan thundered. "Did you know that, everyone?" He let out a cutting laugh. "My father purchased him off a slave ship when he was but a boy. He'll never be anything but a slave.

And yet our father, and now you, Robert, continually encourage him to believe he is something better."

Hearing his vile words, Derryth's pulse increased, and a thin sheen of perspiration rose upon her arms and against the back of her neck. She despised Duncan . . . and pitied him! That he should be so intentionally cruel, out of petty jealousy, made him seem so very pathetic. But she knew Duncan's pettiness made him dangerous, and if she had feared for Cull before, she feared for him doubly so, now that she knew . . . she *knew* she carried his child.

Everyone stood silent, staring at him. Buchan's nostrils flared, but he did not speak. Perhaps she read his expression wrong, but he appeared embarrassed for his son. Behind him, Cull stood unmoving, his stance as relaxed as before, as if Duncan's words did not wound him in the least. With his blue eyes alight and a half-smile on his lips, appeared almost amused.

Duncan strode past Cull, his gaze fixed on Derryth. "Why meet this *nothing* in contest, when I have already won?" His lip curled into a taunting smile. "She may have tied a ribbon on your arm, but it is I who will marry her, and take her each night into my bed."

Derryth flinched at the words, fearing they would provoke Cull's response, and indeed, Cull's eyes went flat and black, and he moved as if to intercept Duncan—

"*No,*" she said, stepping forward.

But the world *turned* suddenly, disappearing from under her feet. She saw nothing more, because the day turned black.

* * *

Cull carried Derryth toward the castle, Duncan forgotten. Everyone followed close behind him.

"Take her into the hall," cried Lady Nester.

"Nay, take her straightaway to her room," Mairead replied.

"Summon my physician," Lord Nester ordered.

To his relief, he felt her move in his arms. Glancing down, he saw her blue eyes looking up at him, hazy and confused. But the color had not returned to her cheeks.

"You fainted, I think," he said.

"I'm sure that is all," she replied, straightening. "You can put me down."

"I will not."

Up the steps of the castle he carried her and inside the great wooden doors, held open by Buchan's guards. Inside, he took the steps upward into the tower. Voices echoed off the stone walls, all around them.

"Careful not to drop her," Ainsley said, sounding insincere.

On the landing where he'd kissed her the night before, he dipped his head.

"Don't be afraid. I'm going to get you out of here," he murmured. "I won't let him marry you."

She peered up at him, her eyes warm and soft. "I can't marry him. I don't love him. He's not the father of my bairn."

He was overtaken then, by women intent on tending to her. They urged him toward her curtained bed, and pulled down the covers, and set about pouring water.

And yet he noted very little of that. All he heard inside his head were the words she'd spoken. Really, just the one. Bairn.

A baby.

"You're certain?" he asked softly, as he lay her down, her head upon the pillow.

"Yes," she whispered back, color flushing her cheeks.

His chest seized tight. He wanted to order them all out of the room . . . to be alone with her, and yet he was pushed . . . jostled toward the door.

He heard Derryth's voice behind him. "I do not need a physician. I did not eat this morning, nor last night. That is all. Yes, truly. Yes, Lady Nester, I'm well."

Cull did not see Derryth again that evening. He overheard that she took her evening meal in her room. Being separated from her put him on edge and no doubt he scowled, for everyone in the great room gave him wide berth. Most especially Ainsley, who'd been casting him wounded looks all night. He was doubly cross for having his efforts to meet with Buchan yet again rebuffed, with another promise of tomorrow.

Tomorrow would come, and he would have his say with the earl, and as honor required him to do, he would formally relinquish his command of the siege at Inverhaven. Then, one way or another, he would get Derryth out of this place. Whether he would return with her to her family—which would be a very complicated decision for him—or take her far from the Highlands remained to be seen. It was his plan that they would make the decision together, after his meeting with Buchan.

A short distance away, the earl played chess with Lord Nester. At the Wolf's every move, those who watched broke out into praise and applause, marveling over his cunning. Duncan sat on the opposite side of the room, throwing dice with a group of men.

Robert appeared out of the shadows, to sit beside Cull on the bench, goblet in hand.

"I can see you are most unhappy," he murmured.

"That I do not deny. Your father rebuffs my attempts to speak with him at every turn."

"Because he knows he does not want to hear what you have to say."

"He will hear it tomorrow. I will wait no longer."

"Aye, I'll stand with y' Cull." He chuckled. "We'll face that storm together. But this night does not have to be so miserable as you're making it out to be."

His hand came down on the bench between them. Shifting toward him, his dark eyes intent in the night, Robert pressed something hard and cool into his hand, which, glancing down, Cull saw to be a key. A key that he knew, without asking, would open the door to Derryth's chamber.

"Don't say I never gave you anything," said Robert. "There are hidden stairs. I'll show you where. You won't be seen."

It was a dangerous gift, but Cull felt no fear. Only a rush of anticipation at being alone with her—of holding the woman who, if he could protect her, would bear his child.

"You have done much to prove yourself as a friend

to me," he said to Robert. "But your own brother has made clear he intends to marry her, so he can have Inverhaven. Your father, while he has not yet agreed to Duncan's demands, will no doubt seek to use her in some way to serve his own purposes. So this key . . . why?"

Robert looked down into his goblet, pensive. "Because you love her, and she loves you."

He closed his eyes. "That I do."

Robert murmured, "I was once in love. With a beautiful young woman who was, to her misfortune, a ward of my father."

Cull turned his face to him. "And?"

It was the first he'd heard of this. Robert and Duncan, like their father, were notorious for their affairs. But there had been some change in Robert. Perhaps this woman was the reason why.

"My father, always the ruthless player, sought to make a game piece of her as well. She was not *good* enough for me, I was told," he muttered. "And he determined that he would use her elsewhere." He leaned forward, and rubbed his thumb across his jaw. "Not good enough for me—what farce. It was I who was not good enough for her."

"What happened?"

"My father all but plundered her inheritance, taking her properties for his own. As part of his campaign against the Kincaids, he betrothed her to a Highlander—the son of one of the lairds who betrayed them the night they were all killed. A pathetic excuse for a man." He looked across the room, at nothing. "She died. *Terribly*, if you must know. And in the two years since, I have . . . tried to forget my anger. The way I still feel. But as time passes, my need for vengeance . . . nay, not vengeance, but to set things *right*, only grows. Perhaps Buchan is my father by blood . . . and Duncan, my brother . . . but they are no family of mine."

Cull had never had a family, and had always envied those who did. But in this moment, he saw that he and Robert were very much the same.

"I don't want the same thing to happen to you and Derryth. Don't allow her to be torn from you. If there is any chance you can . . . defy . . . even triumph over this pit of vipers that is my family, I will help you in any way."

Cull tightened his grip on the key. "Then I would beg one more favor."

Long after the midnight bell tolled, Derryth lay awake, with only a small fire on the hearth to light the room. Even as exhausted as she was from the night before, she could not sleep now.

She was carrying Cull's child. The signs had been there for days, and she'd blamed them on fear and anxiety, but this morning, she'd put them all together. It had been much the same with Elspeth . . . except with Elspeth, there'd been so much joy at realizing.

But Derryth was alone, and separated from Cull, wondering how they would ever be together—and desperately afraid. Even now, loving him, and knowing he loved her, she could not look one day into the future.

A sound came from the small door beside the hearth, one she supposed led to a back passageway but that had always remained locked. Fearful, she sat up, looking that direction. Again a sound . . . a furtive turn of the key, and the scrape of wood against stone. She threw back the covers and stood, searching for anything she might use as a weapon to defend herself.

But before she could, a tall, hulking figure emerged, ducking his head before stepping inside.

"Cull!" she cried. Crossing the floor, she threw herself into his arms. They tightened about her, and he bent to press an urgent kiss against her cheek.

A moment later, she realized he was not alone.

Chapter 19

Robert came into the room behind him, his gaze sharp and clear. Then a smaller, stockier man wearing the garb of a priest, who appeared very nervous to be standing in their presence.

She exhaled . . . realizing . . .

Cull came near, taking her hands. "I told you I would get you out of here, and that I will. All I ask is for one more day to put affairs in order with Buchan, and then we will go—escaping, if necessary."

She nodded, her heart beating fast with excitement and trepidation. "I will wait for you."

"But tonight Derryth . . . marry me," Cull said. He peered down at her in the darkness, his eyes gleaming and his jaw set in a determined line. And yet his hand, which rested at her back, spread wide and his arm pulled her closer, into a tender embrace. "Because you can't marry Duncan if you're married to me. And if I am to die tomorrow . . . or the next day . . . or a fortnight from now, I would have our child know that his mother was married to his father."

If he died?

No, she thought in desperation. He could not die. She loved him too much.

"Yes, I will marry you," she choked out, tears rising in her eyes, her only regret being that she would marry him with her hair in a simple braid and while wearing a night-rail. On second thought, she could imagine nothing more perfect. How precious the memory would always be.

How far they had come from that first moment, when he'd lifted her up out of the mud and carried her into his life. She'd been so miserable at the time. And oh, yes, she was quite miserable still, but how strange life could be, for at the same time, she'd never been happier than in this moment. She did not know what tomorrow would bring, but she had Cull now.

"I've no name to give you, no—" He said the words so solemnly.

"*You* are everything honorable and good, Cull. *You* are what I love. I don't want or need a name," she interrupted, her heart tightening in her chest. "I need *you*."

"Then let us begin," said Robert, urging the priest forward.

Cull took Derryth's hand, and held it between both of his as the words were spoken. She closed her eyes, listening to the powerful words of the priest, and loving the sound of Cull's voice as he repeated them. *Love. Comfort. Cherish.* Then it was her turn.

"Until death, do you part," the priest pronounced.

Her heart beat faster. It was done. She sighed, peering into her husband's gravely serious, handsome face.

Bending, he kissed her, sending a rush of pleasure through her, so different than she'd known before, for along with the passion, there was also a promise of forever—however long their forever might be.

"You may both go now," Cull said to the two men, without taking his eyes off her. "I wish to be alone with my wife."

She knew what his words meant. That they would make love. Already, the flame of desire sparked between them, underscored by the magnitude of what they'd just done. She saw the smoky heat in his eyes, and knew the same to be reflected in her own. She had spent so many nights alone, with only the memory of their time together in his quarters to occupy her mind, and fantasies of being intimate with him again. She had never felt so close to someone. Cull made her happy. He made her brave. Somehow, knowing the danger they placed themselves in by being together made the forbidden moments they would share when they were alone even sweeter. Her pulse jumped in anticipation.

Robert laughed, low in his throat. "Well then . . . congratulations," he said. "And"—his smile faded— "be careful leaving. You must be gone from here before dawn."

The servants would be about, lighting fires and pouring fresh water into basins. Cull followed the priest and Robert to the door, and they disappeared into the passageway. Cull produced a key from somewhere at his waist, with which he locked the door.

Turning to her, he looked at her for a long moment, a half smile rising to his lips, and emotion bright in his eyes. Seeing this, Derryth felt as if her heart doubled in size.

"It seems we are married, Derryth," he said, his voice low and husky.

"We are," she replied.

"How does a husband make love to his wife on their wedding night?"

Happiness flooded through her, sending a flush into her cheeks. "The same way Cull makes love to Derryth. Beautifully."

His eyes darkened with passion, and he closed the distance between them, so handsome she shivered from the sight. He took both of her hands in his.

"I love you," she whispered, peering up into his eyes.

"You won't be sorry," he replied, suddenly serious. "I'll live every day making sure of that."

Raising her hands, he kissed her knuckles . . . her fingertips . . . and her palms. There was so much to fear in their lives, but his unerring strength and honor calmed her.

They would never know true peace as long as Buchan lived. She knew that. But what Cull promised was enough. What mattered was that they loved each other, and that there was trust. The rest they could conquer, day by day.

"As if I needed convincing." She sighed, loving him. "I'm so happy to be your wife."

"Say that again." Bending, he kissed her mouth, as his hands touched her collarbone. Unlacing her night-rail, his hands and fingertips brushed against her skin, sending a rush of arousal spearing through her body.

"You make me happy." Already her breath came in erratic bursts. Would it always be like this? Such excitement from a kiss? From the barest touch?

Her nipples peaked against the fabric, and she let out an uneven breath. He did not push the gown free. Instead, he bent, capturing one tight bud, dampening her skin through the linen, his tongue and lips inflaming her more. She let out a gasp, and swayed against him, her hands seizing his shoulders. In the same moment, he tugged the linen down, freeing her breasts . . . her hips, his hands caressing her everywhere. The garment fell to the floor.

He stepped back, his gaze sweeping admiringly down her body.

"My wife." He moved, circling her, his hands at her waist . . . his garments grazing her skin. "My child."

Their lovemaking before had been so passionate. There was passion between them now, but also something different. With a tenderness and restraint he'd not shown before, he pressed warm, teasing kisses along her shoulder, and her neck, as with steady hands he unbound her hair, setting it free to cascade down her back.

Wanting to touch him too, she turned, grasping the hem of his tunic to push it upward, over his head, kissing his chest, and his nipples, as she revealed his bare skin. He let out an uneven breath. Working the garment upward, over his arms, she glimpsed the slaver's mark that he despised so deeply, tucked high beneath his arm. Pausing, she brushed her fingers across the inky, circular stain, looking boldly upon it for the first time. She pressed her mouth upon it, silently conveying that she loved that part of him too.

He seemed to understand.

"I want y' lass. I want y' so powerfully," he murmured hoarsely, holding her, peering down, his gaze moving over every part of her face and body.

She loved the way he looked at her with such unconcealed longing. And aye, lust. She felt the same lust for him too.

"I want you too."

Stepping back, he removed his boots . . . his trews, before striding naked toward her and gently nudging her backward against the bed, his hands cradling her face, his mouth on hers.

But suddenly, he turned from her—leaving her gasping and wanting. She watched him go, his skin taut and golden in the night. Across the room, he lit another lantern and returning, set it beside the bed, where it joined the one already burning there. His eyes fixed on her, glittering with desire.

"I want to see you," he said. "I want to remember every moment of this night. The way you look now . . . the way you'll look when I'm inside you."

His bold words both pleased her . . . and struck her through the heart.

"Because this night may be our last?" She shook her head. "Nay, I won't believe that—"

"Because it is our wedding night," he interjected fiercely, eyes blazing. "The first of the rest of our lives."

The certainty with which he spoke lit a fire in her

heart. Her eyes fixed on him, she climbed backward into the bed, pushing aside the heavy linens and blankets, and before another breath passed from her lips, he was there, pushing her down onto her back, the bed canopy above him. With open arms, she welcomed him. His weighty, muscled body stretched over her, his hips coming down between her thighs. Her legs hooked round his, and her hips lifted—

"Oh . . . Derryth, the way you move."

Holding her hands above her head, he pinned her against the sheets. Bending, he kissed her with a passion that made her breath hitch in her chest, as his thighs flexed, and he pressed his sex against her—not entering her, but still giving pleasure to them both.

"You're so perfect," he whispered, a ruddy flush darkening his cheeks. "Perfect for me."

"Only you," she replied, stretching beneath him, luxuriating in the pleasure . . . unashamed of her desire, for was not this sort of love and intimate talk meant to be enjoyed between a husband and a wife?

"Aye, only me," he repeated, his impassioned gaze moving over her face. "Only you." He pressed a kiss below her ear. "Watch me make love to you."

Boldly, her gaze followed his to where the light of the lanterns illuminated the primal sight of their bodies. Shifting, he guided himself, slowly prodding her with his crowned tip . . . sweetly teasing her, barely entering before pulling away, leaving her in aroused torment.

"I've never felt anything more right than you beneath me . . . nothing more right than this," he said, kissing her mouth hard, before breaking away to repeat the same disciplined motion again.

Derryth had no such discipline. She grasped his waist, demanding the deeper pleasures she knew he could give.

"Please," she pled softly, bringing him closer with her legs, and lifting her hips.

"Oh, god . . ." The words broke from deep in his chest, and yet still, he denied her . . . but for a moment.

"Ah . . ." he exclaimed, slowly sinking inside her.

This time, her body welcomed him, without pain. There was only a deep *thrum* of pleasure, spiraling out through every part of her.

"Again?" he said, claiming her mouth.

"Aye, *again*," she replied, feverishly, already moving . . . writing beneath him.

Spreading his thighs to widen hers, he thrust once more, filling her completely. A low cry broke from her lips. He grasped her by the waist, suddenly kneeling, pulling her up to straddle him.

He rocked back onto his heels, driving deeper. Stars exploded behind her eyes. Holding her thusly, he thrust rapidly inside her, and soon the canopied space was filled with proof of their pleasure. The creak of the bed . . . their moans and gasps . . . intermingled with the sound of the linen hissing with the urgency of their movements.

"Slower now," he murmured.

He eased her down again onto the pillow, holding her . . . moving with her.

"Come with me, love," he urged.

They arrived together, rising . . . soaring . . . shattering, in passion and in love.

In the moment after, Derryth wavered between absolute bliss and fear that the moment was too perfect. That the door would suddenly burst open and Buchan would be there with soldiers, to drag Cull away. But Cull shifted to lay beside her—his body massive, seemingly hewn from stone. Their breathing slowed, and for a long moment they lay tangled as they were. But within moments, their ardor cooled. The room grew colder . . . and the threat of tomorrow loomed heavy, all around. Perhaps Cull sensed it too, because he pulled the coverlet over them. She clung to him, taking courage from his strength, and knowing he was there beside her, to fight for their future.

"No tears," he murmured.

"No tears," she replied resolutely, blinking them away. "I won't let them take this night from us."

Silence blanketed the room.

"I must go soon."

"I know."

"Before I go, I must tell you . . . I am done with Buchan." He stroked her hair. "After you were taken, I learned that he . . . betrayed my trust. I am a King's Guard, and my men are sworn to serve Scotland. We are not his damned mercenaries. I act on the king and Parliament's orders only, which he led me to believe he'd received. But there was never a final order."

"Is that why you came here, to Carven?"

"Aye, to confront him, and to inform him I and my men will not proceed. But he has refused to see me—because he knows. Instead, through Robert and Duncan he has made it clear he expects me to return, and carry out the farce."

"Why, Cull?" She raised up, holding the linen against her breasts, and turned to peer at him. "Why does he want it to be you so badly who moves against Inverhaven? Why not Duncan or someone else?"

"I do not know. I have asked that question of myself many times." He frowned. "It does not matter. I am done. Tomorrow—regardless of whether he is agreeable—I will tell him I know the truth, and relinquish my command of the siege. Derryth, I do not know what will happen. If Duncan will also withdraw or if they will go forward with their efforts to defeat your clan."

"I feel helpless," she replied, her heart tight in her chest. "My sister Elspeth was very close to giving birth to her and Niall's bairn when I left. I pray all is well with them."

"After tomorrow . . . we will go ourselves and find out."

She looked at him. "What do you mean?"

"I will take you to them," he said, unsmiling. The tone of his voice, resolved. "Though I have relinquished my command of the siege, the men who remain there are largely loyal to me. We will enter the castle under their protection."

"Cull." Tears blurred her eyes. The thought of seeing Elspeth . . .

He pulled her close, against his chest. "You are my wife. It is the right thing to do."

Her love for Cull only grew, that he offered her this gift. Nay, their world was not perfect, and there were so many reasons to be afraid, but she would take whatever chances she could, to see her sister again.

"But you must know that as a King's Guard, we cannot stay there. If there is a battle, I cannot raise arms against the king's son—not without orders to do so."

She nodded. "I understand."

She would not demand that of him. Above all, Cull was an honorable man, and she would not ask him to break the vows he had made—not to her, nor to Scotland.

"Kiss me before I go," he said.

She touched his face, and kissed him, inhaling his breath . . . memorizing the feel of his lips on hers.

Too quickly, he was gone from the bed. Deprived of his heat, a chill moved through her body. He grabbed up his tunic from the floor and pulled it on. Briefly she saw the slaver's mark before it was covered. She sat up and moved to leave the bed, to join him.

"Nay, love," he said tenderly. "You stay there. You're carrying my child, and I want you to sleep." His gaze hardened and his lips thinned. "I don't know what will happen today, but rest now and be ready to depart at a moment's notice."

Once he was dressed, he came to her with her nightrail and assisted her in dressing. "I'd give ye the key to keep, but Robert must return it before dawn before 'tis discovered missing."

"I don't need it. I'm not going anywhere. I'll wait for you." She nodded, reaching for him. "Now kiss me once more."

Then he was gone. Afterward, she lay in the bed, refusing to give in to her fears. Refusing to shed tears.

She was married to Cull the Nameless, who was very possibly Scotland's greatest warrior. Now she must be a warrior too.

Knowing he intended to save her did not ease the determined workings of her mind. She turned restlessly, trying to find some solution that could bring the problems that clouded their lives to an end. Could she herself plead to faraway Parliament for intervention? Would Cull? She feared with the king's illness, those in Edinburgh would show very little interest in Buchan's continued torment of a distant Highland clan.

Why Cull? her mind demanded again. Why had Buchan summoned him to the Highlands to carry out his false mission against the Kincaids?

She fell into an uneasy sleep, and dreamt of Cull as a towheaded boy, trapped in the dark belly of a ship. Cull the slave. Cull the Nameless. With the slaver's mark on his arm, would he ever be free? It bound him not simply to his past, but to Buchan, who had saved him.

The slaver's mark.

The mark on his arm.

The mark on their arms . . . Niall's and Faelan's.

She bolted up, her eyes wide and staring into the dark. Her heart thundered in her chest.

Cull . . . *Cullen*. The murdered Kincaid laird's third and youngest boy had been named Cullen. Her mind counted the years . . . and goose bumps rose on her skin.

She broke away from the bed, dizzied by this possible truth. So agitated, she could not bear the touch of the linens against her skin.

Was it true?

Was Cull the third son?

She paced, seeing nothing of the room about her. Focused entirely on the thoughts in her mind. How would he then have come to be in the possession of a Venetian slaver . . . who had beaten him and tormented him for years, traumatizing him so greatly he had no remembrance of his past?

Because Buchan committed him—a mere child of seven or eight years old—into that horrible life.

Only to have him returned years later, as if by some Devil's agreement.

Cull's mark. She closed her eyes, remembering its shape, the size and shape of a wax seal. She couldn't be sure. She'd never seen Niall's or Faelan's. Indeed, both men guarded their marks like treasure, ensuring no imposter would present himself as their third brother, and that only their true brother would bear the mark.

But Elspeth had described the brothers' tattoos as a wolf's head. Was that what she'd seen? Aye, yes, she thought it was—an old Gaelic design, contained within the bands of a circle.

If so, it provided a cruel and twisted explanation of why Buchan insisted the attack against Inverhaven be led by Cull. He wanted Cull—a warrior of his own creation—to defeat . . . and no doubt kill, his own brothers. Toward what end? Cull's own destruction as well?

She had to tell Cull. But with dawn not yet come, and both doors of her room locked, she was trapped here until morning, when she would be flanked again by Ainsley and Mairead.

A sound came from behind her. The sound of the key turning in the door. But not the smaller door Cull had arrived through.

Ainsley appeared, and strode directly inside—followed by four broad-shouldered men, their faces concealed by dark hoods.

"You're awake, I see," said Ainsley, her lips a hard frown and her eyes gleaming with unspoken intent.

Every muscle in Derryth's body tensed. "Why are you here?"

She was in danger. Ainsley hadn't come alone, and that meant something. Had she brought those men to harm her? Her first thought was for the child she now carried.

"Get dressed," said Ainsley coldly. "You'll need your cloak."

Derryth stepped backward, her heart racing. "I'm not doing anything until you tell me where you are taking me."

"I'm not taking you anywhere, but these men will." Ainsley moved toward one of the men and pushed back his hood, revealing him to be Nathan. "Back to Inverhaven. Back to your clan, where you belong."

Chapter 20

"Why?"

She knew why. To keep her from Cull. Ainsley's actions here were inspired by jealousy. She'd made clear she intended to marry Cull.

"Does it matter why?" Ainsley came close. "You're a prisoner here, against your will. So . . . escape. I am giving you safe passage now." From within the folds of her cloak, she produced a folded piece of parchment, sealed with black wax. "I even have orders here, forged of course, which will allow you to pass through the siege battlements, and into the castle."

Her heart felt torn in two. Return to the Kincaids . . . or stay here? Derryth did not answer. She did not want to leave Cull. He had asked her to wait for him. Nor did she know if she could trust that these men would safely take her anywhere, as Ainsley claimed they would do.

"Your reluctance is very telling," the dark-haired young woman muttered, her eyes narrowing. She moved very close, and spoke in a low voice. "So I'll tell you the truth here. You don't have a choice. If you don't do as I say, you'll—"

"I'll what?" Derryth's eyes widened.

"Well . . . I won't know what happened to you. No one will. You'll simply disappear from this room . . . never to be seen again. 'Twill always be a great mystery. But you won't be forgotten. Stories will be told. Perhaps even ghost stories."

The words chilled Derryth's blood. "You would murder me?"

Tears rose into her eyes, but they were tears of anger. This woman would sentence her to death for loving Cull. Lord, she was sick to death of these Stewarts and their hatred. What would life have been without their plotting and interference? A small inner voice reminded her that she would not have Cull if not for Buchan's hatred of the Kincaids.

But it had been a mistake, that day, for Derryth to be so bold by tying her ribbon around Cull's arm. She'd all but declared a romantic interest in him, for all to see. Derryth should not have forgotten that she was dealing with Buchan's family.

What would Ainsley do if she knew they were married?

Ainsley stared hard at her. "Let's not find out."

Derryth trembled, pondering the choice she'd been given. Without Cull here, she was left to decide what to do. If she somehow were able to tell Cull tomorrow what she believed—that he was the youngest son of the murdered laird, would he believe her, without proof? Proof of which she herself was not certain, having not seen the actual marks on the Braewick brother's themselves? She would not be certain until she spoke to Niall at Inverhaven, and saw his mark.

If Cull did believe her outright, would he insist on confronting Buchan here at Carven, where Buchan controlled everything, including hundreds of men? She could not have him discover the truth about himself . . . that he had brothers . . . and a birthright . . . and yes, a *name*, only to die. Perhaps leaving was the only way.

It was a terrible chance to take, believing that if she left, Cull would follow. But if he were to make a stand against Buchan, she wanted him to make the stand shoulder to shoulder with his brothers.

"Mistress—" said one of the men, shifting urgently.

"Aye." Ainsley circled Derryth, glaring. "We're running out of time."

Derryth snapped, "Give me a moment to dress."

A short time later, she sat atop a horse, dressed in the simple clothes in which she'd arrived—taking nothing else.

"I just want you to know it is nothing against you, Derryth," said Ainsley, stepping back. Her cloak rippled in the night wind. "If we'd met another way, I'm certain we'd have been good friends."

"I disagree," Derryth replied, taking firmer hold of the reins, and turning her animal northward.

Ainsley stepped back, retorting, "Isn't it something that I didn't want you to die? That I gave you this choice at all?"

Derryth ignored her. She had nothing more to say

to her. Now that she sat in the saddle, she was impatient to be home. Impatient to see Elspeth and the baby and everyone there. Impatient to speak to Niall. Impatient to be reunited with Cull, and to give him the truth that he deserved.

Cull. Her heart was half broken over leaving him. She had to believe he would follow.

She looked over her shoulder toward the men who would escort her.

"We'll go quickly. Do try to keep up."

With one last glance at Carven, she jabbed her heels into the palfrey's sides.

"Where is she?" Cull demanded, pushing into Buchan's chambers. There, he found the earl sitting at a table strewn with documents. Ainsley stood just to the side, as if they'd been speaking.

"Where is who?"

Behind him stormed in Duncan, then Robert.

"Derryth MacClaren," bellowed Duncan. "She is gone."

"What do you mean, she is gone?" answered Buchan, his eyes going sharp. He stood, pressing his hands to the top of the table.

Cull paced the length of the table, seething.

"She is not in her room," Robert replied. "And her cloak is gone."

"Who told you this?" Buchan asked, his eyes darkening.

"I did," said Mairead, entering, her face flushed. "I thought . . . well, that perhaps Cull had taken her." She came to stand before Buchan's desk. "Everyone knows that *she* is what Duncan and Cull have been snarling at each other about. That little Highland slut that they've been passing back and forth."

Cull let out a furious snarl of a sound, and glared at Mairead.

She moved closer to the earl.

"Why does everyone care about her so much?" Ainsley cried, color high in her cheeks and her eyes glistening.

Buchan's eyes narrowed on her. "Ainsley . . . do you know something about this?"

"No," she retorted, her eyes widening.

"You're lying," he said.

"You *are* lying," Mairead exclaimed. "I know when you tell lies, and you are not telling the truth now."

"You can have Inverhaven without her," Ainsley exclaimed, rushing toward Cull, and grasping his hands in hers. She looked up at him with a smile and spoke in a low tone, words that only he would hear. "It can be *ours*, together. Think of all that we could accomplish together. My large *tocher* would be yours. You don't need her. Forget her. Tell Father that you want to marry *me*."

Duncan strode forth to glare at his half-sister, and gritted out from between his teeth. "She was not yours to set free."

Cull stared down at her, his every muscle tight with fury. "What did you do with her?"

Ainsley broke away with a hiss. "I gave her a horse, that is all. She is gone. You should thank me. You don't have to marry that Highlander simpleton to have Inverhaven, when you can marry me."

"You sent her off alone?" Cull thundered, his stomach seizing tight with fear. Anything could happen to her. She could be waylaid by miscreants. Attacked. Raped. "With only a horse?"

Ainsley rolled her eyes. "And four men to see that she got where I wished her to be."

"Four men?" he shouted. "Trusted men, or ruffians you recruited off the streets? Can they be trusted?"

"I don't know," she cried. "And I don't care. Why do you care so much?"

Cull strode forward and grasped her wrist. "How long ago?"

"Just after the evening meal before. She's gone too far for you to catch her now."

He knew that wasn't true, because he'd spent the night with Derryth, but he could not exactly announce that now. He could only assume they'd slipped away before dawn, when no one would have seen them. There were too many men, and there would be too many witnesses during the light of day. All he wanted was to get her back. He was finished here. He would say what he had to say, then he would ride.

"You get out," he growled at Ainsley—giving her a small push toward the door. "I would speak alone to your father now."

"Only if it is to tell me that you will be resuming your efforts at Inverhaven."

"How dare you speak to me like that," she replied, bristling.

"Go, Ainsley," said Buchan. "Leave this to me."

He gave Mairead a nudge, and the woman crossed the room, taking Ainsley by the arm. "Come, Ainsley."

"Father!" shouted Ainsley, as she was drawn away. "Remember what you and I spoke of. If you love me at all, you will let me have my way."

In the next moment they were gone, and the door shut by Robert behind them—for Duncan and Robert remained, their faces grave.

"My daughter wishes to marry you," Buchan said. "She is very insistent. She always has been . . . from the first moment she saw you."

Cull strode immediately forward, leaning across the table to glare into Buchan's eyes.

"That won't be possible, because I'm finished with her—and I'm finished with you."

Buchan did not flinch. His expression did not change at all.

"Don't be ridiculous," he replied easily, in a tone of absolute indifference. "And don't throw this chance away. Have you forgotten what you've been offered? Lands. The castle. A name. I can make it all happen. But only if you return to Inverhaven and defeat the Kincaids, as I've told you to do."

"Aye, as *you* told me to do," Cull barked. "Without the king or Parliament's orders."

Buchan's gaze darkened. "When have I ever been bound by their restrictions?"

Robert interjected in a low voice. "But Cull is a King's Guard. *He* is bound by their restrictions."

"You lied to me," alleged Cull.

"You owe me this, Cull. You will do as I say." He rested back in his chair. "If there are questions later . . . if anyone is to be called to answer, it will be me. I take full responsibility."

"No," said Cull. "I will not *collude* with you over some . . . *petty* personal hatred that you have festered over for years—"

"What do you know of it?" the earl snarled, suddenly leaning forward again, his eyes narrowing.

But suddenly Duncan was there beside Cull. "Enough, Father. Forget this lowborn churl! Give the mission to me. I've wanted it from the start. Let me crush the Kincaids. Give Inverhaven—and the Mac-Claren daughter—to me."

"Get out," Buchan ordered. "The both of you." His eyes moved between his sons.

"Father," Duncan exclaimed.

"Go," the earl bellowed.

Both men left—Duncan glaring over his shoulder and Robert's expression conveying concern.

When they were gone, Buchan stood and came out from behind the desk. All vestiges of the sudden fury he'd released moments before, gone, replaced now by dispassionate cold.

"I have always had a tender spot in my heart for you, Cull."

"Then why do you ask this of me?"

"Because I want great things for you. Don't you see that? I can give you what you've always wanted."

But his heart had changed. What were lands and a title . . . a name, without Derryth? Without his child? They were nothing. As if Buchan had somehow picked up on his thoughts, he moved a step closer, speaking in a gentle tone.

"You've come to care for that girl. Derryth Mac-Claren."

Cull's chest grew tight. If the Wolf threatened Derryth's life . . . he would kill the man here and now.

Nay, he could not. He enforced calm on himself. Only calm discipline would see him through this. And perhaps deception on a level to equal Buchan's own.

"All is not lost," said Buchan. "You can have her still. You can have everything still."

"What do you mean?" He looked at the earl with suspicion.

"I know you have no wish to marry Ainsley, and I do not blame you. She is a troublesome girl. So take Inverhaven, and *execute* the two imposters that claim to be Braewicks—who so wrongfully claim those lands . . ."

They were not imposters. But he held that rebuke inside.

"And if I do this?" he said evenly.

"You take all. Inverhaven and the MacClaren girl." Buchan smiled. "But know this. If you do not carry out this order from *me* . . . in gratefulness for all I have done for you in your life . . . I'll kill her myself. Her and the rest of them. Do not be ungrateful, Cull. Let me give you all that you deserve."

Cull closed his eyes and summoned all the strength within him, and turned to the door.

"I will do it."

A brief time later, Cull dressed for travel in his chamber. Robert stared at him in disbelief.

"You're actually going to carry out my father's orders? You intend to kill the Kincaids?"

"Damn your father to hell," Cull muttered darkly,

striding toward the door. "I'm not killing anyone. I'm going to get my wife."

Derryth returned to a castle under siege. Villagers and livestock crowded the courtyard.

It was Faelan and Tara Braewick who greeted her, both drawing her into a tight embrace.

"You are here!" cried Derryth. "But what of Burnbryde Castle?"

"Held by a small force of my men. Burnbryde is nothing if Inverhaven falls. As soon as we heard soldiers approached, we came here with as many warriors and men as we could gather. When the time comes, we will stand with my brother and fight."

"What are *you* doing here?" Tara exclaimed. "How were you able to get through?"

Faelan lectured her sternly. "You should have stayed in Falranroch with Bridget."

"My sister. Niall. I must see them. I'll explain everything then."

Tara lifted a hand to her mouth. "Let us hurry to the tower. You could not have come at a more exciting time. Your sister labors even now. Very soon, the child will be born."

They led her inside, where, like the courtyard, the rooms and corridors of the castle were filled with people, and together, she and Tara rushed up the stairs, leaving Faelan to return to the ramparts.

Entering the laird's chambers, Derryth found her sister in bed, her cheeks flushed. Niall stood on one side of her, peering down at her in concern, while Ina dabbed a cloth on her forehead.

"Sister," Elspeth exclaimed, pushing up from the pillows.

"Nay stay there, do not move," cried Derryth. She moved closer, and perching on the bed, embraced her half-sister. "I cannot believe it. The time has come."

"Why are you here?" Niall demanded. "Why did you leave the safety of Falranroch?"

"We never arrived there. We were captured by Buchan's army, and held prisoner ever since."

"What of Deargh? We simply thought with the siege, that he could not get through."

"He is a prisoner even now out there, in that camp."

Niall's gaze hardened, and his cheeks flooded with color. "I had no idea. If we'd known, I'd have mounted some sort of rescue—"

"How did you break free?" Tara asked, pressing close, her eyes alight with concern. "Were you harmed? Were you mistreated?"

Elspeth let out a sudden cry of pain.

"Later," Derryth exclaimed, grasping her sister's hand, desperate to soothe her. "I will tell you later."

Ina pressed closer. "It will be soon now."

A sound reached Derryth's ears. The sound of a man's heavy boots, rapidly climbing the stairs.

"Laird. You must come. Riders approach the castle."

Derryth leapt up from the bed, her heart spilling over with hope. *Riders.* Was it Cull, already? Of course it was possible. Finding her gone, he would have ridden like the devil to get here. She rushed to the window and peered out, but caught only a glimpse of several horses passing through the gates.

She spun round—

To discover Niall already gone. Her sister sat up in the bed, looking at her, panting heavily. "Derryth, what is it?"

"It is Cull!" she cried, running to the door. "Niall. Wait."

She raced down the stairs, her heart in her throat, never catching sight of her brother-in-law. She hadn't had time to explain. She would never forgive herself if one of them killed the other. In the vestibule, just outside the gathering hall, she encountered Niall's back, and beyond that, a great throng of men. The sounds of swords being drawn echoed against the stones.

"You will wait here, until my laird grants you leave to pass," bellowed a Kincaid warrior.

She glimpsed Cull, tall and bull-like, his expression ferocious. Behind him, in the distance, stood Deargh and the other Kincaids, as well as Fiona, their hands bound like prisoners, their eyes wide—looking bewildered, as if they did not understand what was happening.

"I have brought you your kinsmen as a gesture of goodwill, damn you." Suddenly, Cull's eyes fixed on her. "I just need to see her."

He pushed forward, only to be intercepted by a dozen men, arms extended and weapons drawn.

Travel-worn and exhausted, his eyes burned with something she could only define as intense relief—and anger.

"Cull!" she shouted, pushing past Niall, who seized her. "Nay, Niall. Let him through."

"Why?" he demanded.

Wrenching her arm free, she ran toward Cull and

threw herself into his arms. Like a drop of oil fallen onto water, the Kincaids instantly fell back, staring at her with questioning eyes.

She whirled, pressing her back to Cull's chest, and addressed Niall. "I have something to tell you."

"She is carrying my child," Cull announced behind her, his voice fierce and claiming. His hands held her by the waist.

Eyes wide, she glanced up at him. "That isn't exactly what I was going to say."

"*What?!*" thundered Niall, his face darkening with rage.

Faelan pushed forward to stand by his brother's side, snarling. "I don't believe it."

Suddenly, Elspeth was there, emerging from the stairs, with Tara and Ina helping her. Her eyes found Derryth. "Oh, sister. Is this true?"

"We are also married," Derryth cried, hoping that might diffuse their angry response.

Breathing hard, Elspeth seized her husband's arm. "Give me that sword. I will kill him myself."

But already, Niall and Faelan strode forward, glowering, their hands on the hilts of their swords.

Behind her, Cull yanked his from its sheath. Moving swiftly, he stepped forward to shield her.

"No!" shouted Derryth, pushing around him. "*Cull is your brother.*"

Niall froze, his nostrils flared. "What did you say?"

They all regarded her as if she were mad. Emotions welled up in her chest.

She took a deep breath, and repeated. "I believe he is your brother."

"Why would you say something like that?" Cull murmured tightly, his face peering down at her, half stricken.

"Because I believe 'tis true," she insisted fervently. "Your slaver's mark is no slaver's mark at all, but the mark the Laird Kincaid placed on each of his three sons at their birth. Niall, please look."

"Show me," Niall commanded.

"Please, Cull," Derryth pleaded, looking into his eyes. "Show him your mark."

"It's not true," he said, his eyes glancing to her as if to ask why she had subjected him to this. "But very well, if I must prove it."

With impatient hands, he removed his hauberk and his tunic beneath. Standing bare to everyone's gaze, he wrenched up his arm.

Niall let out a breath . . . and stepped closer, staring hard. Faelan moved close too, resting a hand on Niall's shoulder.

"My god," Niall whispered.

Elspeth let out a sob. "He is your brother?"

"*Cullen*," Faelan declared hoarsely.

"I don't understand," said Cull, his voice hollow.

Chapter 21

Niall moved quickly to wrench his tunic over his head, showing Cull the same mark etched onto his skin. "Do you see? There is the proof. There are only three of us with this mark. No other. You are our brother."

Cull stared at the mark, identical to his own, before looking into their faces. Faces that had belonged to strangers, but that now, in the straight line of their jaws and noses, and the brightness of their blue eyes, mirrored his own.

"I bear the same mark," Faelan uttered low in his throat. "We can summon the council, who will verify it is true. But I don't need them to know who you are. I see our father in your eyes."

The two Braewicks moved closer, each of them placing a hand on Cull's shoulder, gripping him fiercely there.

Niall said, "You are Cullen Braewick, the third and youngest son of the Laird Kincaid."

Derryth appeared at his side again, her eyes flooded with tears. "Buchan must have captured him that night. Niall, he made your brother a slave for many years, and then made a false show of buying his freedom, only to train him as a warrior. For one purpose—"

"The sick bastard! To destroy us all," Niall snarled, before looking to Cull again. "Brother, would you destroy us still?"

The words struck Cull through, like a sword. He had brothers. Family. Kin. But there were no memories. No years of shared history. No trust between them. Buchan had denied them that kinship, and for that, Cull hated him.

That history . . . that brotherly trust would start here. From this moment forward.

"God no, I will not destroy you," Cull replied fiercely, emotion and indignation bright in his eyes. He looked at his brothers. "Perhaps no formal vow has been spoken, but hear me now. You are my brothers. All these Kincaids here, in the castle and on these lands, are my kin. I would defend any, and all of you, to my death."

At that moment, Elspeth let out a tortured sob, followed by a gasp. She bent at the waist.

Cull looked past them all toward Elspeth. "But let's talk about that later. For now, someone please help that woman."

Later that night, Cull watched Derryth in the firelight of the great hall, holding her sister's babe—a healthy, strong-lunged bairn. It was the first moment she'd been able to pry the baby girl away from her doting parents. He could only imagine the joy he would feel seeing her hold their own babe that, God willing, would come sometime after Christmastide next year.

Elspeth sat beside the fire next to her husband, looking radiant but pensive. No doubt the new mother worried over the future of her child.

Niall stood then, and moved to Cull's side. "You know Buchan better than any of us. What do you propose that we do?"

He'd thought heavily upon it the entire afternoon, while waiting for news of the baby. He could think of only one resolution. Derryth moved close, to stand beside him listening.

"I would propose that I send a missive to Buchan at Carven. I will . . . advise him that I have triumphed here, that I have taken Inverhaven, and . . . killed the both of you. I will ask that he travel here to see the results of our victory for himself. I'm still in command of that army out there, and 'twill be no trouble to pull off the farce. And knowing Buchan, I don't believe he'll be able to resist. Robert Stewart is there too, and he will support me in this."

"Robert Stewart?" said Faelan, leaning forward, his expression one of disbelief.

Tara clasped her husband, Faelan's, hand. "He helped me once." To Faelan, she said, "I told you he was different than the others."

Niall nodded. "Send your missive."

The bairn let out a cry, and when no amount of cooing and rocking would soothe her, Derryth returned her to her mother's arms. Cull watched Derryth's every move, his attention captured by the swing of her kirtle and the gleam of her hair. If she had meant everything to him before, she meant even more than that now. She had returned him to his brothers. She had given him a new life. The life that should have been his all along.

Though he would forever deeply grieve the loss of his parents, whom he did not remember, and the life he should have lived here at Inverhaven, he was no longer Cull the Nameless, King's Guard and knight. He was a Kincaid. He would die to protect her. He would die to protect them all, including this castle and these lands.

She turned then, and caught him looking. Coming near, she took his hand and urged him to his feet. "Come, husband. I know you are weary."

"Because of you," he said, pulling her close. "I rode day and night. My destrier is very unhappy with you, I would have you know."

"I shall have to spoil him."

"You knew I would follow."

Rocking up on her toes, she brought him down for a kiss. "I knew you would."

"I love you," he murmured, kissing her cheek.

Several chuckles arose up all around. Glancing around, he discovered all eyes on them. It seemed the Kincaids now took joy and amusement in observing his and Derryth's affection for each other, whereas just hours before they'd been prepared to kill him for it.

"Your chamber is just as you left it, Derryth," Elspeth said innocently, from where she watched, holding her child.

Derryth smiled, and pulled him down to whisper in his ear.

"Come with me now," she said. "I'm curious to know what it's like to make love to a warrior of the clan Kincaid."

A sennight later, Buchan and his personal guard waited outside the gate.

Cull's blood thrummed with anticipation. This morning, he did not wear his warrior's garb. He wore a plaid and tunic, like his brothers. Like a Kincaid.

He nodded to the sentries. "Let them in."

Buchan, Robert, and Duncan passed through.

As planned, the throng of Kincaid warriors surged forward, repelling any further entry by the warriors who accompanied them. Withdrawing just as quickly, before the earl's men could respond, the gates were slammed closed.

Snarling and stunned, his eyes wide, the Wolf circled on his horse, his hand going to his sword. But the surrounding warriors unsaddled and disarmed him, and Duncan as well.

Both men were dragged forth. Behind them, Robert dismounted slowly, still in possession of his sword, his face grim.

Buchan and Duncan men struggled to stand.

"What betrayal is this?" Buchan demanded, his face scarlet with fury. He glanced over his shoulder at Robert.

"Traitor!" Duncan spat in his brother's direction.

Robert's expression did not waver. Instead, he

walked past Buchan and Duncan. Turning, he stood beside Cull and his two brothers.

"'Tis no betrayal at all," said Cull, moving toward Buchan. "'Tis you who betrayed my father, my brothers, and me."

"What did you say?" Buchan smiled then, his lips forming a terrible wolf-like grimace.

"That's right. I know the truth. What I don't know is if you planned for me to kill my brothers, and live on never knowing the truth—that they were my brothers. Or . . . did you expect to kill me too? Perhaps after I did as you wished, you intended to set Duncan upon me? All the while taunting me with the truth . . . that I'd slain my own surviving kin."

The earl's grin flared viciously. "Aye, that was the plan all along."

"But why, Father?" Robert demanded. "Why do you despise them so?"

Buchan seethed at him, lunging forward, but was held back by the warriors who surrounded him. "Do not call me Father, ever again."

"You killed their father. Their mother. Why must you also kill the sons?"

Buchan held silent, his jaw clenched, refusing to speak.

Silence filled the courtyard.

It was Robert who spoke again. "I think that's it, isn't it? You didn't mean for her to die. Y' thought you'd kill her husband, and have her for yourself."

"You don't know what you're talking about," Buchan hissed—but without conviction. His shoulders sagged.

"You . . . who have never truly loved, imagined yourself to love her. And ever since, you hated them all, because she loved them. She didn't love you. She chose to die with her husband."

"*They* killed her," Buchan growled, "not me. What sort of husband allows his wife to stand beside him during a surrender?"

"What sort of man kills another, thinking to take his wife?" Niall growled.

"What happened?" Cull demanded, his hand on the hilt of his sword, hatred simmering in his veins. "Tell us now, or I vow I will slay you and your son right here on these stones. I do not care that you are the king's son. You murdered my mother and father. And then you enslaved me. A mere child."

Buchan sagged between the men who held him. He hung his head, breathing hard. "Aye . . . I was there that night. High upon the hillock, overlooking everything. I had brought some fifty mounted men to support the Alwyn and the MacClaren in taking Inverhaven."

He growled. "She wasn't supposed to die. None of them. Just the laird. But when the Kincaids saw my men coming down the hillside, they changed their minds about surrendering. The fools. They decided to fight."

Robert shifted. "And the sons . . . as long as they live, so does your sin. So does your guilt."

Buchan's lip curled. "Every time I see them, I see their damned father."

Niall drew his sword, and snarled. "I know we agreed otherwise, but he must die."

Cull gripped his arm. "Nay, brother. We will do as we agreed."

"What is that?" Duncan asked, his eyes wild with hate.

"The earl will sign a written confession, detailing all the crimes he has committed against the clan Kincaid. We will send the confession to Edinburgh, and demand intervention. Until then, you will both be imprisoned here in the tower."

Robert moved to stand between them. "Until this morning I believed that to be an acceptable plan, but—"

"But what?" said Cull.

Robert looked long and hard on his father, before speaking again. "You know that I wrote Edinburgh to inquire about the orders my father claimed he'd received to act against the Kincaids. And you know I received a response that those orders had never been issued."

"Aye," said Niall. "What else?"

"I received a second missive last night. Not just a missive, but a formal edict from the king and Parliament. In addition, it is signed by the king's sons, Carrick and Fife."

"You went to my *brothers* on this?" the earl said, the color draining from his face.

Duncan shouted, "I will kill you myself."

"What does the edict say?" asked Niall.

Robert looked directly at Cull. "That in recognition of his faithfulness to the crown, that Cull the Nameless, King's Guard and knight of Scotland, has been named Justiciar of the North. With the king's impending death, they hope he will help to maintain peace in the Highlands. The appointment comes with the bestowal of a title and lands. It's all here, along with the assurance that the appointment will survive the death of the king."

"Why have you done this to me?" Buchan demanded of Robert.

"You know why. If you don't, you're a selfish old fool. I loved her, and you took her from me. She died because of you."

Duncan's eyes widened. "You did this because of a woman?"

"Aye," Robert replied solemnly. "It seems I'm like my father in that way. But not just for her. Because you deserve it, Father. You've destroyed so many lives."

Niall looked at Cull. His frown transformed into a wicked grin. "*Justiciar.* I suppose you think you're really something now."

Faelan pointed his sword between Buchan and Duncan. "You wouldn't dare act against an officer of the king."

Robert looked at Cull. "I would petition you not to kill my father. As powerful as you are now, with this appointment, he does have allies in Parliament who might strike out against you if you act alone. Instead, I ask that you take his confession, which I myself will deliver to my uncles, who I vow will demand that he answer for what he has done. If he is committed to death, let it be done in full accordance with the law, by the judiciary powers of this land."

"'Tis true," Cull said to his brothers. "If we execute him now, we put the future of Inverhaven in jeopardy.

Whereas if we exert a right and just hand, and defer to the ruling courts of the land, I have no doubt we will be found in the right, and have our justice."

Niall looked at Faelan, who scowled but nodded. "I want him dead. But I also want peace. For my children to grow up without fear."

Robert continued. "Take his confession. He will sign it, along with an agreement that he will never step foot on Kincaid lands again. Let Scotland render his final judgment."

"Let us think upon it," said Cull. "Until we decide, take them to the tower."

The next morning, Derryth stood at Cull's side, as Buchan and Duncan were allowed to climb atop their horses, without weapons. Without armed warriors to accompany them. Kincaid villagers and warriors gathered to watch, all around.

After signing the documents, Buchan had refused to speak. Now, he rode away, with his son at his side.

"It's not over," Niall said. "You know that, don't you?"

Cull stared at the earl's back. "When the time is right. He cannot escape this."

The gates closed with a thunderous rattle, and a cheer went up among the people.

Derryth stepped back, tears blurring her vision, as she watched Cull turn to embrace Niall and then Faelan. Turning, the three of them reached for Robert, gripping his shoulders . . . shaking his hands.

"Thank you, Robert," said Cull.

"You're welcome."

Cull turned to Derryth then, and pulled her close. "Come with me."

Together, along with the others, they climbed the stairs, taking to the ramparts. From there they watched, as over the next hours Cull's orders were followed. The tents . . . the catapults . . . the livestock . . . the men . . . all withdrew, disappearing over the horizon.

Twilight painted the rutted, upturned earth.

"What a mess," murmured someone.

Cull drew Derryth close to his side.

"I disagree," he murmured. "I have never seen a more beautiful sight."

She rested her head upon his chest. "I can't believe it. He's finally gone. And you are here. I'm so happy, Cull."

He bent to kiss her. Instantly, the flame of passion flared between them.

"Cullen," she whispered against his lips. "Cullen Kincaid."

He chuckled. "Don't forget the Justiciar of the North part."

"I can't forget. I'll never forget." She turned to look alongside them, at the sight on the rampart. There, Niall and Elspeth embraced, as did Faelan and Tara. And all the others. "Just look at them. I can't imagine a more beautiful sight."

"I can," said Cull, peering down at her. "I'm looking at it right now."

Afterword

After being called on by his brothers and Parliament to answer for his numerous transgressions, Alexander Stewart, the notorious Wolf of Badenach, spent a few more years wreaking havoc with a force of paid mercenaries—even burning the cathedral at Elgin and getting himself excommunicated from the church. It was here that he once more found bitter defeat against the Kincaids, who gathered with other nobles and Highlanders to call the earl to heel.

Afterward, shamed and shunned, he withdrew to the silence and seclusion of Ruthven Castle.

It is said that he lived there quietly until one night when—as legend tells—a man clad all in black arrived at the gates. A mysterious man, whom he invited inside for a game of chess behind the locked doors of his great hall.

That night terrible storms rained down, and lightning crashed, splitting the sky. No one saw the stranger leave, but in the morning the Wolf was discovered dead on the stone floor. But not only dead. The small nails that had held fast the soles of his boots were found strewn on the floor on the opposite side of the room from his remains. That peculiar discovery—and the appearance of his body—led all to conclude that he had somehow been struck by lightning.

Of course, like all legends, there are varying versions of the story.

Some scoff, saying there was no visitor at all. Some even claim that the man in black was the Devil come to drag the Wolf to Hell for his sins. With such wild, varying, and often embellished accounts, the truth of whether a mysterious stranger or the Devil himself entered Ruthven Castle will never be known.

Muddying the waters even further, some swear there was not only one visitor that night . . .

But three.

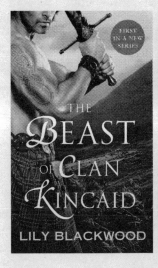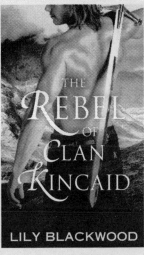
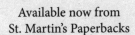